THE LIAR SOCIETY
THE LIES THAT BIND

LISA & LAURA ROECKER

To Joni Roecker, for being the Regulator and a closet Pub Mom

Copyright © 2012 by Lisa Roecker and Laura Roecker
Cover and internal design © 2012 by Sourcebooks, Inc.
Series design by The Book Designers
Cover image © Marie Killen/ Getty Images, Karlova Irina / Shutterstock

Sourcebooks and the colophon are registered trademarks of Sourcebooks, Inc.

All rights reserved. No part of this book may be reproduced in any form or by any electronic or mechanical means including information storage and retrieval systems—except in the case of brief quotations embodied in critical articles or reviews—without permission in writing from its publisher, Sourcebooks, Inc.

The characters and events portrayed in this book are fictitious or are used fictitiously. Any similarity to real persons, living or dead, is purely coincidental and not intended by the author.

Published by Sourcebooks Fire, an imprint of Sourcebooks, Inc.
P.O. Box 4410, Naperville, Illinois 60567-4410
(630) 961-3900
Fax: (630) 961-2168
teenfire.sourcebooks.com

Library of Congress Cataloging-in-Publication data is on file with the publisher.

Printed and bound in the United States of America.
VP 10 9 8 7 6 5 4 3 2 1

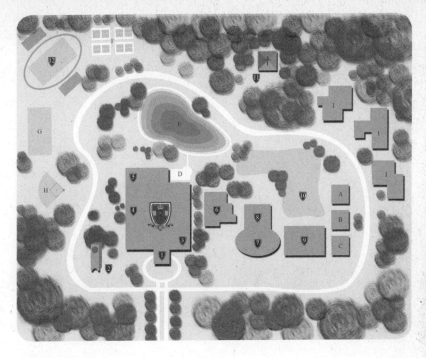

Legend

Station 1. Main Entrance. *Aut disce aut discede.* "Either learn or leave."

Station 2. Clock Tower. *Tempus edax rerum.* "Time is the devourer of all things."

Station 3. School Office. *Faber est suae quisque fortunae.* "Every man is the artisan of his own fortune."

Station 4. Main Computer Lab. *Liberae sunt nostrae cogitationes.* "Our thoughts are free."

Station 5. Detention. *Abyssus abyssum invocat.* "Hell invokes hell."

Station 6. Alumni Hall. *Respice, adspice, prospice.* "Look to the past, the present, the future."

Station 7. Hayden Center for the Arts, Art Wing. *Ars longa vita brevis.* "Art is long, life is short."

Station 8. Hayden Center for the Arts, Auditorium. *Acta est fabula, plaudite.* "The play is over, applaud!"

Station 9. Pemberly Brown Library. *Scientia est potentia.* "Knowledge is power."

Station 10. Garden, Farrow's Arches. *Amor vincit omnia.* "Love conquers all."

Station 11. Pemberly Chapel. *Ad vitam aeternam.* "To eternal life."

Station 12. Pemberly Brown Cemetery. *Pax aeterna.* "To eternal peace."

A. Cornelius Dormitory
B. Vanderplume Dormitory
C. Longacre Dormitory
D. Courtyard
E. Pemberly Brown Lake
F. Tennis Courts
G. Lacrosse Field
H. Baseball Field
I. Buildings of Brown

Chapter 1

They ascended the steps into the clock tower one by one, their red robes billowing in the night like drops of blood.

I shouldn't have been there crouched behind a snow-covered pine tree. I shouldn't have stood watching as boys dressed in black tied blindfolds tightly around the heads of boys dressed in red. I shouldn't have gasped when I saw them being led one by one to stand in each of the ancient windows of the clock tower. My parents would kill me. Liam would dump me. Hell, even Seth would probably be mad enough to permanently revoke my invitation to his tree house. I had made them all a promise.

Let sleeping societies lie.

But the Brotherhood had been responsible for killing my best friend, Grace, and when I heard whispers of a Sacramentum at Station 2—the huge clock tower that measured our hours served at Pemberly Brown Academy like an enormous brick warden—I knew I had to go.

The only things Pemberly Brown took more seriously than its ranking on the *Forbes* list of top Ivy League feeder schools were the crazy traditions commonly referred to as Sacramenta. But this one hadn't been broadcast over the school's social network, Amicus, or sent out via mass text. This was a private, Brotherhood-only ceremony. After three months of arriving at school at the butt crack of dawn to plant the mini-recorder my parents gave me for my tenth birthday in the boys' bathroom where Bradley Farrow and Alistair Reynolds stopped every morning before first period, I had finally gotten some useful information. Too bad it required me freezing to death in the middle of the night in January to record some ridiculous prank. But if this is what it took to prove that the Brotherhood not only existed but also put its members in danger, then so be it.

My hand shook with cold and nerves as I pointed my phone in the direction of the tower and hit the Record button. But when I saw the first boy stand in the window closest to the ground, his back to the sky, his arms stretched wide, my hand stopped shaking. All my muscles tensed in anticipation of what was going to happen next. The night seemed to stand still, noiseless. There were no whispers, no snapping branches, not even a cough as the first boy stood poised on the window's ledge.

"*Inexstinctum!*"

The boy's voice rang clear and strong in the night, the Latin tugging me back into an ancient time. *Inexstinctum*, meaning "that which is never extinguished." And that's when I remembered the legend about the boy who burned for Brown.

Back in the day, Pemberly Brown was two different schools. Pemberly recruited girls from some of the most powerful families across the country, and the Brown School for Boys was an extremely exclusive, all-boys prep school. When the schools were combined in the '50s, the transition to coed wasn't exactly a smooth one. The boys weren't prepared to share their school or campus with the fairer sex, especially not the beloved clock tower.

One of the more misogynistic blokes said he'd rather see it burned to the ground than invaded by skirts. And supposedly he tried to do just that. Sadly, he must have been lacking some serious IQ points, because in all his righteous, antifeminist fervor, he forgot to save himself a way out of the burning building. Rumor has it that he had to jump from the top window in a ball of flames.

I had no idea if the story was true, but given the fact that the Brotherhood was founded to protect male interests in the face of that very feminine invasion, I knew exactly what was going to happen next.

That idiot was going to jump. I had to bite back a scream when I saw him fall to the ground, a red comet against a pitch-black sky. The lowest window was only two stories up, but it was still a good twenty feet above the ground. Enough to break a leg or even snap your neck if you landed the wrong way. I stood there for a beat, hand out, phone still recording, muscles tensed and ready to run.

But then the boy bounced.

I had been so busy watching the boys in red ascend the stairs of the clock tower that I had completely missed the boys in black standing below with what looked like a huge trampoline. Before the first boy had even stood up, there was another cry of *"Inexstinctum!"* And down came the boy in the second window, like something out of a movie. One by one, the red-cloaked figures fell backward from the clock tower into the night.

Twelve boys.

Twelve chances to die.

And I had it all on tape. Surely if I presented this to Ms. D., Pemberly Brown's head of security and all-around Brotherhood-hating badass, she'd take it to the school board and they'd finally dissolve the Brotherhood for good. Maybe then I'd feel like there was justice for what they'd done to Grace.

I had to tip my phone toward the sky to catch the last Brother's fall. He was the unlucky one who had to climb all the way to the top of the tower. It was at least one hundred feet to the ground, and trampoline or no trampoline, that was a long way down.

He stood in the opening with his back to the ground for a good twenty seconds. For a moment, I wondered if he'd have the nerve to fall at all, but then the first syllable left his lips and I watched him stumble backward into the night. "*Inex—*"

"*Consumptus!*" All at once a chorus of girls emerged from the trees surrounding the clock tower, robes of white billowing around their forms. The Sisterhood. "*Consumptus! Consumptus!*" The girls chanted in unison. Extinguish! Extinguish! Extinguish!

Everything happened so quickly. The boy in red fell from the window, but the boys manning the trampoline must have been distracted by the battle cry from the girls. They weren't positioned correctly, and instead of bouncing right in the middle like his Brothers before him, the final boy caught the edge of the trampoline and bounced onto the ground with a sickening snap of bone.

"What the hell?" One of the boys manning the trampoline ripped off his hood, revealing the smooth brown skull of Bradley Farrow. "Alistair! Are you okay? What the hell?" Red and black swarmed around Alistair despite protests to give him space and call 911.

Realizing that their little prank had gone too far, the girls began to scatter. One of them headed straight toward my hideout, ducked behind my tree, and collided with me. Her wide eyes were like liquid gold.

"Kate? What the hell are you…?"

Naomi Farrow, Bradley Farrow's younger sister and my ex-doubles partner. Figures. I put my fingers to my lips and nodded toward the clock tower. The show wasn't over yet. Bradley had caught one of the white-clad girls, and her hood had fallen down her back, revealing long, jet-black hair and a trademark sneer. Beefany Giordano. Well, technically her real name was Bethany, but Grace, Maddie, and I always called her Beefany because she was taller and stronger than 90 percent of the boys on our admittedly pathetic football team.

"What the…my wrist is seriously broken." Alistair was standing now, cradling his left hand in the crook of his arm, his eyes wild and accusing. Even from my post at the tree, I could feel his anger, his absolute disgust. And it was all directed at Beefany. I was surprised she was still standing.

"You had it coming after what you pulled at Candela." I had to hand it to Beefany; she didn't even pretend to feel bad about the turn of events. The girl had guts. In the same way the Brotherhood had formed to protect the interests of the all-boys school, the Sisterhood kept alive the feminist spirit of the original all-girls school.

The Sisterhood had built the tunnels underneath the school generations ago, giving them unprecedented access to everything at Pemberly Brown. The Sisterhood had traded secrets for answer keys. And the Sisterhood had somehow managed to hack the password for every Pemberly Brown email account, including faculty.

And at Pemberly Brown, *Sciencia est potentia*. "Knowledge is power." As a result, the Brotherhood had been fighting to wrest power from the Sisterhood for the past forty years. And this past fall, they'd actually won. No thanks to me.

But I wasn't ready to think about what had happened the night I'd found out how Grace really died. I wasn't ready to remember the moment I realized how she'd been sending me emails even though she'd been dead for over a year. The only thing I wanted to do tonight was to finally get some proof to end the societies for good.

I wasn't stupid. I kept my phone trained on Alistair and Beefany as they screamed at each other in the dead of the night. I was so focused on recording every single moment that I forgot Naomi Farrow was crouching next to me. Well, until she grabbed my phone out of my hand and deleted the entire thing.

"Are you kidding me?" I hissed, grabbing my phone back from her. "I stood out here all night to get that footage. What's your problem?"

"You don't want to mess with them, Kate." She gave me the same sympathetic look she used to flash after kicking my ass in tennis. "You're never going to win."

I rolled my eyes and sighed, looking back to the boys huddled around Alistair. If it weren't for his broken wrist, he definitely would have thrown a punch at Beefany. Alistair Reynolds was not the kind of guy who was afraid to hit a girl. Sadly, I'd learned that lesson firsthand.

I never would have said it out loud, could barely admit it to myself, but I wondered if Naomi was right, if I was fighting a losing battle. I squeezed the phone in my hand, furious with myself for being careless and annoyed with Naomi for her misguided attempt to protect me.

"Well, this has been fun, boys," Beefany called out. "But I've gotta run. I'm sure you understand." She broke away from the Brotherhood, white robe and slightly hysterical giggles trailing in her wake.

"You better run!" Alistair shrieked. "You're finished! I swear to God, you're dead! You wouldn't be the first Sister to get burned."

Naomi and I just looked at each other for a moment, eyes wide and unblinking. Grace. Alistair was referring to Grace.

Screw the odds. Screw winning. The Brotherhood was going down.

Chapter 2

The clock tower showed six minutes after ten. The famous Pemberly Brown landmark had graced the cover of thousands of school brochures, and just looking at it reminded me how close I'd come the night before to having actual, irrefutable proof of the school's secret societies. I had made it my mission to destroy them and I'd failed. Again.

To add insult to injury, Pemberly Brown was finally breaking ground on a new wing of the school funded by donations made in Grace's name. The Farrows had pushed for the reconstruction of the chapel, but the Lees had the final say, and to them, a chapel would have brought back everything they were trying so hard to forget. So even though it was Saturday morning, all of the school's students and faculty were gathering for the dedication ceremony.

And I was late.

My mom would be twisting her rings nervously, a fake smile plastered across her face. Seats would be filled and mine would be empty. People would whisper excitedly about whether the broken best friend would come. I wasn't ready for any of it. When Grace's parents had asked me to say a few words at the ceremony, I'd agreed immediately, but I hadn't really thought about what it would feel like to be here and to be forced to talk about her in front of the entire school.

If I were smart, I would have spent last night writing the most amazing speech of all time, but sadly I was a complete idiot who had opted to spend her evening chasing rich boys in red robes reenacting scenes from an MTV reality show.

I guess being late was the least of my worries.

The site of the ruined chapel came into view and I hung back, observing from a distance. I hoped that if I watched for a few minutes, I'd feel like I'd been there a while, as though I'd gotten that awkward beginning part over with. Women eyed each other and whispered to friends, hands cupped close to their mouths. Men shook hands; guys punched shoulders; girls waved each other over and saved seats.

And then my eyes landed on them: Taylor Wright, Bethany Giordano, Alistair Reynolds, and Bradley Farrow. All of them sat front and center. You'd never have guessed that they were on opposite sides of warring secret societies unless, of course, you knew the story behind the cast cradling Alistair's left arm. You'd also never guess that each of them had a hand in killing my best friend almost a year and a half ago.

My hand flew to my neck, grabbing for Grace's pearls. I had slipped them over my neck in the dark, silent morning to remind myself of the real reason I was here today. My truth.

"Kate?" I jumped at the sound of my dad's voice. The notes in my hand were crumpled and I felt disoriented, like I'd just woken up from some sort of dream. "We've been looking all over the place." His forehead was wrinkled, as usual. I wondered how many wrinkles I had put there. "You ready?"

I mumbled something in response and briefly considered ditching my notes and sprinting into the thick woods that edged the site of Grace's future wing. Why did I put myself in these situations? I wasn't ready yet. I wasn't sure I'd ever be.

"It's time." He placed his hand on my shoulder and nodded toward the first row of pristine white chairs where my mom was waiting, a jacket slung over the back of a chair to save my place. The chairs were arranged around a gaping hole in the ground. A ridiculous white ribbon bordered the opening in an effort to soften our memories of what had happened here that night. It didn't work. The flames that had consumed that old chapel and turned my world to ash were seared in my memory forever.

A large glass vase stood empty on a table next to the podium. After the memorial, 157 written memories, sentiments, apologies, and secrets would be dropped inside, one from each of Grace's classmates, another Pemberly Brown tradition. Mine was crumpled, the ink smeared in spots, probably illegible, which in my mind was better. Grace was the only person who needed to know what it said, and I wanted to believe that wherever she was, she already knew what I had to say.

As we wound our way to our seats, I tried to ignore the way the whispers stopped when I came close or the way fingers discreetly pointed in my direction. I took a deep breath and exhaled slowly.

Dr. Prozac, my pet name for the shrink my parents forced me to see once a month, would be so proud.

"Kate." Liam Gilmour always said my name like a statement, never a question. On this frigid January morning it sounded more like an affirmation.

"Hey, I'm so glad you're here," I said, trying with every last ounce of my being to sound genuine and calm and *okay*. That was the most common question I got. Are you okay? And I'd almost figured out how to fake it.

Liam grabbed my hand and squeezed, seeing right through me. His blue button-down was untucked and wrinkled, but I could tell he'd tried to dress up, which meant much more than anything he could say. The sun glinted off his perfectly messy hair, all shiny golden brown—the kind of color women spent a fortune trying to achieve in expensive salons.

I turned Liam's wrist over in my hand so I could see the simple orange bracelet everyone wore in honor of Grace. The Concilium, Pemberly Brown's version of a student council, had asked me her favorite color. Liam was without a doubt one of the best things that had happened to me since Grace died, but something about seeing him wearing that orange band around his wrist reminded me that Grace was truly gone. The finality of it blindsided me.

Liam would never know Grace. He would know things about her. Like the fact that her favorite color was orange, or that she loved to stay up late and watch trashy TV while slurping Diet Coke through Twizzler straws. But he would never be forced to sit through one of her endless knock-knock jokes. He'd never have one of her world-famous playlists dedicated to him. Liam would never really know my best friend.

My eyes filled with tears, and a couple of them spilled over and splashed down on his wrist.

"Hey." He pulled me into his chest in spite of the fact that my mom and dad were standing less than two feet away. He cupped my cheek and forced me to look into his light eyes. "You're going to be fine."

"Kate…" My mom tugged me away from Liam. "It's almost time. We have to sit down." The satisfaction in her tone reminded me that she still wasn't totally sold on my smexy, rumpled boyfriend. I gave him a lingering kiss on the lips so she'd know I was on to her. I heard Liam laugh quietly as our lips met. He knew exactly what I was up to.

"I'll see you after, okay?" he whispered.

"Okay." I trotted dutifully after my parents to find our reserved seats.

"Oh, look, there are the Allens." My mom tilted her head their way, and I looked over just in time to see Seth's mom lick her finger and swipe it across his face. He noticed me watching, and his cheeks burned redder than his flaming curls before he slapped his mother's hand away. I shot him a sympathetic smile, and he immediately mouthed what looked like "I love you" at me. It might have been borderline romantic if he didn't have something brown smeared across his upper lip, no doubt the spot Mrs. Allen had been after.

"When are you going to give that poor kid a chance?" My dad elbowed me, a smirk pulling at the corner of his mouth.

"Um, try never." I tried to infuse the appropriate level of disgust in my tone but failed miserably. The truth was that Seth was my best friend in the whole world. For a while he had been my only friend. I wouldn't even be here if not for him, so it was kind of impossible not to love him. Cheeto breath and all.

I was snapped out of my reverie when Headmaster Sinclair took the stage. His hair appeared thinner, the sprinkling of gray throughout more apparent. A hush swept across the grounds before he even uttered a sound. His pinched face was all anyone needed to quiet down.

"On behalf of Pemberly Brown Academy, I'd like to welcome you to the Grace Elizabeth Lee Memorial dedication ceremony. As all of you know, at the beginning of last school year, our entire community was shaken to its core." His voice remained steady, cold almost, the words memorized to the point of losing all meaning. A secretary had probably prepared his introduction. "Grace was an exceptional student, friend, daughter, the list goes on, and she was taken far too soon in a tragic accident that will never be forgotten."

I couldn't help but notice how he hung on the word "accident." It felt especially meant for me. "But part of moving forward is letting go." Sinclair's eyes flicked onto my own for a split second, so quickly that I wondered if it had even happened at all. "While at the same time always remembering. This new space will help us do exactly that."

The headmaster cleared his throat, looking down for a moment before his gaze met the eyes of the crowd once again. "With that said, Grace's family and I thought there was no one better suited to share her favorite Grace memory than Kate Lowry, Grace's best friend. Kate?"

I'd never heard my name sound so sugar-coated, especially out of his mouth. It made me nauseous. Even more so when I watched him drop a tiny folded piece of paper into the glass vase. It didn't seem fair that his "memory" got to be first. Headmaster Sinclair was one of the Brotherhood's most powerful alumni, and he had been instrumental in covering up the truth behind Grace's death last year. The fact that he was at her memorial ceremony pretending to honor her memory made me want to pummel him until there was nothing left except a bloody pair of bifocals. But I wasn't in the mood to make a scene. Grace deserved more than that.

Instead, I approached the podium and settled for squeezing him hard enough to crack a rib when he wrapped his arms around me in a chilly embrace. Before lowering the microphone, I fished the worn paper from the bottom of my pocket and dropped it into the vase. An illusion of balance was restored.

"Careful," he hissed. I gave him a demure smile that translated into something slightly more profane than "screw you." The microphone let out a squeal when I angled it down, and it was as if all two hundred people in the crowd cringed at once. It all seemed so surreal then. Grace's picture, bare branches scraping the sun-drenched sky, an entire community gathered in mourning. How had I ended up here? Liam must have recognized the panic written across my face because he gave me a wink. And then I got my footing.

I could do this. I had to do this. For Grace.

"As most of you know, Grace Lee was my best friend." The strength of my voice surprised me. It must have surprised my parents too, because they beamed with pride. A little bit of sadness was mixed in, but mostly pride. "When somebody dies, it's hard to find the right words. People say the same things—'She's in a better place, I'm so sorry, I know how you feel, I'm praying for you, thinking of you.' I used to say that stuff too, because it's just what you say."

I wasn't even looking at my notes anymore. The only things that seemed to make sense were the words coming out of my mouth.

Seth caught my eye and gave me a little thumbs-up. His small gesture gave me the courage I needed to continue.

"And after a while people start talking about moving on and going back to normal. But it's not that easy." Obviously. I had faded pink hair and brown roots. And that was only on the outside.

"Grace and I were like the same person. Everything I remember is connected to her."

I picked up the framed picture of Grace. "This was taken on our first day of upper school at Pemberly Brown." I paused for a minute, not sure how to put into words what that morning had felt like, why this picture was so important to me. It had been such an ordinary moment. Grace's long, dark hair cascaded down her back in waves, and her almond-shaped eyes were laughing.

"I love this picture, this memory, because it captured the moment before…well, before anything, really. There was all this anticipation. All this hope. I guess it's just how I want to remember Grace." I mumbled the last words, feeling stupid for even saying them out loud.

My eyes locked with Liam's and he smiled, cheering me on from his seat. But I couldn't seem to stop my eyes from raking through the crowd, sifting through the expectant faces until they landed on Bradley Farrow. His mocha skin had turned the color of ash, and his golden eyes were heavy and sad. And just like that, every last one of my words vanished into thin air.

"So, yeah, we should all remember her this way and keep her memory alive." Good lord, that sounded just as idiotic in my head as it did over the microphone, but I couldn't seem to stop myself from saying it. "So thanks. We're now going to hear from some of Grace's other friends."

I shuffled back to my seat, cursing Bradley Farrow for being a living, breathing reminder of all the ways I'd failed Grace. But today wasn't about Bradley. It wasn't even about me. It was about Grace.

I managed to tune out all the noise and focus on the other students sharing their memories of Grace. As I listened, my eyes heavy with tears, I felt thankful that I had the strength to stay, that I didn't take off into the woods or stand up and scream at the unfairness of the world. As much as I hated to admit it, the broken parts of my heart seemed to be coming together, forming a thick, dark scar. Maybe that's what moving on felt like.

After everyone said their piece, the president of the school board stood to make the dedication.

"Thank you, students, for that spirited memorial to your friend. I'm sure she would have appreciated it." She cleared her throat and shuffled her note cards.

"As you all know, in honor of Grace's memory, the Lees have made an extremely generous endowment to Pemberly Brown.

These funds will be used to build a new wing of our school to accommodate our growing student body."

The audience politely applauded, but the president just cleared her throat.

"These funds were donated on the condition that any student found accessing restricted areas of the school or trespassing on school property after school hours will be immediately expelled. We will not suffer another tragedy."

She paused briefly, as though waiting for applause, but the crowd was silent. Was she really saying what it sounded like she was saying? Most of the Sacramentum ceremonies were so old and so respected that even teachers turned a blind eye.

As I digested this new information, I felt my phone buzz twice against my thigh. When I reached to look at the text, I saw all of the other students surreptitiously doing the same.

Obsideo tonight. Station 12. Sunset. Don't be late.

Chapter 3

Within seconds, the energy on the grounds shifted. Students were already buzzing about the invite. No doubt the new rules about being in restricted areas of campus after hours would only heighten the excitement. Clueless to the change, my parents attempted to steer me toward the Allens, but I hung back, clutching at my stomach. I wasn't ready to field Seth's questions about the new school rules or Obsideo and especially not about Grace. I needed time to process.

My mom rushed back to me, her face twisted with worry. "Kate, what is it?"

"I don't feel good all of a sudden. Can we go home?" I wrapped my arms around my middle, holding on for dear life.

"Sweetie, you're freezing. I'll get your coat." Before I could tell my mom I hadn't brought a coat and wouldn't be caught dead in one of hers, she returned, holding out a jacket I recognized immediately. But not because it belonged to either of us.

I felt the color leave my face. "Where did you get that?"

My mom's forehead wrinkled. "Honey, you left it on your seat."

I closed my eyes for a second and heard Grace's infectious laugh, watched as she shrugged into the orange fleece, pulling the sleeves down over her hands. A wave of dizziness had me swaying on my feet, and my mom put her hands on my shoulders to steady me as I opened my eyes. The material was soft between my fingers, and I was barely able to resist holding it up to my face to see if it still smelled like Grace's spicy perfume.

"Greg, she's had enough. We need to get Kate home."

And just like that, my parents led me to the car, no questions asked. That's kind of how we operated. They didn't ask; I didn't tell. It actually came in quite handy.

The second we got home, I raced up the stairs to my room, flipped open my laptop, and began typing.

> To: GraceLee@pemberlybrown.edu
> Sent: Sat 1/10 12:26 PM
> From: KateLowry@pemberlybrown.edu
> Subject: Obsideo
>
> Grace,
> Your coat. Why is this happening to me? Am I imagining it? Is someone messing with me? Maybe it's your parents; your mom was always so worried about us being cold. I don't know. This just doesn't make any sense. Sometimes I feel like you're still here, just on vacation or transferred to another school. And seeing your jacket, smelling your perfume, it feels like you just forgot it in my locker or loaned it to me for Obsideo.

Obsideo…Do you remember trying to sneak in when we were in eighth grade? We sat by the mausoleum and listened to them say every single name. I don't think I even listened.

It just wasn't real then, you know? They were just names. But now they'll be saying your name. And I just can't be there to hear them say it. I'm not ready. I guess a big part of me still wants to believe you just forgot your jacket in my locker and then moved away, you know?

I hate this,
Kate

I saved the email to Grace in a folder in my inbox and flopped back onto my bed. I'd gotten into the habit of emailing her after she died a year and a half ago. I used to actually send them, but now I was too paranoid to hit Send. The societies were always watching, waiting. They regularly hacked into email accounts to get whatever info they could. There's no way I would ever give them the satisfaction now.

I liked writing down all the stuff I would have talked to Grace about if she were still alive. It was comforting somehow. And it still felt like somehow Grace was reading them.

I looked at the phone on my bed; the text about Obsideo was still up on the screen. Obsideo, meaning "to haunt." Translation: PB students gathered at Station 12, the Pemberly Brown cemetery, in the dead of winter at sunset and drank cheap beer out of red plastic cups, pretending to pay tribute to the dead, specifically the Pemberly Brown dead. The list was pages long and included students from the graduating class of 1950, the year our school was founded, on through the decades. Cancer, car wrecks, heart attacks, four plane crashes, a couple suicides, and one freak hiking accident had all conspired to end the lives of various alumni throughout the years.

During our first Obsideo, Grace, Maddie, and I had huddled together, shivering in tank tops and skinny jeans, half listening to the names like everyone else. The names were all vaguely familiar, faceless members of our school's folklore and the inspiration for countless school traditions. Maybe that's why I never really thought about their being dead—the stories made them feel alive.

I needed time to process. Or maybe it was the nagging feeling that no one ever *really* died at Pemberly Brown.

I dropped my phone and headed back to my desk. I couldn't *not* log onto Amicus to see what was going on.

The Obsideo RSVP list was blowing up—totally predictable, given the announcement this morning. When were adults going to learn that forbidding kids to do stuff only made them want to do it more? It's called reverse psychology, folks. Look it up.

My heart sunk a little when I saw that Liam had responded Yes. Part of me wanted to be there with him. To feel him squeeze my hand when they read Grace's name for the first time.

And then I saw Bethany "Beefany" Giordano's RSVP pop up with a comment.

RIP Grace.

All of the muscles in my body tensed at the same time. No way was I going to Obsideo.

The *Twilight Zone* theme song sounded from my phone, and Seth's picture appeared on the screen.

"I'll pick you up at four," my dorky next-door neighbor breathed into the phone before I'd even had a chance to say hello. He sounded like he'd just come off the treadmill.

I chose to ignore his assumption that I was going to this stupid thing. "Why are you so out of breath?"

"What do you mean?" he huffed.

"You're breathing so heavy. It's distracting."

"It's just how I breathe, okay? So see you in a couple hours."

"I actually don't need a ride."

"Ahh," he said, Darth Vader–like breaths filling the silence. "You have plans with BJ. He's the only other person who hasn't replied yet."

"Who?" I asked, wondering where this could possibly be going and how some unfortunate soul had wound up with such a tragic nickname.

"You know, English class. The super-smart one."

"Uh, you mean Brad?"

"Yeah, Brad James—BJ."

I didn't bother taking the time to explain to Seth just how wrong that nickname was. Of course I knew who Brad was. He and his sister, Jen, were basically connected at the hip in the creepiest way imaginable. I glanced at the RSVP list again. Both of their names appeared on the No Reply list after mine. Not surprising, considering that the last party they went to ended with Alistair Reynolds offering them one hundred dollars to make out. Keeping it classy. That's just how we roll at Pemberly Brown.

"Just don't start calling him BJ in public, okay?" I said, clicking through the comments again.

"But why not? His middle name is James!"

Just then my phone signaled another call, and when I looked at the screen, I saw the goofy picture of Liam pretending he was going to eat my parents' mistletoe. I remembered punching him playfully in the arm and then snapping the shot. It made me laugh every time he called.

"Listen, I have to go, but have fun tonight."

"If you change your mind, the white bullet leaves at four sharp." I pictured Mrs. Allen's white minivan. Not exactly a selling point. "Oh, and Kate?" Seth asked, still breathing heavy. It sounded like he was eating the phone, which, with his appetite, wouldn't be out of the realm of possibility. "You gotta at least give it a shot tonight. Grace would want you to be there."

My phone beeped again.

"I know," was all I could come up with to say.

I clicked over to Liam and couldn't help but smile. "Yes?"

"You left in a rush this afternoon and you haven't RSVP'd yet," he said. I could hear tapping as he scrolled through the RSVP list.

"Don't you have anything better to do than stalk me? Besides, I already have plans," I said, smiling, which totally gave me away. I examined a strand of hair for split ends.

"Hot date?"

"Yes, actually. The name's BJ. Sister's chaperoning. It's going to be epic."

Liam snorted. "Get dressed. I'll pick you up."

I wished I could just say yes, pick out an outfit, and slap on some makeup. Maybe even have a quick argument with my parents about curfew. But I didn't really care about clothes or makeup, and my parents weren't exactly big on curfews, not that Liam would ever let me break one anyway.

I sat up in bed and rolled one of Grace's pearls between my fingers. Before the email that had changed my life a few months ago, I'd kept the pearls shoved at the bottom of a box at the top of my closet beneath piles of books and old clothes and yearbooks. Just imagining the pearls used to make me feel like someone had punched me in the stomach and simultaneously sucked the remaining air out of my lungs for good measure. Now wearing them felt more like pressing a finger into a bruise on my thigh, a conscious, almost pleasant reminder that I was hurt. Honestly, I was relieved to feel something when I looked at the necklace Grace had worn every day of her life. Because nothing scared me more than the thought of not feeling anything at all.

I heard shuffling on the other end of the phone. Liam was clearly planning on pulling the classic hang-up-and-I'll-be-pulling-into-your-driveway-any-minute move. I opened my mouth to stop him when a message box popped up on my computer screen. It was from Beefany. Not only could she take any guy in an arm-wrestling match and win, but she was also a card-carrying member of the Sisterhood.

Her lame-ass RIP comment was bad enough; I couldn't believe she had the nerve to message me on Amicus.

> BethanyGiordano: You need to come to Obsideo.

I imagined myself among the gravestones.

> BethanyGiordano: No one blames you for anything.

I saw myself listening to someone recite the names on the list.

> BethanyGiordano: It's tradition.

I imagined hearing Grace's name read aloud in the darkness, letting the tears slip down my cheeks, praying it would be too dark for anyone to notice.

I'd spent months in therapy with Dr. Prozac to prove to myself that none of those things were my fault. I didn't have to prove it to anyone else.

> BethanyGiordano: She'd want you there.

"Kate? Who's messaging you?" Liam asked, startling me. I'd forgotten he was even on the phone.

"I'll call you back," I said, tossing the phone on my bed.

I had to read the words on the screen three times before I fully processed them. Outrage bubbled up in my chest, knocking the wind out of my lungs. I couldn't believe that Bethany freaking Giordano was playing the Grace card. Who the hell did she think she was?

I slammed my laptop shut, harder than I should have, causing one of the picture frames on the shelf above me to wobble and collapse. All of the frames in my room were like little time capsules containing years' worth of pictures sandwiched on top of each other. I'd just changed this one out last month with a picture of Seth, Liam, and me before Homecoming. It had replaced a picture of Grace and me dressed up for Halloween one year. And I didn't need to open the back to know the rest featured Grace as well. They all did. Maybe she was trying to tell me something.

"Go to Obsideo" or "Don't go to Obsideo" or, most likely, "Don't slam your laptop shut."

I picked up the frame and repositioned it on the shelf next to the place where all of my required reading books for school went to die. They all featured crisp pages devoid of any notes or earmarks and perfectly straight spines without creases. Well, all of them except one.

Which of these things is not like the others, I thought as I slid the book off the shelf. I held my breath as though a part of me already knew what was coming, an instinctual coping strategy.

Remember Me by Christopher Pike, a classic, Grace's favorite. It had probably been read at least a dozen times by all of us and whoever had owned it before. Grace's mom loved garage sales, and although we turned our noses up at her box of fifty-cent books, we secretly devoured them during sleepovers.

Sure enough, when I opened the front cover, Grace's name was scrawled in orange ink. I fell back into the chair as my phone vibrated from my desk and Liam's ridiculous picture appeared on the screen again. I pressed Ignore as I tried to wrap my head around how Grace's book had ended up on my shelf. I must have borrowed it, never returned it, shoved it on the shelf after she died, forgotten about it in my haze. My stomach twisted as I fanned through the pages. And that's when I saw it. On page 56, Grace's handwriting was clear as day, orange and bubbly like always.

> Someone has to remember.

I threw the book across the room like it was on fire, my hands shaking, then rushed to open my bedroom door. Something about being alone in my room made the entire situation that much scarier.

"Mom?" I called. "Dad?"

"Right here, honey." My mom materialized at my door with unsettling speed. "How're you doing?" She smoothed my pink ponytail and I wriggled away from her. Not wanting to be alone but not wanting to be with her either. "We were just going to go pick up some dinner. Why don't you come?"

The way I saw it, I had a few options:

1. I could tell my mom about the weird message in the book. That was easily ruled out on the grounds that it would probably result in more time with Dr. Prozac.
2. I could stay here and be left with the creepy message in Grace's book all alone. *Riiight.* That was off the table, because I'm not

one of those stupid girls in horror movies who open the basement door to investigate a creepy moaning noise. I liked to think I was too smart to fall into that trap. Unfortunately that really only left me with one choice.

"Actually, I'm going to hang out with Seth tonight, if that's okay."

My mom's whole face brightened the way it did every time she heard Seth Allen's name. "Of course, honey. Spending time with friends is so important right now. Just make sure you're home by eleven." She kissed me on the forehead and walked downstairs.

I walked back to my desk, lifted the screen of my computer, and clicked the Yes button before I could even think about what that really meant—how one of Beefany's minions would "accidentally" spill her drink on me, or how Alistair Reynolds would inevitably crack jokes about my hair. Because none of that really mattered when you had just read some secret message in your dead best friend's book that may or may not have been some sort of weird coincidence. I watched as my name disappeared from No Reply and materialized on the Will Attend list and wondered if that's what Grace would have wanted.

I could almost hear my classmates repeating the Obsideo motto: *Vivere disce, cogita mori.* "Learn to live, remember death." They'd say the words, but would anyone really mean them? Would anyone there really be remembering Grace?

Someone has to remember.

And it would have to be me.

My phone vibrated again and I swallowed back a scream, feeling ridiculous and scared and nervous and entirely exhausted by the past ten minutes.

"So you decided to cancel on BJ. Good choice." I could tell Liam was smiling by the sound of his voice. It calmed my nerves and made me feel like I'd made the right decision.

"His sister pulled out. It was a non-starter." The words were light, but the delivery was off. My voice shook, a classic tell.

But if Liam noticed, he didn't say. Because that's just the way he was.

"I'll see you soon," he said before hanging up.

I folded and refolded the soft, orange fleece on my bed, smoothing the material into a perfect square. My heart thumped to life again as I approached the discarded book in the corner of my room, but I swallowed my fear and picked it up. The book and sweater had to be signs. Not scary, just signs. I placed the book on top of the sweater and considered adding Grace's pearls for good measure, a tower of Grace, but I kept them around my neck instead. I'd need a little piece of her tonight.

Learn to live. Remember Grace.

I pressed my fingers into the imagined bruise on my leg, surrendering to the ache.

Chapter 4

The large hands on the clock tower showed 4:47, which meant we were early, just in time for the pre-party that would no doubt be in full swing on the green. Winter had snuck back up on us as the sun hung low in the sky. Our breath hung in the air, while our fingers were numb to the bone. The memorial, the speeches, the crisp sunshine of the day all seemed far away as we snuck back onto campus. The president's threat, however, trailed us like a shadow.

A wrought-iron fence lined the perimeter of the century-old cemetery. The ubiquitous Pemberly Brown crest decorated the gates, and I ran my fingers over the prestigious-looking key that was supposed to represent the act of unlocking knowledge, ironic considering that the gates were always supposed to be locked at dark. The block print was clear: "Cemetery closes at dusk; trespassers will be prosecuted."

Yet another one of Pemberly Brown's rules that had been made to be broken. No one was ever really prosecuted for trespassing. Especially during a Sacramentum. The truth was that the administration honored the age-old traditions more than the student body. They turned a blind eye, leaving a door ajar, a gate unlocked. But then again, why wouldn't they? Pemberly Brown was built on these quirky after-hours affairs. Which made the announcement at Grace's memorial even more baffling.

Sure, the Lees probably had their hearts in the right place—they didn't want another tragic death at Pemberly Brown—but it was kind of shocking that the school had gone along with the Lees' wishes. They might as well have listed Sacramenta ceremonies in the brochure. "For an annual tuition that costs more than a BMW, your kid can chant Latin and party in graveyards with the nation's elite." They'd probably even throw in a picture of the burnt-down chapel to really give the hard sell.

I swallowed the bitterness in my mouth. Tonight was about remembering my best friend. The whole expulsion thing had to be an empty threat, and judging by the turnout tonight, I wasn't the only person who felt that way.

I could barely bring myself to slap the bronze plaque as we walked through the gates. *Pax aeterna*. "To eternal peace." I squeezed my eyes shut as my palm met the cold metal and prayed that Grace had found some sort of peace. Wherever she was. I sucked in a lungful of frigid air and braced myself for what lay ahead.

Liam squeezed my hand as we stepped through the gates, sensing my apprehension. "We can go home if you want. Get out of here and pretend that we go to a public school where students hang out at normal places, like malls."

I laughed a little at the thought of hipper-than-thou Liam

shopping at American Eagle. "No, I think I need to be here. Someone has to be, you know?" I looked up at him, seeing how his eyelashes made little crescent shadows under his eyes.

"I'm glad you're doing this, Kate. I knew you'd do the right thing."

I messed with the pearls around my neck, unsure how to answer. "Sounds like everyone is really taking that new school rule to heart, huh?" I laughed, deciding to try to keep things light as much as possible. A mass of students was all headed in the same direction, some holding hands, some hooked together by the arm and laughing.

We wound our way deeper into the cemetery, headed north to where the memorial garden led to the grave sites. I found it kind of shocking that people wanted to spend eternity buried at the same place where they served detention, but a surprising number of alumni thought PB was the perfect resting place.

As a result, the cemetery was as picturesque and overly groomed as the rest of campus. During the daylight hours, the grassy hills and carved stone benches made it feel more like a park than a graveyard. But the atmosphere shifted as darkness descended. The granite eyes of angels and gargoyles seemed to follow our every move; shadowy figures darted between graves, and soft voices hissed from the shadows. Even more reason to be thankful I had Liam at my side.

People were everywhere. Turns out those dark figures were actually second-year girls huddled close together, blowing into their bare hands for warmth. Guys wearing hats and ski jackets circled around them like sharks, shoving each other and laughing. Plastic red cups dotted the third- and fourth-year circles, while first- and second-years inched around the perimeter with hungry eyes.

I tugged at my scarf and felt the heat of hundreds of eyes staring at me as we walked through the party. Whispers followed me like ninja paparazzi, and I wanted nothing more than to go back to the warmth of Liam's Jeep and pretend this had never happened. Speaking about my best friend at her memorial during the daylight hours was one thing. Attending an after-hours, forbidden ceremony that might or might not get us expelled was completely different.

But the moment I felt Liam's fingers wrap around mine again, gently urging me forward, I threw my shoulders back and lifted my pink head just a little bit higher. If anyone had a right to be here, it was me. I just had to find somewhere I could blend. Kind of a tall order for a girl with a fading pink ponytail.

I was beyond grateful when all heads turned to the far-right corner of the crowd.

A circle had formed. Kids on the outside stood on tippy-toes trying to peer in, while the lucky few along the inside raised their fists, screamed excitedly, clapped, and laughed. I had my suspicions about who the crowd had formed around, and it was confirmed when every few seconds I caught a flash of spiky, blond, overly gelled hair. Ben Montrose.

Ben was from some uppity private school in Southern California, but he was more *Jersey Shore* than *O.C.* Unless, of course, surfers gelled individual strands of hair at precarious angles and ripped baby trees out of the ground to demonstrate brute strength. But somehow that image didn't quite jibe with all the *90210* reruns I'd been watching. I had the dubious honor of being Ben's lab partner, which had resulted in a perpetual headache the entire span of Chem on account of his unique ability to force me to roll my eyes approximately every three seconds.

"For the love of God, please tell me he's not walking over hot coals or something. Remember a couple of months ago when he broke his hand trying to prove he could karate-chop a brick in half?"

"How could I forget? He walked around with a Prada cast for the next three weeks." Liam stepped aside just in time for me to catch a rather sarcastic round of applause.

"I actually feel sort of sorry for him. I've tried explaining that people aren't really laughing with him, but the entire concept seems foreign to him."

"How's that saying go again? 'He who laughs last laughs longest'?" Liam's tone was full of mock solemnity.

"You just made that up, didn't you?"

"Absolutely not. I read it on a Bazooka gum wrapper. The word of the gum." Liam saluted and I laughed.

"You know I'm laughing at you right now, not with you. Just for the record."

"Yeah, yeah." Liam wrapped his arms around me, and I felt his mouth nip at my earlobe. I had to hand it to the guy; he knew how to get a girl to start taking him seriously.

"You guys are so cute. I just wish I had my camera." Before I even turned to take in his expensive shirt beneath an open jacket or the rich color of his skin, I knew it was him. Maybe it was the way he lingered on the word "camera," or maybe it was just because seeing Bradley brought me back to the night of Grace's death. Either way, interactions with Bradley were more ambush than amiable. "Hey, Kate, toss me your phone and I'll get some footage of you two lovebirds. Your phone has a video camera, right?"

My brain lit up with all kinds of four-letter words. Bradley was one of those guys who had passed tall, dark, and handsome and slid right into towering, black, and devastatingly hot. His dark features split into a cocky grin as he taunted me. Bradley and his sister, Naomi, the girl who'd deleted my evidence last night, were from one of the richest, most established families at Pemberly Brown. Their great-grandfather had been the first African American to attend school here, and after founding one of the biggest real-estate development companies in Ohio, he had become one of the school's most valuable benefactors.

"What's your deal, man? We're just hanging out. No offense, but no one invited you." Liam took a couple of steps toward Bradley.

"Oh, that's right. Kate knows a thing or two about invitations. Why don't you tell him what you and your Sisters were looking for last night? Naomi says you're their resident videographer."

"Dude, I have no idea what you're talking about, and I'm guessing Kate doesn't either. Just lay off, Bradley. Can't you see she's having a tough day?" Liam took another two steps toward Bradley.

I yanked on Liam's jacket and inserted myself between the boys. Bradley's golden eyes were framed by eyelashes that were short and thick, like fanned-out paintbrushes. He smelled exactly the same as I remembered, like mint and sandalwood.

"Enough." It was all I could manage without going into detail about my actions the night before.

All of the anger leaked out of Bradley's face and his eyes softened, almost pleaded. "What are you doing with them, Kate? I can't believe that after everything that happened, you're getting involved again. We need to sit down and talk…"

The word "talk" sent me crashing back to reality. The last time Bradley Farrow had wanted to "talk" was the night Grace died. "I have nothing to say to you." I turned away from him so quickly that I felt the ends of my pink ponytail whip his cheeks. I grabbed Liam by the arm and hauled him around the corner of the mausoleum.

"What the hell is going on, Kate? Were you seriously with the Sisterhood last night? You promised this would stop. You promised you were done with revenge."

I braced myself against the wall, my forehead touching the smooth marble and slowly bringing my body temperature back to normal.

"I promised you that I wouldn't get hurt and I didn't. But, Liam, they had people jumping out of the clock tower. They could have killed someone again. I had it on tape and it would have been all over for the Brotherhood, but then—"

"Stop. I don't want to hear it, Kate." I expected Liam to walk away, but instead he grabbed my hands and pulled me toward him. "You know I worry about you, like, constantly, right? Even when you're not trying to fight a bunch of meaty assholes who think they own our school."

"I know." I tried to grab his hand, but he jerked away and headed back toward the party. For a second I thought about following him, but instead I closed my eyes, sank down to the ground, and rested my head on my knees, hating myself, hating our school, hating this night. But then somehow the memory of Grace, Maddie, and me sneaking into Obsideo in eighth grade snaked through the bars of my hatred like smoke through a grate.

Grace had spent hours picking out our outfits. Considering the fact that we had to be dressed in head-to-toe black, you'd think that would make things easy, but according to Grace, looking fashionable was never supposed to be easy.

She forced me into the softest black sweater dress with quarter-length sleeves in spite of my repeated protests that my forearms were going to freeze. Maddie still had all of her baby fat, leaving her at least two or three sizes larger than Grace and me, but Grace still managed to sausage her into a cute pair of skinny black jeans.

Grace tried to talk us into stealing black stilettos from her mom's enormous shoe collection, but I patently refused to suffer for fashion and opted for my black riding boots instead. As a result, I was the one laughing the loudest when Grace and Maddie toppled to the ground after one of the first-year boys popped out from behind a gravestone and sent us running back toward Grace's house.

The memory reminded me why I had come tonight. Grace. The note she'd scrawled in our favorite book. *Remember Me*. Isn't that all any of us wanted? To be remembered?

I opened my eyes and swiped my phone to life. 5:04 p.m. A sliver of sun clung to the horizon, which meant it was almost time for the ceremony. I hurried to my feet. This was stupid. I had to find Liam, I had to explain. He'd understand eventually. He had to.

And that's when I saw her. Standing behind the same gravestone where she'd stumbled almost a year and a half ago. Her long, dark hair hung down to the center of her back, and her plaid skirt grazed her thighs slightly higher than the rest of us dared. For a second the world went completely still. All I could hear was the blood pumping in my ears, and all I could see was my dead best friend's ghost standing three feet away from me.

Grace was back.

Chapter 5

Dark patches blurred the edges of my vision. The shock of seeing Grace again seemed to have turned everything to jelly, even my eyesight.

I felt myself falling, and it seemed to take extra time for my body to meet the ground, as though I were sinking to the bottom of a pool instead of tumbling back through air.

When I came to, I felt someone's arms around me and heard whispers.

"Kate? Kate? Are you okay? Answer me! Kate!" It was Liam's voice. He'd come to my rescue as usual. I wanted to open my eyes, to tell him I was fine. But I was too scared of what I'd see.

"Is she okay?" a girl's voice I didn't recognize asked softly.

"Everyone give me some space. I know CPR. I think she needs the breath of life." I recognized that squeaky voice right away.

My eyes flew open. "I'm fine! I'm fine!" I managed to croak.

"Works every time," Seth snorted.

My eyes flicked from Seth's hazel ones to Liam's furrowed brow. And then I saw her.

Only it wasn't Grace. Just some first-year with long, dark hair.

"What happened?" Liam's arms were wrapped around me, and he slowly brought me up to a seated position.

"I just lost my footing. I'm fine now." The wet grass had soaked through my jeans, and I scrambled to stand up. I was sure everyone would be pointing and whispering about my little episode, but the party was still behind us. Thankfully Seth, Liam, and Faux-Grace were the only people who had witnessed my short trip down Lunatic Lane.

"Maybe this wasn't such a good idea…" Liam gripped my elbow, and the warmth of his hands helped clear my head.

"No, no. I'm fine now. Seriously."

Someone needs to remember.

I was still a little light-headed, and I was 99 percent sure my left butt cheek was frozen solid, but I couldn't leave. I'd already failed Grace so many different times in so many different ways. But this was something I could do. Something I could control. It was a small thing, but it was all I had.

I felt a clammy hand on my forehead.

"No fever," Seth noted cheerfully.

I batted his hand away. "I'm fine." I widened my eyes and tried to give him my mom's patented death stare, but I felt my mouth start to give in to a smile instead.

"Next time I'm giving you the breath of life. No arguments. I've been looking for a good excuse to use the CPR skills I picked up at that junior baby-sitting course my mom made me take at the library." With one enormous bite, he finished off a candy bar that had literally appeared out of thin air. "You're sure you're all right?"

He said the words through a mouthful of Snickers, and once I got past the fact that he'd just sprayed me with chocolate-nut saliva, I realized there was genuine concern in his eyes. I melted a little more.

In spite of his frequent offers to administer mouth-to-mouth, Seth was the closest thing I had to a best friend. Maddie was still refusing to answer any of my calls or even respond to any of my emails. Granted, she was in some kind of intense inpatient program for refusing to ingest actual food for the past year and a half, so chatting with her ex-bestie probably wasn't at the top of her priority list. But still.

"I'm fine. Really. The mere threat of mouth-to-mouth probably saved me from slipping into a coma."

"That's what I'm here for," Seth replied cheerfully. Liam rolled his eyes in my direction, but he was smiling. Some guys might get jealous if a scrawny redhead was constantly hitting on their girlfriend, but Liam was not one of those guys.

The cemetery was almost completely dark now, the aged, moss-covered gravestones lit only by the flicker of an occasional flashlight. Somehow the frigid air seemed to make the rising moon burn brighter in the sky, casting an eerie glow on the faces milling around the statues. I scanned the crowd and caught sight of a girl from my English class who was pointing at me, gesturing at her hair, and then laughing with the girl standing next to her. My hand instinctively flew up to my pink ponytail and smoothed the strands self-consciously. It wasn't easy being different at Pemberly Brown, but I'd learned from experience that it was significantly easier than trying to fit in.

A loud yelp sounded behind me, and I turned quickly to see Beefany pounding Alistair Reynolds on his good arm. Judging by the way Alistair was massaging his shoulder, her fists lived up to her nickname.

"You bastard!" she shrieked and struck him again, this time in the center of his chest. She knocked all the air out of him and he fell back, steadying himself on a stone bench.

"Calm your shit. I was just having some fun." Alistair laughed cruelly, and my back went stiff at the sound. Alistair was the leader of the Brotherhood. The fact that he was here instead of rotting in some cell in juvie was a constant reminder that I'd failed to bring Grace's killers to justice. Everyone else thought the fire had been an accident, but I knew better.

More than anything in the world, I wanted to walk over there and slap that pretty-boy smirk right off his face. I lurched toward him involuntarily and immediately felt Liam's arm slide around my waist.

"Don't," he said. Never had there been so much meaning packed into one tiny word. The anger was back in his eyes. And on some level I had to admit that I understood. The last time we'd gotten involved, it had ended with me nearly getting charged with manslaughter and Liam almost getting killed. Safe to say things hadn't exactly gone as planned.

But I wasn't ready to give up on justice. And nothing made me want to fight back more than watching Alistair dude-hug Bradley. My eyes narrowed as the boys bumped shoulders while Liam's voice reduced to a low drone I was barely conscious of. Watching them left me feeling light-headed all over again, and I swayed on my feet.

"Kate!" Liam grabbed me by the elbow and turned me around so the boys were out of my line of sight. "They're getting ready to start," he said tersely.

"Oh, right. Sure." I looked in the direction he was pointing and saw a fourth-year dressed in a white robe. She was standing on one of the benches and was flanked by two first-years who appeared to be freezing their butts off in outfits better suited for summer. The younger girls trained twin flashlights on the fourth-year to create a flickering spotlight as Porter Reynolds, Alistair's younger brother and wannabe rock star, gently strummed on his guitar.

"You can't keep doing this," Liam added under his breath. "You've gotta just let it go."

Tears sprang to my eyes, and I wiped them away with the backs of my hands.

"I know this isn't easy for you, but Grace wouldn't want you putting yourself at risk for them." He cupped my face in his hands and used his thumbs to wipe away fresh tears before they even had a chance to fall. "You're never going to win this. If you had a chance, they wouldn't bother playing."

"I know." And I did. There was no doubt in my mind that Liam was right. But that didn't make it any easier to give up.

The fourth-year's voice began to ring out over the crowd, carried through the quiet cemetery by the sharp winter wind. "*Ad perpetuam memoriam; ad vitam aeternam.*" In perpetual memorial; to eternal life. She began to slowly read off the list of names, the paper fluttering in the breeze. Some—like Abigail Moore, a woman who'd fallen victim to a Sisterhood initiation gone wrong in the '50s —I recognized, but most were just an endless series of first names that sounded like last names followed by thirds, fourths, or even fifths, depending on how long the family had been rich.

I remembered hearing the same monotonous list of names with Grace and Maddie while we hid behind the mausoleum. It felt like a million years ago that we'd barely listened to the endless litany of Pemberly Brown's fallen students, too busy ogling fourth-years and giggling from the shadows. It was as though instead of names we were hearing the words "This will never happen to you" over and over and over again.

But here I was, about fourteen months later. Grace-less.

My entire body stiffened when I finally heard the fourth-year call out Henry Rowenstock's name. He'd died of leukemia when we were in lower school, and his name had been last on the list a couple years ago, so that could only mean one thing. Liam squeezed my hand as the fourth-year took a huge breath.

Seth looked down at his feet, and I felt the entire crowd shift and turn toward me. No matter how hard I tried to fight them, the tears still pooled in my eyes, and my throat began to close up as the girl wrapped her lips around Grace's name. But just as the sound left her lips and I prepared to hear my best friend's name, a piercing scream shattered the night instead.

Chapter 6

The sound tore through the quiet like shards of glass exploding at an accident scene. This wasn't the playful shriek of a girl who had been startled; this was the sound of someone completely terrified.

My senses went into overdrive, my body preparing to respond even before my brain could determine what to do. Liam's hand went slack in mine. I heard the swift intake of air as the crowd gasped collectively, and my eyes instantly adjusted to the darkness as the flashlights clattered to the ground, leaving shadows where there once had been light.

And then, chaos.

Everything shifted. Voices muted, colors blurred, and yet my nose filled with a stench so powerful that I felt my lungs burn.

Smoke.

And then the graveyard evaporated and I was watching my best friend burn to death in a collapsing chapel. People moved all around me, just as they had the night of Grace's death, and yet I stood still, my muscles frozen in time, waiting.

"We're leaving."

I felt Liam tug my arm.

"Do not let go of my hand."

I felt my legs bend, my feet begin to move.

"This was a bad idea." Liam swore under his breath as he dragged me through the crowd. A train of first-years held hands parallel with us, their cheeks flushed with excitement. A group of guys darted away from the direction of the crowd, disappearing deeper into the pitch black. Taylor circled on her tiptoes, screaming a name I couldn't make out. It could have been last fall. It could have been that night. She could have been calling Grace.

Someone was in trouble.

I ripped my arm from beneath Liam's grip. His forehead wrinkled. "What are you doing?"

He reached for my arm and tried to move forward with the crowd again. When he realized I wasn't moving with him, he stopped. I watched as his face twisted with emotion—first confusion, then disbelief, and then anger when he realized what I intended to do. But that scream echoed through my ears again and I saw Grace's handwriting in that book. I couldn't walk away. Not tonight.

Liam shook his head, his longish hair making it impossible to see his eyes, but I didn't need to see them to know that they'd turned the stormy gray color that meant he was severely pissed off. "You can't keep doing this. It's not your problem."

I hated making him angry, hated that I was disappointing the guy who had pulled me to the surface and saved me from the overwhelming loneliness and depression I was drowning in after

Grace died. Liam's intentions were good. He had my best interests at heart. Always. But he would never understand what it felt like to watch your best friend die. He would never feel the consuming need for justice. He'd never be haunted by ghosts, real or imagined, looking for peace.

Honestly, I hoped he never would.

I scanned the cemetery again, searching for where the scream had come from.

"*They're* not your problem." Liam was almost shouting now. He jerked his head toward Taylor. Her light eyes shone in the dark and her blond hair practically glowed. Panic radiated off her in waves as she called out. This time I heard the name. Bethany. She was searching for Bethany. "This is probably another one of their stupid pranks. Let's just go."

I watched Taylor for a beat longer. She had friends at her side, cloned girls who wore their hair the same, mimicked her clothes, and attempted to copy the essential eau de Taylor that made her queen bitch of Pemberly Brown. But they never really got it right. They were trying too hard, caring too much, taking themselves too seriously. They all looked pretty freaked out, but Liam was probably right. It was probably just another ridiculous prank pulled by the societies. They were at war. This kind of stuff happened all the time.

I wanted nothing more than to walk away with Liam, to make him happy and forget this entire night had ever happened. If I was the kind of girl who believed in signs or omens, I would have seen all of this as a big, flashing neon sign from the universe telling me to get the hell out of there.

But my gut was telling me that something had just gone very, very wrong. Whoever had screamed had cleared practically the entire school off the grounds in a matter of seconds. I shook my head. It *had* to be a joke, because if it wasn't a joke…

Liam noticed my hesitation and softened. "Come on. It's fine, Kate. Everyone's always messing around on nights like this. We'll get something to eat. Everything is fine. I promise."

My stomach growled at the mention of food. Apparently I'd turned into one of those girls who eats her feelings. But Liam was right. PB students were notorious for this kind of jackassery. I turned back toward Taylor one last time. I could have continued that way, hemming and hawing, looking back and looking forward, but I had to make a choice. Choose the girl who'd sucked me in a few months ago, who, according to Liam, had used me to get what she wanted, or choose the boy who kept trying to pull me forward out of the drama and into that fresh start everyone was always talking about.

"You know what? Food actually sounds good." It might not have been my most convincing performance, but I could almost feel the tension leave Liam's shoulders. It was so easy for him to walk away, so easy for everyone. If only it could be easy for me.

At this point the cemetery had pretty much cleared out, except for Taylor and her minions. Liam pulled me closer, tucking me under his arm as he guided me toward the gates. I settled into his rhythm, enjoying the way he made me feel safe, protected from all of the drama for once. His distinct smell of boy deodorant mixed with whatever laundry detergent his mom used instantly comforted me, offering the illusion of ease. He smelled safe and solid.

As we made our way toward Liam's car, I did my best to focus on the ground in front of my feet instead of the shadowy gravestones surrounding us. The imposing stone monuments that had looked regal on our walk to the ceremony now looked foreboding as they hovered over us in the darkness. It wasn't so much knowing what was buried beneath them that freaked me out, but wondering who or what might be lurking behind them. Ghosts had always scared the crap out of me, but the past few months had taught me to be much more wary of the living.

My eyes picked out a figure bent over a grave. I stopped, straining to see in the darkness, but I didn't say anything. I thought maybe I was the only one who saw it. Another hallucination. But Liam craned his neck and narrowed his eyes as well.

"What the hell?" Liam said, instinctively pulling me behind him.

The person's head was bent, as though in prayer, and the large statue next to the figure cast a shadow over the person's face, making it impossible to discern any features.

"You okay?" Not exactly the best question to ask a person kneeling next to a grave in the dead of the night, but it was the best I could do under pressure.

She lifted her head.

"I'm sorry. It's me. I just…" I recognized her voice right away. It was my old best friend, Maddie.

Chapter 7

The night of the fire last fall, I hadn't just lost Grace. I'd lost Maddie. She'd sworn off food, sworn off the truth, but most of all she'd sworn off me. Too bad secrets never stayed buried and best friends were impossible to ditch.

"Maddie?" I couldn't stop her name from sounding like a question, even though I had no doubt that it was her. "I thought you were at…"

"I'm done with the program." She stepped forward now and caught the dim glow of one of the lights illuminating the path. She looked different than she had two months ago. Her hair was curly again, and even in the dark, I could tell that she had color in her cheeks. And while she was still thin, she looked good. She looked like Maddie. I was torn somewhere between wanting to hug her and wanting to hate her for not being Grace.

"I'm glad you're…" I hesitated, unsure how to finish the sentence. Here? Home? Healthy? There was so much I wanted to say.

I didn't get the chance to finish because a car horn tore through the silence. Seth's red head hung out the driver's side window. "Kate! Liam!" Seth screamed, cupping his hands over his lips. "I've been looking for you guys everywhere! Maddie's back!" His voice cracked on the word "back."

"He doesn't miss a thing, does he?" Liam whispered, which made me smile and eased the tension that filled the frigid air between Maddie and me. She shifted her weight from foot to foot.

"We were just going to get something to eat. You want to come? I mean, if you don't have anything else to do and you're…um, hungry." I couldn't believe that I'd broken out the h-word in front of a recovering anorexic. I couldn't believe I'd even invited her.

I should hate her. I should ignore her. But I couldn't do either of those things, because a long time ago we had been best friends. And maybe if I could figure out how to swallow the lump of anger that seemed to clog my throat whenever I thought about all of the screened phone calls and unreturned emails I'd sent her after Grace died, maybe we could be friends again.

"Sure?" Maddie tugged at the hem of her wool coat. Her eyes were still haunted, and she looked like she'd rather be lost in the graveyard alone than stuck in this awkward conversation. I wanted to say something to make things normal again.

"Awesome," I replied, nodding so hard I might have slipped a disk. Wow. Awesome? Really? That's what you're going with when your ex-best friend comes back from rehab?

"Awesome!" Liam said, with a smirk in my direction. "You guys choose the place and we'll follow. But let's go. I'm starving."

I punched Liam in the arm and caught Maddie smiling a little. She laughed as I rolled my eyes for her benefit. It was a moment like millions of others we'd shared when Grace called her boyfriends dopey nicknames or when my dad insisted on bringing me my lunch on the school bus in his bathrobe. It wasn't much, but it was a start.

As we made our way to Liam's Jeep, I snuck a quick peek back to see if Taylor was still looking for Bethany, but no one was there. Just the black rolling hills dotted with graves and statues that glowed in the moonlight.

The scream that had shattered Obsideo still echoed in my head and I shivered, goose bumps snaking up my spine. Tonight I'd found my best friend, but I couldn't quite shake the feeling that someone else had been lost.

Chapter 8

The Imperial Wok was completely empty except for two women in their mid-fifties wearing matching blue nylon tracksuits and reading romance novels with shirtless men in compromising positions on the covers. The walls were covered with dingy red wallpaper, and the black enameled tables were chipped and sticky with soy sauce. Fortunately, what the restaurant lacked in glitz it made up for in deep-fried cuisine.

The four of us were seated awkwardly in a horseshoe-shaped booth with cracked vinyl cushions spewing foam batting. Liam twirled his straw around in his water glass. Maddie tugged at her sweater while glancing longingly at the exit. I cleared my throat, trying to figure out how to break the ice. The only person completely unfazed by this dinner of epically awkward proportions was, of course, Seth. He hadn't stopped talking since we walked into the restaurant.

"Well, I just want you to be prepared in case some guy runs up to you and tells you his baby isn't breathing and tries to lure you into his van. You remember my friend ConspiracyLuvR? He just sent me an email, and this guy's killed like twenty girls in the past month."

Seth shook his head and frowned, an action that made him look like a very tiny fifty-year-old man. "We all heard the scream tonight. Maybe it wasn't a joke."

I rolled my eyes. We'd already discussed the scream ad nauseam. Maddie said she saw girls messing around behind one of the mausoleums, and Liam said he'd bet all the money he made last month designing band posters that it was some upperclassman screwing with the social underlings of the school. All of that—on top of the fact that this was the fourth or fifth cautionary tale Seth had shared with our table tonight—made it physically impossible for me to bite my tongue.

I took a deep breath, gearing up as Liam shot me his "Go easy on him, tiger" look. "Seth, you know that's just an urban legend, right? I mean, I'm guessing that if some lunatic killed twenty people, the paper probably wouldn't have run that story about the weatherman's new baby on the front page."

I heard a tiny laugh from Maddie's direction and began talking faster. "And why do serial killers always use vans? If I were a serial killer, I'd totally go for a Prius or something. No one expects a serial killer to be environmentally friendly."

"Oh, ha-ha, Kate. Very funny. For your information, serial killers use conversion vans because there aren't any windows. Duh." Seth sounded like he was quoting from Serial Killer 101. Honestly, I wouldn't put it past him.

And then I heard it. Maddie snorted. The sound whooshed me back to eighth grade during one of our sleepovers. Grace had just pulled off one of her legendary "Singers Anonymous" prank phone calls. I could almost smell the fabric softener Mrs. Greene used on the pillowcases that Maddie and I had to bury our faces in to muffle our laughter.

And then I remembered another Maddie. The girl I'd seen outside the computer lab the morning after I'd dyed my hair pink for the first time. Grace had only been dead a couple of months at that point and I was drowning, clawing at Maddie with texts, voice mails, emails, praying that she'd help keep me afloat.

I'd walked toward her that morning wondering if she'd remembered Grace's fifteenth birthday, praying that she'd look at me, that we'd finally be able to talk about the pain of losing our best friend. But she was flanked by Taylor Wright and Beefany Giordano. I saw Beefany gesture wildly at her hair and hiss something at Taylor and Maddie.

And time stopped.

Something about the fact that they were talking about me—my hair, my complete inability to move on and fit in at this miserable private school—turned my legs to stone. There was a brief moment when Maddie didn't respond at all. Her eyes were full of something that looked like an apology, but before I could even register what was happening, she began to laugh. The sound was hard and cruel, so far from a snort that it almost sounded like it had come from an entirely different person. I guess maybe it had.

The combined weight of both of the memories knocked the smile off my face. And all of a sudden I was angry again. I vaguely heard Liam asking if I was okay, but I ignored him and slid out of the booth, heading for the front door. It was all too much. Having Maddie there with me and Seth and Liam. Sitting at our table.

Snorting at our jokes. After all this time, after all she'd done, was it so wrong to think that she didn't deserve us?

The frigid winter air was like a slap on the face. I sat on the curb outside the restaurant, the wet concrete soaking through my still-damp jeans. I rested my head on my knees and took deep breaths, an exercise that would have made good old Dr. Prozac proud. Too bad my parents had finally agreed that I could stop seeing him now that I was "showing signs of reengaging with the world." If they could see me now, they'd have my butt back in his office faster than you could say "Zanax."

I felt a timid hand on my shoulder, too delicate to be Liam, too hesitant to be Seth.

"Kate?" Maddie's voice trembled a little as she bent beside me. "You okay?"

I slowly lifted my head and willed myself to look at her. Her hair was back to a frizzy brown halo of ringlets, and her eyes were warm, a light honey brown, just like when we were little. But her face was now gaunt, and the deep circles under her eyes reminded me that a lot had happened since our days of sleepovers and best-friend necklaces.

"I'm fine. I guess I just needed some air. I..." I wanted to say more, to tell her the truth. That she'd hurt me and I couldn't wrap my head around how to forgive her. But the words wouldn't come.

"I'm supposed to talk about stuff. Part of the program," Maddie said. *That makes two of us*, I thought as I watched her pick old polish from her nails. "I know we can't go back to the way things used to be. At least not right away. But I miss you." She now pulled at a loose string on the sleeve of her sweater, still unable to meet my eyes.

"My parents didn't want me to come back to PB, you know. They thought it might be easier if I had a fresh start. Somewhere new." She looked up and over my shoulder, shook her head, and then finally looked at me. "But I had to come back. I messed up. I have to at least try to make it right." Her eyes were shiny in the light streaming out the restaurant windows.

"I miss you too, but…" I cleared my throat, trying to force the words to come. "I don't know. It's just hard having you back. You remind me…" I let my voice trail off. I didn't need to finish that sentence for Maddie. She knew better than anyone what it was like to try to live your life with a piece of your heart missing.

"I know. But promise me you'll try, okay?" She grabbed my arm and pulled me up off the ground. "We're the only ones who really remember her."

I placed my hands beside me on the cold concrete, about to push myself up from the curb, but stopped short. *Someone has to remember.* The words from the book were eerily similar to Maddie's. As it registered, I cocked my head, completely focused on processing this new information.

But Maddie was already standing, her hand outstretched to help me up, her eyes glassy after mentioning Grace. It must have been a coincidence. A fluke. So I let her take my hand. I let her help me up. And I let her hug me.

Because regardless of who had left me that book, I needed Maddie. She was that last thread, however frayed and weakened, that bound me to Grace. Surely I could figure out a way to make it stronger.

"Now, promise me you aren't gonna stare at me while I eat, okay? Everyone does that now and it totally freaks me out."

"Only if you pretend not to notice my roots." I bowed my head and displayed my inches of brown in their full glory. As much as I loved the pink, maintenance was a bitch.

"Eh." Maddie shrugged her shoulders. "You could pull anything off. Besides, rumor has it pink is the new blond."

We were both laughing as we walked back to our table in the restaurant.

"Girl problems?" Seth asked between mouthfuls of mu shu pork. Mental note: Time to think of a new excuse.

"Something like that." I gave Liam's thigh a quick squeeze as we sat down.

"I saved you a fortune cookie." Liam tossed a cookie onto my plate and cocked his head in Seth's direction. "This guy went to town on the rest of them."

"What? My mom always says it's good luck to eat them first." Seth had a piece of pork stuck between his front teeth.

"Really?" That struck me as a very un–Mrs. Allen opinion.

"Yeah, I totally made that up. But it sounds true, right?" Seth grinned and I pulled on my ear, our agreed-upon code for when he had food stuck in his teeth. He turned ten shades of red and excused himself to the bathroom while I cracked open my fortune cookie and popped a piece of the sweet, papery cookie into my mouth.

But the cookie turned to sandpaper when I recognized Grace's loopy orange handwriting on the tiny slip of paper curling between my fingers.

Another Sister gone while the Brothers walk free.

Chapter 9

A piece of cookie lodged in my throat as the words on the fortune played over and over again in my mind. I managed to choke down some water and get the coughing under control right around the same time Seth returned from the bathroom and threatened to administer the breath of life—again.

"Better?" Liam asked.

Tears streamed down my cheeks, and I was pretty sure my complexion was as pasty as the rice Seth was semi-successfully shoving into his mouth with chopsticks.

"No," I managed to croak. "I…don't feel good." Story of my life.

Liam dug a twenty out of his pocket and threw it on the table, ushering me out of the booth. He apologized for both of us and left Maddie and Seth appearing a little shell-shocked. I was too freaked out to care. I had to get out of there, and I wasn't prepared to explain why. I wasn't sure I'd ever be.

"What's wrong?" Liam asked for the tenth time despite me repeatedly mumbling some lame excuse about a headache. He reached across the dashboard to turn down the volume on the local college radio station.

"I just need to lie down, that's all." I stared out the window, knowing that if Liam saw the look on my face he'd see right through me.

"Look, I saw everything. We need to talk."

A wave of relief washed over me. I didn't have to do this by myself. He'd seen the fortune. He'd help. I began to launch my explanation about the fleece, the book, the fortune, everything. "I don't know where the mess—"

But Liam interrupted me. "But you do know, Kate, that's the whole problem. As far as I'm concerned we got off easy when we made it out of those tunnels alive." His fingers gripped the steering wheel so tightly that his knuckles turned white. "I know how you must feel about Grace, but I see the way you look at those girls and it has to stop. It's too risky. They're dangerous and you already know too much."

The fortune was damp in the palm of my hand, and I did my best to keep the flash of anger out of my voice.

"You have no idea how I feel."

Liam pulled into my driveway and yanked up the parking brake on his Jeep. He shook his head slowly and grabbed my hand.

"I have no idea?" His eyes grew wide, and even in the darkness I could tell they were more gray than greenish-blue. Anger had muddled them once again. "What's done is done. There's nothing you can do to bring her back."

My back stiffened and I reached for the door. There's no way I was going to sit there and listen to Liam pretend he knew what this was like for me. As if he knew how it felt to watch the people who had killed Grace mess around at parties every weekend or how it felt to be tricked, fooled, and made to feel like an idiot.

But Liam knew me too well, and before I could open the door, he'd already grabbed my arm and pulled me close to him.

"It would kill me if something happened to you. You know that, right?"

I nodded and examined the salt crusting around the toes of my riding boots. I knew Liam cared about me and I knew he wanted me safe, but there were some things he would never, ever be able to understand.

His lips brushed against mine, but I pulled away. He had good intentions, but his words still stung. Unfortunately, my move didn't go over well.

A short laugh left his lips, even though none of this was funny, and he shook his head. "I'll see you tomorrow morning, right?"

"Sure. Whatever," I answered at the same time I pulled the handle on the door and stepped down. I knew he was upset, but the tiny slip of paper in my palm meant I had more important things to deal with at the moment. I just needed some time to think. If I could figure out what was going on and pull together some type of plan, Liam would understand eventually. He'd have to.

"I'm sorry," I said before closing the door. Those words were never quite enough, and I could tell by the way he reversed down the driveway that we weren't done discussing any of this. I stood outside until his taillights disappeared down my winding street and then headed into the house.

My dad's voice rang out when I was halfway up the stairs. "Nice try, Kate." He flipped on the hall light, illuminating his disappointed face—a combination of wrinkly forehead mixed with narrowed eyes, his chin lowered slightly.

"Oh, sorry. Did you want to talk?" My dad had majorly cut back his hours at the law firm after my involvement in uncovering the truth this past fall. Apparently, underground sword fights raised a few red flags. Although, I wasn't entirely sure if my dad's recent interest in my life was because he was genuinely worried about me or if my mom had somehow guilted him into it. Probably a combination of both.

"You know you can invite Liam in every once in a while instead of steaming up the windows of his car every night."

He did *not* just say that. I kept walking up the stairs. "Noted."

"Is that Kate?" My mom's voice sounded distant. She was probably already in bed. Her life was made up of work and sleep, rinse and repeat.

"Yes, Beth, she's home," he called up the stairs. Lowering his voice, he said, "Did Mrs. Allen see you two necking?" My dad looked furtively up the stairs as I tried to hide the fact that his use of the word "necking" had triggered my gag reflex. "Your mother will kill me if Mrs. Allen calls again."

I chose to let a fake vomiting noise serve as my response. I was pretty sure my dad mumbled something about respect and figuring out how to breed a culture of fear in our home, but I couldn't be entirely sure, because I'd already slammed the door to my room. Daddy-daughter conversation could wait. The slip of paper burning a hole in my palm, however, could not.

I sat down at my computer and immediately pulled up Amicus. Pemberly Brown would be buzzing about whatever had happened tonight at Obsideo.

I scrolled through some new messages—one from Maddie asking if I had plans for tomorrow, one from my super-annoying lab partner, Ben, and a couple from Seth hypothesizing that perhaps I was allergic to MSG. Apparently, his dad was and always had to run to the bathroom after eating Chinese food. Pretty much TMI defined.

But the last message made my breath catch, my pulse quicken a beat after.

Taylor's name was foreign on my message page. It looked out of place beside Seth's and outright foreboding next to the subject line, which read, "We Need to Talk." I couldn't click fast enough. But when I did and the message expanded, the body of the message was entirely blank except for Taylor's signature—her name typed in pink cursive. A familiar feeling took root at the base of my stomach, wrapping tightly around my insides like ivy. Fear.

Something was wrong, really wrong, if she was sending me emails. I thought of the fortune I'd gotten at the restaurant and couldn't suppress the tiny shiver of déjà vu that tickled the back of my neck. I closed her message and clicked on the All-School tab. The page was littered with mini-conversations about Obsideo, and they all revolved around one event: the scream.

> I heard a first-year was raped.

> I saw someone wearing a mask.

Has anyone talked to Alyssa Jacobs?

Someone told me it was a fourth-year prank.

I heard a gunshot as everyone ran away.

Who's talked to Alistair?

A bunch of us are missing money! Check your purses.

Bethany, message me if you see this.

Most of the messages were the usual combination of nonsense and drama found on Amicus, but the last message stuck out like a scholarship student at the "cool" table. Taylor never posted on All-School. In fact, she almost never posted anything on Amicus at all. As PB's reigning queen bee, she tended to keep her distance from the commoners. While everyone else posted details of what they ate for lunch or random pix of their friends, Taylor had offered nothing except for her plea to Bethany.

I clicked on the link to Bethany's page, and again my head began buzzing. Apparently all of Bethany's friends were looking for her.

B, where are you? Return my texts, you biatch.

If you're hooking up with you-know-who, I'm gonna kick your ass.

Bethany, CALL ME.

Um…is this a joke? Where are you? We've been waiting an hour.

I hope you got a ride home. Almost missed curfew and had to leave. Where were you?

Bethany, hellooooo? You there?

The messages spanned pages, and I felt the fear creep higher up the back of my throat. The scream from Obsideo rang in my ears again. If Bethany really was missing and the scream belonged to her…No. It was all just a misunderstanding. It had to be. Beefany was more than capable of taking care of herself.

My phone buzzed on my desk and I jumped. I had one new message from an unknown number, making my stomach muscles heave.

I closed my eyes for a second. If I opened the message, there would be no turning back. I'd be in. But if my finger slipped and hit Delete, it's not like things would go back to normal. Another text would come, or someone would show up at my house, or I'd start seeing people who weren't really there or getting emails from Grace. For whatever reason, I was involved.

My eyes opened and I clicked the message. I'd deal with whatever this was—for better or for worse.

For worse.

It was a picture of Bethany, her eyes wild, her mouth gagged.

End the Sisterhood, or lose another.

In that instant, a few things became clear as day despite my foggy brain.

Bethany could not take care of herself. What happened to Grace could happen to another girl. I had the power to stop it from happening. And more than anything else, I was going to need help.

Chapter 10

Unlike 99 percent of kids my age, I didn't have to be dragged out of bed that Sunday morning. I'd spent what was left of the night watching the numbers on my clock dissolve into each other, waiting for a new day that I hoped would bring me answers. After packing my bag, I fabricated a class project and managed to score a ride to the library with my dad. There was only one person who would know how to handle a text with a picture of a missing girl and a ransom demand of ending a secret society, and that was Ms. D. (Officer D. if you pissed her off.)

Station 9, the PB library, was my favorite building on campus and like the clock tower was featured as one of Pemberly Brown's most notable landmarks. The gigantic, repurposed Tudor mansion had been built for Pemberly's original headmistress and featured all sorts of hidden passageways and secret nooks. Ivy blanketed the surface, even in the winter months, and the building stood proud at the highest point on campus. Since it was the only building open twenty-four hours a day, a constant stream of kids trickled through the front doors at any given hour. Most were armed with heavy bags stuffed with actual work and what I considered the luxury of being able to tell their parents the truth.

Two years ago, I might have walked in their shoes, but as I waved good-bye to my dad, I realized I'd never again be one of those kids. The kind who could look their parents in the eye and tell them exactly what they were doing, where they were going. Well, at least not until I dealt with the warring societies that seemed determined to destroy my life.

Ms. D. was not at her normal post reading the morning paper, and the quiet was unsettling as I breezed through the door. Normally she'd make a joke without looking up, welcoming me as if she'd been waiting all morning for the moment I'd arrive. Today, the silence just added to the already cavernous pit in the bottom of my stomach. I craned my neck to peer through the hallway back to her personal office and saw Ms. D. rubbing at her eyes, her glasses resting on the desk in front of her. It looked like she'd had just as long a night as me.

A former PB history teacher, Ms. D. was now in charge of campus security. She was what my mom referred to as "big boned," and although she was in her late sixties, she still beat most of the boys on campus in the annual arm-wrestling matches at the end of every school year. She also happened to be an alumna of the Sisterhood. Unfortunately now that Headmaster Sinclair, one of the Brotherhood's more dickish alumni, was running the show at Pemberly Brown, she was demoted to night watchwoman. It was bullshit, obviously. But Ms. D. stuck around to keep an eye on the girls.

In the past, things had been pretty even, with the Sisterhood controlling the tunnels and all of the priceless information in the headquarters while the Brotherhood controlled the school administration via Headmaster Sinclair. But now that the Brotherhood had taken over everything, the balance of power was heavily weighted in the Brotherhood's favor, and if their most recent exploits were any indication, they were getting reckless.

I pushed around the front desk and spilled into her office. "Ms. D., I've got to talk to you. It's happening aga…" The words died on my lips the second I realized we weren't alone.

Ms. D. raked a hand through her closely cropped gray hair and shook her head briskly. "Kate, you know Taylor Wright." The girl standing in front of the huge desk whirled around. The first thing I noticed was that she wasn't perfect. I realize that doesn't sound like groundbreaking information, but it kind of was for Taylor Wright. Taylor was queen bitch of Pemberly Brown, the reigning princess of perfection. Her nails were always manicured in an understated ballet-slipper pink, her lips always glossed, her clothing pristine.

But today Taylor's shirt was rumpled as though it'd been pulled from the bottom of the laundry bin or even slept in. Her white-blond hair appeared tangled, and tiny crescents of purple ringed her bloodshot eyes.

"What the hell…" I said, my brows pulled together, eyes narrowed.

"Before you begin streaming vulgarities, you need to understand that something awful has happened." Taylor cut me off, her soft voice enunciating every syllable like a stage actor. I think that was the most consecutive words she'd ever said to me. The princess of perfection preferred to maintain an icy indifference to her subjects, and that didn't involve a whole lot of small talk.

"Now, now, Taylor. Slow down. There's no reason to drag Kate into this. She's not in the Sisterhood and we can't risk—"

"What risk exactly? The risk of expulsion to save my best friend's life? She was there too that night, Dorothy. She heard Alistair's threat. He said he was going to kill her." Taylor's voice was hysterical, and all at once I realized that I wasn't the only one who'd gotten that picture last night.

I grabbed my phone from my pocket and pulled up the picture. I held the phone out so Taylor and Ms. D. could see it.

"Bethany," I whispered.

Ms. D. sighed and the chair squeaked beneath her as she sank deeper in. Taylor's face lit up. "They sent it to you too. You are already involved. If we confront them together, they will have to listen. They will have to—"

Apparently it was Ms. D.'s turn to interrupt. She lifted her hand to silence Taylor. Remarkably, it worked. In that moment, I had a whole new respect for Ms. D. I mean, I always knew she was a badass, but I had no idea she was capable of controlling *the* Taylor Wright. To be perfectly honest, up until that moment, I never realized Taylor could be controlled.

"Now, if I'm understanding this properly, you two were both on campus after hours participating in the very secret ceremonies that the school board president discussed at Grace's memorial."

Taylor and I nodded mutely.

"And it appears that Bethany was abducted by the Brotherhood at one of these events."

We nodded again.

"As I'm sure you can both imagine, nothing would make the administration of this school happier than making an example out of students who disobey their new rule. And no one would make a better example than the two of you. Kate, you practically have a target tattooed on your forehead." I considered my pink hair and bumpy history, especially with Headmaster Sinclair, and knew she was right.

"And Taylor…" Ms. D. put her glasses back on and turned in her seat. "You are a leader in this school, so in their mind, publicly disciplining you for participating in unsanctioned after-hours activities would pretty much guarantee no student would disobey their rules again." Ms. D. shook her head and turned back to her computer. "The alternative is giving the Brotherhood what they want and dismantling the Sisterhood for good." Ms. D. looked at Taylor and shook her head. "I think we can all agree that this isn't an option."

"But why not? What do you really have to lose?" I couldn't stop the words from tumbling out of my mouth. The only thing Ms. D. and I ever disagreed on was the Sisterhood. She wanted me to join. To become one of the girls who protected the legacy of Sisterhood that the founders of Pemberly had established all those years ago.

After everything with Grace, Taylor had issued a standing invitation for me to join. And most girls would have jumped at the chance. On top of being the most popular girls in school, the

Sisterhood had access to information and a powerful alumnae network that could pull unimaginable strings. They never failed a test because they always had the answers beforehand, and none of them ever got rejected from colleges or clubs because there was always someone to make sure they got in.

Being a Sister gave you complete access to pretty much anything you could ever want.

But none of that mattered. Not when I remembered the role they had played in Grace's death.

"That is never going to happen, Kate. Never." Taylor's voice was barely above a whisper, but somehow her words still managed to scare me a little. When it came to the Sisterhood, Taylor was like a terrorist—willing to die for the cause.

Ms. D. nodded briskly. "You're going to have to let me handle this, girls." She said the words as she typed into the system. "Hmm," she said, "I see they're already one step ahead of us. Bethany has an excused absence all week, supposedly called in by her parents."

"Impossible! Her parents are in Europe. It was forged by the Brotherhood. Obviously." Taylor's voice was steeped in frustration as she rose out of her seat, both hands on the desk for leverage.

"No, no, it's actually better this way. The less the school administration knows about this, the better. I'll have to go directly to the headmaster and tell him what his boys have been up to. Hopefully the security footage from that night will convince him it's in his best interest to force them to cooperate. We'll get her home."

I sagged with relief. Ms. D. had everything under control. I knew she'd know exactly what to do. Unfortunately, Taylor hadn't taken the news quite as well. She looked positively manic.

"Are you crazy? They have stolen my best friend. She has been tied up in a chair or locked in one of their disgusting closets, and you expect me to just sit tight while you negotiate with Sinclair? We have to find her before they make good on their threat." It was the first time I ever remembered not having to strain to hear exactly what she was saying, Taylor's stilted words dominating the small room.

Ms. D. appeared unfazed by Taylor's diatribe. "These are teenage boys we're dealing with here, Taylor. Not serial killers. Certainly accidents have happened in the past." Ms. D. shot me an uneasy look. "But I'm confident they mean Bethany no harm. This is just more of their antics and games. I will figure out a way to get Bethany home safely without you two getting expelled."

An ironic "Amen, sister" was on the tip of my tongue, but I snapped my mouth shut when I saw the look on Taylor's face. Her eyes were bright with unshed tears. Her hands shook and her lower lip quivered. But it was the tremor in her voice that got me. "I have to save her. You do not understand. This is my fault, and I need to save her."

Oh God, I knew that tremor. I'd heard it in my own voice the night I lost Grace. And then I thought of the look on Grace's parents' faces at the memorial. I thought about the way her handwriting had looked in her favorite book, begging to be remembered. I thought about how much she'd loved this stupid jacket I was wearing.

And in that moment, as much as I hated to admit it, I realized that Taylor was right. The Brotherhood had taken another victim, and we had to at least try to find her. This was my first chance to finish what the Brotherhood had started a year and a half ago. My first chance to put things right.

"Thanks for taking care of this, Ms. D. Keep me posted." I kept my tone light and did my best to ignore the shock and grief on Taylor's face as I walked back toward the library.

"Kate, wait," Taylor said, rushing out of Ms. D.'s office after me. I could barely turn around. It's not that we were on bad terms. I had to admit, after everything that had happened with Taylor in the fall, I didn't really hate her anymore. But we lived in two different worlds, and it was easier when we kept our distance.

"You heard Ms. D. She's got it under control." I said the words but didn't believe them for one second.

"It is just that if anyone would understand, it is you."

You don't say.

"Look, Taylor, I'll let you know if I get any more messages. I have to go."

I left her standing outside the library, tears streaming down her cheeks, and felt a quick stab of remorse, but I was already planning my next move. Bethany's house. Stat. Taylor would only slow me down, and something told me time was of the essence.

Chapter 11

As I pulled up Bethany's contact information on Amicus and plugged her address into my phone, a call came in from Liam. The second I saw his name, my stomach dropped. I was supposed to meet him at Jack's Deli for breakfast. Crap. Crap. Crap.

"I'm so sorry," I said without even saying hello. "I have this project and I forgot to call and, oh, Liam, I'm sorry." Liam and I had an unofficial breakfast date every Sunday morning—the kind you know will happen without even having to ask, because he always pulls up in his Jeep at the same time, with the same smile, headed in the same direction. To make matters five million times worse, he had even unofficially reminded me last night. I was the worst.

"I get it. You forgot. It's not a big deal. The streak was bound to be broken."

Burned.

"I officially suck." I pulled the phone away from my ear to catch a quick glimpse of the map and continued down Marchmont. If only Liam knew exactly how much I sucked.

"You're not all bad," Liam said, and I could hear the smile in his voice.

Forgiven.

"Plus, there's always lunch. Are you still on campus? I'll pick you up."

My first reaction was to duck, crouch behind the closest bush, fall to the ground on my belly, and army crawl to cover. I looked around frantically, as if thinking Liam might catch me in my lie and dump me immediately. "Um, I'm actually nowhere near being finished." I scoured my brain for an excuse to end the phone call as soon as humanly possible. "But I'll call you when I'm done, okay?"

Please say okay, please say okay, please say okay.

"Um…okay," Liam agreed in a halting voice, but I knew him well enough to know he didn't really agree at all.

We hung up just as I approached Beef…er, Bethany's front door. It didn't quite feel right referring to her by her nickname when she was actively missing. Once she was safe, maybe. I rang the doorbell even though I felt pretty sure no one would answer. Taylor had said Bethany's parents were out of town, and if Bethany really was missing, I assumed she wouldn't be darting to open the door anytime soon. But still I waited, because I hadn't really planned past ringing the doorbell.

No footsteps. No sounds.

I cupped my hands around my eyes and peered through the glass panes situated at the side of the door. Looked like a normal house. Huge foyer. Stairs to the right. Dining room. Kitchen toward the back. And that's when I noticed the flowers. On the table, a vase was tipped over, the flowers splayed across the wood, a few on the floor within a puddle of water. That was weird. Who left for out of town without picking up a knocked-over vase? Or how would a vase get knocked over in an empty house?

I tensed, the muscles in my arms stiffening. I knocked automatically on the window but got the same response.

Nothing.

I tried the door, which was locked, of course, so I went around to the back of the house, my senses heightened. It occurred to me that I probably shouldn't be there alone, but I reminded myself that I'd only seen a tipped-over vase. It wasn't like I'd seen a puddle of blood. And then one of the back doors came into view. Instead of being locked tight like the others, this one was slightly ajar.

My heart pumped furiously. Fight or flight? I stepped forward. Apparently I was fighting. I pushed the door open wider with my foot. If I kept one foot firmly planted on the back patio, I could escape if I needed to. At least that's what I told myself.

"Hello?" After I said it, I realized maybe that wasn't the smartest thing to do. By calling out, I'd just announced my presence to whoever had left that door open, if they were still there.

Nothing.

I poked my head in, and Bethany's kitchen and family room came into full view. I didn't know how the Giordanos kept their house, but I was pretty sure it didn't normally look like this. Just about every drawer was pulled open, and the contents spilled across granite counters and hardwood floors. Stools along the breakfast bar were overturned, and a few kitchen chairs lay on their side. My hands shook as I pulled the phone from my pocket and called the police. This was not right.

"Nine-one-one, what is the location of your emergency?"

"Um…I'm at 6711 Marchmont in Shaker Heights. I need to report a break-in." My voice shook and I had to crouch to keep from feeling like I was going to pass out. "And a missing person." And God only knew what else. Ms. D. was not going to be happy, but this had gone far enough. I mean, did we really know for sure that the Brotherhood had taken Bethany? Sure, they had a motive to abduct her, but I couldn't imagine why they'd want to trash her house. I was scared.

I heard typing as the dispatcher tracked my location and began a case file. "Do you know if anyone is still in the house?"

"No, I don't think so. But I don't know. I'm kind of freaking out," I whispered. I moved farther away from the door at the thought of someone still being inside.

"Okay, I'm dispatching officers to the house right now. Don't hang up. I need you to keep talking to me until they arrive."

Within minutes I heard sirens, and a wave of relief crashed over me. And then dread because I knew how much explaining I would have to do. Not only to the police, but to my parents and Liam and everyone else. I rushed back around to the front of the house and met my dispatched officer. And I should have known right when I dialed a nine and then a one and then a one exactly who would be sent—because that's just how it works out if you're Kate Lowry. It was Detective Livingston.

The relief I'd felt just seconds before was replaced with frustration.

I found myself thinking back to being in Detective Livingston's office after I'd discovered exactly how Grace had died, after I'd handed him all of the proof about the societies and what they'd done to my friend, after he'd threatened to charge me with assault if I didn't leave the Brotherhood alone.

But this was different. It had to be. He and his partner rushed past me and secured the area. They spent about ten minutes in the house before they came back outside.

"Sit tight," Detective Livingston said, his smile pulled in all the wrong ways. "I just have to call this in and I'll be right with you."

There was absolutely nothing that man could have said that would make me trust him. Or sit tight. I waited a beat and then followed him toward the side of the house, where he whispered into his phone.

"Yeah, looks like someone tore the place up." I edged closer to him, determined to hear every word. "Looks like someone was looking for something…Yeah, uh-huh…It's definitely the same girl. Yup, we've got the other one with us." Wait, the other one? What was he talking about?

He turned back toward the chair where they'd left me sitting in the front yard when they went in the house, clearly looking for me. I prayed he wouldn't turn toward the bushes I was crouching behind. My prayers were answered when he started walking again. "Okay, if you're sure. Thanks, Captain." He ended the call and I scrambled back to the front yard before he caught me eavesdropping.

"It's Kate Lowry, right?" Detective Livingston said, sugar sweet, tucking his phone back in the pocket of his uniform.

"Uh, yeah. It's just that, my…um…friend is missing and there's been all this weird stuff going on, and when I came to look for her, it looked like someone broke in. And I'm scared for her." Tears welled in my eyes as I spoke, which made me want to scream. I just needed him to believe me. I needed him to *do something*.

"Well, it looks like unforced entry. Whoever broke in had a key. Just some minor damage. More like some type of prank than anything else."

Right.

"It's up to you if you want to come down to the station to make an official statement, but we'd have to call your parents." He leaned in close to whisper his next words. His breath was hot in my ear and stank of coffee and the cheap peppermints my great-grandmother used to keep in her purse. "But between you and me, I'd probably just head on home. The captain pulled some strings to stop them from pressing charges against you in the fall, but if you piss him off, those strings are real easy to unpull, if you get my drift."

Yeah, I got the drift all right. Detective Livingston was the Brotherhood's bitch. I thought about requesting a different officer to handle the case. Maybe a woman would listen to me. I mean, if the Brotherhood had people inside at the station, surely the Sisterhood had an alumna or two who'd be willing to help me.

And then I remembered Ms. D. She had specifically warned us about this. How deep did the corruption run? Pretty damn deep. She was right. We were on our own.

"Come on, you look like you could use a ride home. I'll drop you off at the corner of your street so your parents don't see."

As much as I wanted to tell him exactly where he could put his offer for a ride, it was freezing and I was exhausted. I headed to his car without a word, only to find another passenger waiting in the backseat. Taylor. She was the "other one" the detective was referring to. She looked even worse than before, if that was possible. Her hair was pulled back now, and her eyes were rimmed in red as though she'd just finished crying.

The detective opened the door for me, and as soon as he shut it, Taylor launched into an explanation. "I was already at the station when you called," she whispered. "I had one officer convinced this was real. That Bethany needed help. And then he came back with Detective Livingston, and I knew it was all over."

"Don't you guys have someone in the Sisterhood who can help?" I asked, my eyes narrowed at Detective Livingston, who was outside the car, signaling to his partner.

Taylor shook her head. "We did, but when they found out who she was, they fired her. They haven't hired a woman since."

Detective Livingston swung open the front door and gave us a long look in the rearview mirror. "I see you two know each other."

We nodded.

"And I trust we won't be hearing from you two again." He smirked at his partner, who ducked his head as he climbed in the car.

I just looked out the window. They couldn't arrest me for refusing to agree with their asinine statements. Apparently I was right, because when neither of us responded, the police officer just sighed and pulled his car out of the driveway. As we were turning onto Taylor's street, my phone buzzed in my pocket. I pulled it out and saw a text from Taylor.

Help me find her. Please.

I looked up and saw her blue eyes burning with the question: will you help? I turned toward the window and focused on the snow-covered trees as we pulled closer to Taylor's house. Trying to find Bethany on my own was one thing, but teaming up with Taylor was something else entirely. Particularly since she had the power to end this if she really wanted her friend back. All she had to do was dismantle the Sisterhood. The fact that it wasn't even an option made me hate Taylor. I would have done anything to save Grace. Anything.

The officer, true to his word, stopped a few houses away from hers to let her out. Detective Livingston put the car in park and walked around to Taylor's door to let her out.

"Remember our deal."

"I remember." Taylor's voice echoed with defeat, and I thought about that picture of Bethany, her trashed kitchen, her scream at Obsideo. I took my phone out of my pocket and tapped in the words as fast as I could so I wouldn't second-guess myself.

Station 5 2morrow @open. We talk to Alistair.

I thought I would feel the sickness of regret the second I hit Send, but instead I felt something else entirely. I felt strong. I felt powerful. I felt ready to take on the Brotherhood. And for the first time ever, I felt like I might actually win.

Chapter 12

By the time Detective Livingston pulled onto my street, the sun was low in the sky, spreading a golden glow over the towering trees lining the street. My house was dark and silent, no downstairs lights on, no smiling parents making Sunday dinner in the kitchen.

I used the spare key hidden behind a fake rock to slip in the side door and found a note waiting for me on the kitchen counter. My parents had been invited to a last-minute work dinner, and I was supposed to reheat leftovers for dinner. Guess I should have had the cops drop me off in my driveway. At least it would have given Mrs. Allen something to gossip about at step aerobics that week.

I dumped my parka and boots in the middle of the hardwood floor in the kitchen solely to piss my mom off. The thing about my parents was that even though I didn't want them around bugging me and asking me questions, I still sort of wanted them around.

My eyes caught on the chairs lining our counter. They looked exactly like the ones Bethany had at her house, only ours weren't tipped over. A vase of calla lilies sat in the middle of our kitchen table, but all I could see were the broken stems of the flowers heaped on the floor at Bethany's house. That's when I decided it might be a good idea to turn on some lights and set the alarm. You know, just in case.

After the house was blazing and I'd spent ten minutes pushing leftover pad thai around on my plate, I decided I needed a project. Not homework. Something that would take my mind off all of this Bethany crap. Something epic. Something that would somehow reflect the strange combination of fear and excitement that was churning around in my brain.

I caught a glimpse of myself in the mirror that hung next to the kitchen table. At least three inches of brown roots circled my scalp, the most brown I'd seen on my head since Grace died. As much as the roots drove my mom crazy, I could tell she was secretly praying that I'd let the pink go, holding her breath as she delicately suggested making an appointment with a professional to get the ends cleaned up. And for a while I was actually considering her offer.

But that was before.

I threw my dishes in the dishwasher and made my way up to my bathroom. In the tiny closet next to the shower, I pushed aside all of the towels, extra soap, and shampoo that lined the shelf to reveal the rainbow of hair dyes I'd bought following Grace's death.

We were driving home after her funeral and I thought I was going to throw up, so my parents pulled over at the drugstore so I could get some air. The second I'd left the car, my brain switched to autopilot, guiding me along the same route that it had memorized back when Grace, Maddie, and I used to ride our bikes to that store over the summer. The second we were allowed into town by ourselves, fistfuls of baby-sitting money stuffed into nylon wallets and purses, we'd head straight to the candy aisle, giddy with excitement over yet another sugar-fueled sleepover.

But as we got older, we slowly began bypassing the candy and heading straight for the Wet n Wild. Blue nail polish, silver eye shadow, and bubblegum-pink lip gloss quickly replaced Sour Patch Kids and Skittles. But before we'd leave the store, Maddie and I would always find Grace in the same place. She'd be standing in front of the boxes of hair dye, one hand on her hip, glossy, black hair spilling down her back.

"How much would you pay me?" she'd say, holding up a box featuring a platinum-haired goddess and a cheesy slogan about blonds having more fun.

We'd laugh and each hold up a box of our own. I'd choose brown, barely any different than my natural color, and Maddie the standard caramel highlights. But none of us ever had the guts. We were too afraid of our parents and what everyone at school would think. Instead, we'd shove the boxes haphazardly back on the shelf and grab the latest issue of *US Weekly* at the register. By the time we left, we'd have blown hours and all of our money on false promises and empty calories.

But the day of Grace's funeral was different. Instead of just ogling all of the colored dyes, I grabbed one of every color and paid for them. Neither of my parents commented when I returned to the car with a bag, but when I came to the breakfast table with pink hair the next morning they had plenty to say.

Tonight, I prepared my hair for the dye without a second

thought, spreading the bleach from root to tip like icing. After rinsing, I grabbed the first box I saw, ripped into it, and slipped my fingers into the plastic gloves. I rushed to prepare the solution and applied the color frantically, as if the faster I worked, the faster this broken, uneasy feeling would go away. Although I should have known better.

The dye stung my eyes and the tears came involuntarily.

I bent my head over the sink and got to work, only briefly wondering what everyone would think. My parents, Maddie, Seth, Taylor. And Liam. Would they know just by looking at me that something else had happened? Would they understand? But then I thought of Grace and now Bethany. Honestly, I wasn't really sure it mattered.

My fingertips tingled with anticipation as colored water slipped down the drain and my hair darkened. Looking at myself in the mirror with my dark, wet hair, it was impossible to see what the true color was, and for a second, the years slipped away and I looked like the girl I'd been before Grace died. But when I started to blow-dry the strands, they lightened to their new color.

I had felt a satisfying mixture of anger and hope when I'd first combed through the bright pink strands all those months ago, and tonight was no different. But this time I managed to surprise even myself when I swiped the steam off the mirror. Gone was the quick glimpse of the old me, gone was the tired-looking girl with faded pink hair and brown roots.

This girl was bold, powerful.

Icy blue.

Served cold, just like revenge.

> To: GraceLee@pemberlybrown.edu
> Sent: Mon 1/12 3:57 AM
> From: KateLowry@pemberlybrown.edu
> Subject: Change
>
> Grace,
>
> I've gone blue. Something tells me you'd love it. This is one of those nights when I wish I could pick up the phone, touch your name, and see your ridiculous picture as the phone rings. I still call you sometimes, just to pretend. But tonight I can't bring myself to do it. The out-of-service message might kill me.
>
> I wonder if you were here if you'd be dying your hair too. You always said you wanted orange streaks. Remember when you used to say, "Friends don't let friends dye their hair alone"? I wish I still had a friend like that.
>
> I'm getting messages in your handwriting, and they're making me feel crazy, because they can't be real. I know they can't be real. But on some level I wish they were. Maybe that's the craziest part of all.
>
> Do you hate me for helping the Sisterhood? Honestly, I sort of hate myself. But then maybe you understand. Bethany is missing and I see so much of myself in Taylor. I remember exactly how all of this felt, and it's pretty much impossible for me to just sit back and

let them destroy her. It feels like I finally have the chance to make things right, and there's no way I'm going to mess that up again.

So I've been wearing your pearls again. They make me feel strong. Liam doesn't want me involved. He'll never understand. It's not like before. This time I know I can't bring you back. But I might be able to stop it from happening again. I have to at least try. I know you'd want me to at least try.

Chapter 13

After all the drama of the previous day, it was no wonder that when I finally crawled into bed, I fell into the type of sleep where you wake up in the same position you fell asleep in.

When I did wake up, my heart was pounding. I had been in the middle of a dream. Grace and I were on a cliff. We were talking and laughing until Bethany showed up and pushed me off. In retrospect, I guess being startled awake was way better than actually plummeting to my death, but still a crappy way to wake up on a day I already wasn't quite ready to face.

You would have thought she saw the ghost of Grace herself the way my mom gasped when she took in my streaky blue hair. I could handle the fight, the angry words screamed back and forth, my dad's failed attempts to calm everyone down and remind my mom that it was only hair, that it would grow out. But what was harder to swallow was her defeat, when she shook her head slowly, her eyes downcast, the wrinkles around her mouth deeper suddenly. I wasn't immune to the shame of disappointing my parents. I would have given anything to walk downstairs showcasing normal-colored hair like any other girl at Pemberly Brown. But for a reason I couldn't begin to explain, mine had to be blue.

By the time I made it to school, I felt like I'd already run some sort of messed-up marathon. I was approximately ninety-seven minutes late and hesitating at the front entrance. When I finally forced myself to pull the heavy doors open, warm air crashed over me and I was greeted with the familiar eau de PB. It was a mixture of freshly ground coffee, expensive perfume, and the ancient leather that clung to every surface.

Normal high schools reeked of disinfectant, glue, and a noxious combination of every available Axe body spray. But the hallowed halls of Pemberly Brown were never sullied by scents so common. Pemberly Brown smelled like privilege.

The bell rang and I did my best to melt into the crowds of students pouring into the hallways, but as usual I failed miserably. The whispers began almost immediately, like a little spark. I was used to them by now. They rolled right over me, beading on my skin like raindrops on a windshield. Lucky for me, I was whisper resistant. Well, except when it came to one very important person: Liam.

I still felt guilty about missing our breakfast yesterday and avoiding him for the rest of the day so I wouldn't have to tell him what was going on with Bethany and Taylor. I wasn't lying to him. Not exactly. But I was hiding things, and that just felt wrong. Plus I couldn't really fathom how he'd react to my hair color du jour. So I did what I always did when I was faced with conflicting emotions—I hid. Well, not literally, but avoiding someone was easy when you knew exactly where he'd be between every class.

But I could only avoid him for so long. It was lunchtime and I had fifteen minutes before I had to meet Taylor for our little tête à tête with Alistair. I knew Liam would already be in the cafeteria saving me a seat. I could only hope that by the time I actually found him, the whispers would have made their way to him and would have become so diluted that he'd anticipate a bald head with a giant hand flipping the bird tattooed on my scalp. For once, the gross exaggeration of the Pemberly Brown gossip machine might actually work in my favor. I mean, blue hair was nothing compared to *no* hair.

I made my way into the cafeteria and stood in the lunch line weaving through the entrance. I played with the pearls around my neck with one hand as I balanced my lunch tray with the other. The pearls felt like some sort of life preserver keeping me afloat as I paddled out into uncertain waters again.

I loaded my tray with a slice of pizza (protein), an ice cream bar covered in tiny chocolate and vanilla cake crumbs (dairy), and Tater Tots (vegetable) and journeyed across the cafeteria toward our usual table. I spotted Liam huddled with a group of his music-obsessed friends. They were all talking excitedly about something, probably some new jam band they'd all discovered or a bouncer who barely looked at IDs at Tim's, the eighteen-and-over club. I watched him, waiting for him to feel my stare. And then he saw me. He stopped talking, and even from a distance, I could see his eyes flicking back and forth, taking in my new look.

I wasn't patient enough to try to read his mind, so I ignored all of the whispers and all of the looks and marched right up to my boyfriend and kissed him. And not one of those weirdly chaste, closed-mouth kisses. A real, honest-to-goodness, so-hot-it-might-get-me-a-demerit-for-PDA kiss. The moment I felt his lips open to mine, my knees went weak and I leaned even closer to him. But it ended all too soon when he pushed me gently away and gave me a hard look.

I could tell he had a million questions about my hair, where I'd been, and why I was avoiding him, but before he said a word, his lip pulled up on one side. I knew it was only a matter of seconds before the other side followed and we were in full-force cocky, mega-swoon grin territory. He shook his head slowly.

"Blue," he said, lifting a long strand and smoothing it between his fingers.

"Blue," I said, looking up into his ridiculously gorgeous eyes. If I looked closely enough, I could pick out flecks of blue and green and gray and brown. They were my favorite part about him, constantly changing so you never knew what you were going to get.

He moved aside the hair covering my ear and leaned in close, his breath warm against my neck but still able to prick goose bumps along my arms and legs. "Hot."

"I know, right?" Suddenly, I felt like an idiot for avoiding him all morning. Liam didn't need to know why I'd suddenly dyed my hair. I was under no obligation to tell him anything about the Sisterhood or Bethany's disappearance. I could keep us separate. Sacred.

"What the…?" A voice squeaked behind me, stopping me

mid-thought. I pulled away from Liam and spun to face the other boy who, whether I liked to admit it or not, mattered. A lot. "You're blue." Seth's voice squeaked again.

"Pretty much," I said, running my fingers through my hair. My mom always tried to threaten that one of these days the strands would just go on strike and fall out after one too many bad dye jobs. But my hair had never felt softer. And I had to admit I was having a particularly fabulous hair day for my big debut.

Seth narrowed his eyes, looking from me to Liam and back, and I could almost hear the gears churning in his brain. Finally he said, "Cool," and walked off to buy another school lunch.

"Hurry up and eat. I want you to hear this song, but I left my music in the Jeep. We can head out during open period." Liam's arm slid around my waist, and he steered me toward our usual table at the back of the cafeteria.

"Actually, I have to—"

"Holla!" And the moment was interrupted. It was Ben, of course. His hair was intentionally messy, all weird, overly gelled, evenly distributed spikes, and his designer khakis (who knew they even made designer khakis?) still had creases from hanging on the rack at the mall. His shirt was a wrinkled mess, probably the kind that had been painstakingly creased with a special iron by some cracked-out designer, but in reality he looked like he'd slept the night in a sketchy van.

Slung across his body was a bright orange man bag, which he adjusted carefully, flexing his biceps. Two very sad realities about that fugly bag struck me in that moment.

1. It probably cost more than my entire wardrobe.
2. In spite of his nonstop workouts and protein shakes, Ben was still probably small enough to fit inside of it.

"You know what they say, blue is the new pink," I said, predicting the direction of the conversation.

"What? Oh, yeah, I thought I noticed something different about you, but my stylist says orange is really big this season." Apparently I had predicted incorrectly, and omigod, the boy had a stylist. A really, really bad stylist. Ben barely gave my hair a second glance as he patted his man bag and began looking around for someone more important. The boy had a serious case of wandering-eye syndrome. He was constantly searching the vicinity for popular kids he could somehow latch onto or a conversation he could overhear and weasel his way into.

I rolled my eyes and occupied myself with examining his too-tan-for-an-Ohio-winter skin. He must go tanning. Of course he went tanning. His skin matched his bag.

After he'd exhausted his surrounding options, he turned back to me and flashed his Chemistry textbook. "We still on for open? I gots to get a B on this lab."

One of the many annoying things about Ben Montrose was his five-year lag time on teen slang. Maybe his parents forced him to watch too much Disney Channel in Cali when he was young or something. That kind of exposure could really warp a young mind.

I noticed Liam watching us. He winked at me as if to give me permission to talk to another guy, which I completely did not need. Especially considering the other guy was Ben.

And then she was next to me.

"It's 12:05," Taylor hissed. Before turning to her, I noticed a shadow cross over Liam's face when he saw us talking. This was not going to end well. Lame boys were one thing; members of a secret society, completely different.

"Sorry, Ben, this will only take a minute." But Ben just stood there with a strange look of euphoria on his face and immediately went back to not-so-subtly flexing his muscles. That is the impact Taylor Wright had on social-climbing d-bags.

I pulled Taylor by the arm so we were a few feet away. "We still have time. Detention runs for all of open." Alistair basically spent every free period, as well as mornings and afternoons, rotting in detention. No one knew what he did to land himself in there, but it was as constant as the slapping of hands against the station plaques. "And McAdams sleeps on the job. We'll be fine."

"I saw you kissing your boyfriend and I thought you changed your mind. They're saying Bethany's on a yoga retreat, Kate." Taylor's eyes glimmered with unshed tears, and I could see myself in their reflection. I remembered how it felt to hear the rumors and half-truths about Grace after she died.

"Fine, let's just go. McAdams is probably already sleeping."

When I turned back to Ben, he was staring at Taylor with that same dopey expression on his face. Well, at least he wouldn't give me a hard time about ditching.

"Ben, I gotta run. You're on your own."

"Taylor." His voice was barely above a whisper, and he didn't even glance in my direction.

"So, um, you'll finish up the lab, right?"

"Shiny." He lifted his hand in the air.

I decided to take that as a yes. "I totally owe you one."

He didn't bother responding. Now Liam was a different story.

He was by my side within seconds. "What are you doing?" His voice was loud and clear, despite the fact that Taylor was only a few feet away. So much for keeping things separate.

"It's nothing," I whispered, hoping he'd match the level. "I just…I forgot that we sort of have this thing to do during open. It's for Concilium, and if I skip out again, it'll go on my transcript, and… you know." I looked straight past him as the lie left my lips, praying he wouldn't call me out on it. But he didn't say a word. I met his eyes again, but they were focused on my neck. More specifically, on Grace's pearls. Crap.

"You haven't worn those in a while." He lifted them with one finger as though they might burn.

I didn't feel like answering to him. It wasn't his fault that he cared, but it was also none of his business when I chose to wear my dead best friend's jewelry. I slipped into emotional shutdown mode as easily as into a broken-in pair of jeans.

"Guess I'll just talk to you later then?" I couldn't help it. I turned back to Taylor without waiting for a response.

She reached out her hand, a weak smile pulling at her lips, and I realized how much she needed me right now. And although that was hard to understand or even to admit, it felt good. Not good enough to hold hands, though—that was just weird.

But that didn't stop Taylor. She grabbed my hand and yanked

me behind her, her deceptively strong fingers clamped around mine. She dragged me toward the double doors at the entrance to the cafeteria.

When I turned back to look at Liam, he looked stunned, like I'd slapped him across the face.

And that look on his face mattered. But finding Bethany mattered more.

Chapter 14

We traveled the empty hallways to Station 5, PB's official detention room, and I slapped the plaque at the door automatically. *Abyssus abyssum invocate.* "Hell invokes hell." True to Pemberly Brown form, no one could remember where the rituals came from, and hitting the signs marking the twelve stations for good luck came just as automatically as the rest.

I liked to pretend that I was above all of the ridiculous, antiquated crap that my self-obsessed private school passed off as tradition, but today I wasn't in the mood to tempt fate. Taylor ran her fingers over the bronze, and it surprised me that girls like Taylor even bothered. Then again, we could use all the luck we could get.

Or maybe she was just thinking about all the Sisterhood had lost over the past few months. The twelve stations also served as the markers to the underground tunnels the Sisterhood had built when Pemberly and Brown first merged in the '50s. They'd controlled the tunnels for years, using them to navigate the campus after hours from their underground headquarters. But now the Brotherhood had taken over and changed the locks, like some advanced breed of squatters, and by the looks of things, they weren't going anywhere anytime soon.

In the detention room, half the chairs were full of kids sleeping, texting, staring off into space, or even reading. Alistair was one of the sleepers. I shoved Taylor through the doorway. If McAdams was awake, she was the better candidate to do the talking. McAdams and I weren't exactly best buds, since I'd spent my fair share of free periods in detention rotting along with Alistair.

"Kate!" she protested, stumbling into the classroom. "I am… um…sorry, Mr. McAdams?"

I heard an unintelligible grunt from behind the door and assumed it was McAdams. I could see a few kids lift their heads, including Alistair, who glared in Taylor's direction. Psycho much?

"Mrs. Newbury in the office sent me here to get Alistair. I think she has a message for him."

I was very impressed with Taylor's improv. I didn't know she had it in her.

"I hope you have a note, Ms. Wright," McAdams grumbled, more bear than man.

"She was in the middle of her lunch and said to apologize. It will just take a second."

Even though I could only see the back of her head, I could tell she was smiling, which I knew must have been incredibly difficult to pull off at the moment. The girl was good. I also knew she'd hooked McAdams. No one could resist Taylor Wright's smile. Especially not an underpaid widower in his early sixties.

Another gurgle and Alistair was free.

"Thanks for the free pass, T.," he said, pushing past Taylor and into the hallway. "Sorry I've gotta run." Then his eyes landed on me, and he looked back at Taylor and started laughing. "Nice hair, freak show." In terms of greetings, I had to admit that was actually one of Alistair's more friendly salutations. "See ya around."

Wow. I never knew that level of dickery actually existed.

"We got your text," I called out to him as he walked. That stopped him in his tracks just like I knew it would.

"Well, at least we're not beating around the bush anymore. I suppose you're here to tell me that you've disbanded the Sisterhood?"

"Do not be ridiculous," Taylor snapped. "We are here to give you one last chance to let Bethany go. Or else."

Alistair laughed. "Or else what? You'll tell that fat-ass security guard to beat us in an arm-wrestling match? Ooh, scary."

Never in my life have I wanted to punch someone more than in that moment. Alistair Reynolds was the worst kind of asshole. The kind who had never been put in his place. The kind with actual power.

"Let me know when you're ready to turn over your little robes and necklaces, and then we'll talk. But you better hurry, because I heard your friend wasn't feeling too hot this morning, and now that I think of it, I'm not sure anyone remembered to feed her."

Taylor ran up to Alistair and went straight for his face, her hands ready to claw his eyes out. He managed to grab her right hand, but with a broken wrist he couldn't stop her left hand from drawing four lines of blood down the side of his cheek.

He cupped his fingers over the wound and, without a word, turned his head, his eyes like flint.

For one long moment I thought he was going to backhand her. But Taylor just stood up and walked back down the hallway. Her arm bumped mine as she passed me, and I could see the struggle in her face as she tried to hold back tears. I could tell by the look on her face that if she even uttered a single word, the floodgates would open and every emotion she'd bottled up over the past few days would come pouring out all at once. And if Taylor was anything like me, tears would make her feel weak, defeated. She picked up her pace and pushed into the closest girls' bathroom and was gone.

So that went well.

I made my way over to Alistair, who hadn't moved an inch.

"This isn't going to end well. You might as well just tell me where she is."

"You want to know the truth, Lowry? I have no idea where they hid her. It's not my job to know. This whole thing wasn't even my idea." It was strange, but Alistair almost sounded like he was telling the truth.

"You honestly expect me to believe that as president of the Brotherhood you have no idea where they're hiding the girl you're holding for ransom?"

"I don't expect you to believe anything, but you should know that I'm not the president anymore. And like I said, this isn't my plan, so I'm doing my best just to stay the hell out of it."

Alistair turned in the other direction and began walking, his hand still pressed tightly against his cheek. As I watched him go, I saw a piece of notebook paper flutter to the ground.

For a moment I held my breath, sure he'd notice that he'd

dropped it, but he kept walking. The second he rounded the corner, I snatched up the piece of paper. I figured with my luck it would be something stupid, like his Latin homework, but I was wrong.

The piece of notebook paper had clearly been ripped from a journal of some sort. There were cutouts of beautiful girls in bathing suits and words pasted across their faces.

> Too young to die, too old to live.
> Gone. Gone. Gone.
> Tick tock, time's out.

I examined the girls in the pictures, trying to see if any of them looked like Bethany or even Taylor. Maybe this was some kind of hit list the Brotherhood had created? But these girls just looked like a bunch of models randomly snipped from magazines. I carefully folded the paper and slipped it into the pocket of my uniform skirt. And just as I was about to push into the girls' bathroom to check on Taylor, I caught a flash of plaid at the end of the hallway, light spilling in from the huge bay window behind the girl. But there was no mistaking her.

She was taller than Grace, and while their hair color was the same, it hung differently down her back. For a split second, I lost my place. I felt like months had been ripped away from me, that I was back at square one. But this flash of a girl was new. I'd only caught a glimpse, but there was no mistaking her thick hair, her height, her swagger.

It was Bethany.

Chapter 15

The bell rang and kids poured into the hallway, a sea of plaid and khaki. I pushed through, showered with nasty looks and sarcastic laughs. I screamed her name, forcing my legs into action as I turned the corner after her. "Bethany, wait!"

But when I made it to the bay window, the hall was almost clear of students who'd already found their way into classrooms and she was gone.

I collapsed onto the window's wooden ledge and let myself slip back into that place where I'd seen Grace so many times before, the darker place where nothing seemed to matter. Dr. P., my parents, Liam, Seth, so many people counted on me to stay normal. I had promised all of them at one point or another that I'd stay away from the Sisterhood and the Brotherhood, that I'd ignore the ghosts or the hallucinations, whatever you wanted to call the things I saw that weren't really there.

But when I thought of leaving it all behind, ignoring Taylor, forgetting the picture of Bethany and her trashed house, my throat burned. I reached into my pocket and pulled out the paper again, wondering what it all meant. I could help Taylor find Bethany. I could be there for her so she wouldn't have to go through the most terrifying, lonely, heartbreaking moment of her life alone.

Or I could walk away.

My stomach knotted when I noticed the time. Doors were clicking shut, teachers launching into lectures. I was headed into demerit territory. I slid down from the window seat and considered going back for Taylor. But based on her dealings with McAdams, Taylor wasn't quite as prone to demerits. I didn't have that same luxury. And then I heard my name called from down the hall.

For a split second I thought it was Bethany and my entire body clenched, the slip of paper floating to the ground. But it was just Maddie, rushing down the hall toward me, her uniform still hanging off her thin form despite her having put on some weight. I held Grace's pearls and bent to retrieve the paper just as Maddie made it to my side.

"Someone said they saw you out here. Richardson's about to write a demerit, but I told her you needed help. What's going on?" Maddie was out of breath as though her trip down the hall had taken everything out of her.

I tried to discreetly fold the paper. "Um…yeah, I'm fine. I just didn't feel good. I needed to sit down for a second." Maddie's eyes zeroed in on the paper. "But I'm okay now. You can go back to class."

I went to shove the paper back in my pocket, but it was snatched from my hands before I could stop her. "Where the hell did you get that?" she asked.

"I, um…well, I just found it in the hall, and I thought it looked interesting."

"So you have no idea where this came from?" An angry flush colored Maddie's cheeks.

"I…well, yeah. I guess. What is it? Do you recognize it?"

Maddie shook her head and stuffed the paper into her uniform pocket. "No, I don't recognize it. Just looks private, that's all."

She was lying, obviously. And all of a sudden, Maddie's homecoming seemed a little too coincidental. I mean, she magically showed up the same night Bethany disappeared. She hated Bethany almost as much as I did, maybe even more after enduring a year of her endless manipulations and lies while the Sisterhood and Brotherhood covered up what really happened to Grace. And now she was lying to me about some weird coded document Alistair was carrying around with strange phrases covering girls' faces. And, of course, there were the messages blatantly blaming everything on the Brotherhood and written in our dead best friend's handwriting.

It just didn't add up. Or maybe it did. I've always sucked at math.

"You coming?" Maddie asked, headed in the direction of Richardson's classroom. Staring at her for a second longer than was natural, I finally nodded.

I wasn't sure what I wanted more—to find Bethany or to finally get a second chance with my best friend.

I never could have guessed that I'd have to choose between the two.

Chapter 16

I tried to convince myself that it was normal to ride my fugly bike to Maddie's house at 11:00 p.m. I tried to pretend that I was just a concerned friend who wanted to make sure her old bestie was adjusting to life outside of rehab. I was counting on this being a very boring stakeout, but when I saw a tiny dark-haired figure make her way out onto the roof, I knew I was wrong. Or right. Honestly, I wasn't sure which.

Either way, my heart sank as I watched Maddie climb down the trellis on the side of the house. She paused for a minute and dug a piece of paper out of her pocket. It was the same weird page of pictures that Alistair had dropped earlier. I was right. It was some sort of code, or maybe even a map. As I watched her clamber onto her old orange bike, I guessed it was probably the latter. Seeing Maddie on that bike brought back memories of long bike rides to the pool and handlebars sticky with Dairy Queen ice cream. For a second, the frosty January air disappeared, and I could almost smell the charcoal-barbecue, fresh-cut-grass smell of summer.

But there was no time for memories. Maddie had always been

the fastest of all of us, and apparently that hadn't changed over the past few years. I raced off in the direction of PB's campus, keeping a safe distance between us but never losing sight of my old friend.

My heart stopped dead in my chest when I heard a car approach. The engine slowed to an idle, and I fully expected to see some black car with tinted windows stalking me like something out of a movie.

The moment I saw the bright white minivan was the perfect mixture of extreme relief and extreme annoyance. The driver's side window rolled down, and a head of curly red ringlets popped out of the car.

"What the heck are you doing out here?"

"Seth! You're killing me. Ever heard of inside voices?" I hissed, the bike wobbling beneath me as I attempted to steer and talk at the same time.

"But we're outside." He looked genuinely confused as he slurped noisily on what looked like a large chocolate milk shake. "I saw you sneaking around from my treehou…I mean, my observatory, and I thought I'd come keep you company."

I squeezed the brakes on my bike and skidded to a stop, stretching my neck to be sure I still had a visual on Maddie. "Seth, that was over an hour ago. Have you been watching me this entire time?"

"Maybe." Even in the darkness I could see the red flush travel up his cheeks.

I looked down the road again and saw that Maddie had disappeared.

"Crap! I lost her."

"Why are you stalking Maddie anyway? Not that I was like stalking you…I mean, stalking is such a strong word. Watching…

watching is better. Why was I watching you…er, why were you watching Maddie?" The tips of Seth's ears were now so red I thought they might burst into flames.

"Enough!" I sounded harsher than I meant to, but I was nervous about losing Maddie. With my luck she was probably dragging Bethany's lifeless body out of some secret lair or hooking up with Alistair, and I was missing everything. Ugh. "Look, I'm sorry I snapped at you, but this is important. We have to follow Maddie."

"Well, why don't we just offer her a ride?" Seth popped the trunk of the minivan. "I mean, with the storage capacity in this bad boy, I'm sure I could get both of your bikes in here."

"No!" Seth looked taken aback at my response. "I mean, she doesn't know I'm here, and it's kind of a long story. Can we just go? Please?"

"Sure. On one condition. You explain everything on the way." Seth waggled his eyebrows at me, and I knew he wasn't going to move an inch until I agreed and Maddie was already out of sight. Plus it's not like I had to tell him everything, just enough to keep him moving.

"Fine! Fine. You win."

I threw my bike into the back of his car with a clang. I'm pretty sure I saw a couple of screws roll underneath the van, but I'd worry about that later. Right now, my main goal was to follow Maddie.

As Maddie rode toward Pemberly Brown, I told Seth that I was worried about her getting involved with the societies again and that I'd seen her with a weird document I thought was some sort of map. All of which was true, just not the entire truth. We sat at the edge of the parking lot watching Maddie lean her bike up against the side of Station 8, Hayden Auditorium.

"*Acta est fabula, plaudit*," I whispered.

"The play is over, applaud!" Seth translated the station motto for me. "You think she's involved in some sort of undercover performing-arts troupe?"

I couldn't help but smile as I pictured Maddie secretly performing scenes from *Romeo and Juliet* in the dead of the night with other hardcore theater geeks. Unfortunately, I had a feeling that Maddie's late-night journey to campus involved something much more sinister.

We watched as she tried to open the front door. It must have been locked, because she then made her way around the side of the building.

"Come on." I flung open my door and slunk out, running with my head bent to take up as little space as possible until I could take cover in the surrounding trees. Seth did the same, although he fell flat on his face two or three times before we finally stood side by side, huffing and puffing. At first I thought I was seeing things. Maddie looked left and right suspiciously and then finally flipped over a rock, expertly revealing a small keypad. After punching in a code, she flung open a hatch door flush with the ground and hidden by snow-covered moss and then disappeared. I heard Seth gasp.

"She got in." His voice was breathless and at least an octave higher than it normally was. "She's in the tunnels. But how..."

I didn't wait to hear him finish. I was already off and running, desperate to get to the door before it locked again. My fingers dug into the grass, and I felt the wood underneath my fingernails as I pulled as hard as I could. The door swung open a breath before I heard the dull clicking noise of the mechanical lock sliding back into place.

I felt Seth's hot breath on my neck as we peered down into the darkness.

"How do we unlock the tunnels? I mean, they are locked, right? We have to follow her. We can't leave her alone. She'll just repeat all her same mistakes and then stop eating and then go back to skinny-girl rehab and then probably just die. I mean, that's what happens when you stop eating. You just die, right?" I wasn't sure if Seth was panting from physical exertion or because he hadn't stopped to take a single breath while talking.

"Right." I said it mostly to shut him up. "Follow me. But be quiet, okay?"

He nodded and I began climbing down the stairs into the ancient tunnels that ran beneath our school. Seth eased the trapdoor shut and we were thrust into a deep, velvety darkness.

"What happened to the lights?" Seth's whisper bordered on panic. "There used to be lights down here."

I shushed him. We didn't have time to rehash everything that had changed about the tunnels—the new hatch that had seemingly appeared out of nowhere, the lack of flickering sconces, the fact that Maddie knew exactly how to get in. Instead, I held my cell phone out in front of me as a makeshift flashlight, and we made our way slowly down the stairs. My fingers trailed along the rough brick walls as we descended deeper and deeper beneath the earth.

As soon as I felt my foot hit solid ground, I froze, listening. I could barely make out the sound of footsteps to my right.

We padded quietly in the direction of the noise, and I prayed that we'd figure out how to get out of here. The walls of the tunnel seemed to tighten the farther we moved away from the stairs. Claustrophobia wrapped long fingers around my neck and chest, slowly squeezing until the air burst from my mouth in short gasps. My throat began to close, my breath rasping audibly in the stony silence.

I leaned my cheek against the wall, hoping the cold bricks would calm me down or at least put out the fire burning on my cheeks, but it only served to remind me that we were fifty feet underground. Enclosed in a narrow tube of brick-lined concrete. Nothing surrounding us except dirt. The panic tasted like bile on my tongue, and a cry rose up and out of my lungs.

"Shhh!" Seth grabbed my arm, stopping me short. "I think she's going up."

The footsteps did sound different, lighter somehow. When we heard a door creak open and then slam shut, we broke into a run.

"Over here!" I whispered. My phone barely illuminated a staircase to our right.

We ran up the stairs and flung open the door at the top. I had no idea what we were going to find, but I was past the point of sneaking around. I just needed to get the hell out of those tunnels.

But when I heaved my body up and out through the door, I was thrust into darkness so dense and so black that I felt like I'd been blindfolded.

I held my phone out in front of me like a beacon, but it was immediately knocked out of my hand. A scream bubbled up in my throat and I opened my mouth to let it out. I knew I had to stop, but the panic was choking me. And then someone's hand closed roughly over my mouth.

I did the only thing I could think to do. I bit down. Hard. The hiss of pain from behind me brought me grim satisfaction until I realized it had come from Seth. He let out a tiny yelp before yanking me to the ground and prodding me forward to crawl.

I couldn't see two inches in front of my face, but I could tell by the scratched hardwood floors beneath my fingers that we had found our way not only into the auditorium, but onto the stage itself. Tiny gusts of air washing over us indicated movement, and I could tell that there were a lot of people doing the moving. And there was a rhythm to their movement. Calculated somehow. They swarmed like malevolent ghosts, brushing against my arms and legs and cheeks as they moved around us. The only sound was the swish of fabric and the muted padding of bare footsteps.

Seth gripped my hand, prodding me forward until we reached one of the perimeter walls. I was reminded of all the late summer nights when Grace, Maddie, and I would sneak out of Maddie's house, creeping down to the lake at the center of her neighborhood. We would jump off the dock and into the cool, black water, stifling screams and giggles, not knowing which way was down or up, left or right. The blackness was all-encompassing, like a shroud. Exactly like this.

"Now what?" I hissed.

"We have to find Maddie."

A scream, shrill and panicked, bounced off the surrounding walls.

"That's her! We have to do something." Seth tried to yank me up, but I refused to move.

He was right; that was Maddie's voice. I'd recognize it anywhere, had it memorized after hundreds of lame haunted houses and late-night encounters with the Ouija board. But why was she screaming? I thought she was here to meet Alistair. To torture Bethany. The fortune, her weird reaction to Alistair's letter, her convenient return to Pemberly Brown the night Bethany disappeared—all signs pointed to Maddie Greene teaming up with the Brotherhood again to destroy the Sisterhood once and for all.

The robed figures were running now, chanting something low and quiet in rhythm with their steps.

"*Sacrificum. Sacrificum. Sacrificum.*" The chanting grew louder and louder, and the figures moved faster and faster. They were frenzied ghosts, wreaking havoc, shouting, and laughing cruelly as they danced in the darkness.

Seth's hand dug into mine, and I felt thankful not to have to be here alone. I had a friend willing to stay by my side, even through the scary stuff. That one moment seemed to stretch out for hours.

And then without warning a spotlight flipped on.

I blinked, blinded by the glaring light. Black spots blurred my vision, but I heard a door swing open, then peals of laughter and footsteps.

By the time my vision cleared, the black figures had disappeared. Instead there were boys filing in through the double doors and down the aisles, pointing and staring. At first I couldn't see what they were looking at, but then I saw her.

Maddie, pale and alone, stood center stage handcuffed to a chair. She was completely naked except for her babyish polka-dotted underwear and what looked like one of her old training bras. Tears ran down her face as the boys laughed and pointed, but it wasn't until she turned around that I saw that someone had scrawled something across her back in bright red marker.

Proditor.

Traitor.

Chapter 17

Every muscle in my body tensed with rage. I was ashamed that just moments ago I had been ready to accuse Maddie of kidnapping Bethany or even of murder. But seeing her tear-stained cheeks, the way her back hunched over in shame, I knew she could never have hurt Bethany.

Bradley Farrow kneeled in front of Maddie, red marker in hand, adjusting her handcuffs. And despite the blackness still curling in at the edge of my vision, despite Seth's attempt to pull back on my hand, I shot forward.

Because even though she'd lied, screwed me over, and ditched me, she didn't deserve this.

"Get away from her!" It wasn't my voice. I mean, I guess it was, but it didn't sound like me. Honestly it sort of sounded like the voice of the devil from one of those creepy movies about possessed people. At least that's how it sounded in my head. Either way, the sound of the words coming out of my mouth made all the heads in the room turn. Satisfaction settled over me, but there was no time to bask in the afterglow. I had work to do.

I scrambled across the stage and knocked the marker from Bradley's hand. He grabbed my wrist, his golden eyes wide and shocked, but I ignored his silent plea and slammed my elbow into his stomach, smiling when I felt my bone pushing into his flesh. Bradley doubled over, lost his footing, and fell to the floor.

Alistair pulled himself onto the stage, rage twisting his pretty-little-rich-boy features. I knew for a fact he didn't subscribe to that whole "never hit a girl" rule. But it didn't matter. The only thing that mattered right now was Maddie.

She had curled into herself as best she could, attempting to cover her exposed body with her hands bound behind her, which was pretty much impossible. Her head was turned to the left as far as it would go, the tendons in her neck strained to their breaking point. Some of the boys had the decency to look away. Maybe in the light, the prank looked different, more serious. Maybe they regretted what they'd done.

"Who has the key?" I screamed. Seth had rushed beside me now, ripping his jacket off to cover Maddie's naked shoulders. Next, he stripped off his shirt, his skinny, white torso nearly as blinding as the spotlight. He made a valiant effort at securing his T-shirt to Maddie's legs, but it kept falling off and a few snickers drifted up from the crowd.

I shook my head and tossed the shirt back to him. "Let's just get her down from here, okay?"

"On it." He slipped the shirt back on and got to work looking for something that might pick the lock on the cuffs.

Bradley looked down at his feet and I knew he was hiding something. "Give it to me! You piece of…"

Alistair moved forward again, slowly, like he was dealing with a rabid dog. "Relax, Kate. Settle down. It was just a joke." His voice was slippery, patronizing. The carefully modulated words made me foam at the mouth. The only thing worse than having your friend publicly humiliated, naked, and crying was having some asshat tell you to settle down. I could practically feel the sick pleasure of my knee connecting with his groin.

"I swear to God, Kate, I had nothing to do with this." Bradley shook his head adamantly. "They shoved the key and marker in my hands. I swear to God." In that moment, I didn't think; I just jumped down, plowing into Bradley headfirst. He scrambled backward, getting to his feet and holding the key out for me.

"Someone just handed it to me. It was dark. I didn't see…I was going to get her down!" His light brown skin was flawless even in the harsh light, and his eyes were begging for me to believe him.

"It's not like she didn't deserve it," Alistair said, raising his eyebrows and cocking his head. A fresh stream of tears spilled down Maddie's cheeks as Bradley shot him a look. "What?" he said with a shrug.

I took a deep breath. I couldn't beat him here—as much as I wanted to pummel him to a pulp.

Instead, I grabbed the key and threw it to Seth, who dropped it, of course, but then successfully unlocked Maddie. She immediately went down onto all fours, her hands moving around the ground, looking for something until she finally produced a small cloth-covered notebook. It fell open, revealing pages and pages of Maddie's neat cursive handwriting interspersed with pictures of girls with words over their faces.

"My journal. They stole it and told me they'd copy it and send it to everyone in the school if I didn't show up tonight." My arms flew around her in a tight hug, partly for comfort and partly to shield her from the crowd of people. She shoved her head into the nook between my neck and shoulder, her back convulsing as she cried. With nothing more to see, the boys began to file out, until there was just one person left standing in the auditorium.

Liam.

I didn't try to hide my shock at seeing him here. His lips were a straight line, his eyes heavy with disappointment. Disappointment in me? In the guys involved? In himself for being there?

Well, two could play at that game. He was here. Just standing in this room made him an accomplice to this atrocity. What did that say about him? About us?

"I got a text to be here," he said softly. "I didn't know it was this." His arms swept around the room, but his eyes were locked on Maddie.

A knot formed in my throat, and I felt like I was either going to throw up or burst into tears. I wasn't sure which was worse. There was so much to say, but I had no words.

Bradley hovered in the doorway and opened his mouth to say something, but he changed his mind and snapped it shut.

"Are you coming, Kate?" Seth called from the back of the room, holding Maddie up like a rag doll. She still hadn't lifted her head, and I wondered if she ever would again. If this didn't send Maddie spiraling back into whatever anguish she'd recently surfaced from, I didn't know what would.

I rushed toward them just as my phone vibrated in my pocket. Praying that my parents hadn't discovered my absence, I lifted it out and saw six missed calls and one new text. In all my rage, I hadn't even felt it vibrate.

All six calls were from my mom. The text was from an unknown sender.

> The play is over, applaud.

Chapter 18

I couldn't go home. I couldn't even bring myself to answer my phone, but if I screened another call from my parents I had no doubt they'd go all *Hunger Games* on my ass and hunt me down via hovercraft. My bike rattled in the back of Seth's mom's van as we made our way to Maddie's neighborhood. Why weren't his parents calling every five minutes? Mrs. Allen was probably just relieved Seth had an "active social life." She always said the term with implied air quotes, and it never failed to bring to mind senior citizens zipping around on those creepy geriatric scooters.

The truth was that my parents operated on two extremes. They went from obsessed to negligent in the time it took to say "baggage." Apparently tonight they were obsessed. Ever since I'd started seeing Dr. P., books with titles like *Talkin' 2 Your Teen: How 2 Jive with Ur Offspring* littered my parents' nightstands. Brutal.

"I have to call my mom. Don't talk." I turned to Seth as I said it, knowing full well I didn't have to worry about Maddie. She was curled up in the backseat, head tucked into her chest. I clicked on my home number and put the phone to my ear. It didn't even ring once before I heard them pick up.

"Where in the hell have you been?" Not Mom. Dad. Not good.

"Dad, I'm sorry. It was just…it was Maddie and I didn't know what to do and I tried to wake you guys up, but I seriously shook you for like five minutes and she was crying and I had to help her. I sent a text. Didn't you see the text?" I clicked random buttons on my phone, shaking it around in my hands a bit. "I'm looking at it right now." The lies spewed out of my mouth like vomit.

My dad breathed heavily into the phone, and I knew he was shaking his head. I could hear my mom in the background, frantic, asking question after question. Finally, I heard a click as she picked up the extension in the office.

"There is absolutely no excuse for this behavior. I don't care what you think you have to take care of. You are fifteen, Kate, fifteen. We didn't know what happened! And here we tried to call and you didn't even answer your phone!" Her voice broke and I felt my heart pull a little. I never thought they'd find out. They never woke up. My luck had officially run out.

"Mom, it was *Maddie*," I said, knowing the name would remind her of everything that used to be. How could it not? I silently cursed myself for not keeping my hair brown. Brown hair definitely would have helped smooth things over at a time like this. Blue? Not so much. "She needed me." I wished that was the whole story and felt another wave of guilt when I remembered what had really made me set out on my bike tonight. Some friend.

My mom inhaled deeply and exhaled slowly. A yoga breath. Always a good sign. She was pulling herself together. "You may think this behavior is coolio," she paused, letting her lame slang sink in, "but it leaves your dad and me feeling like we've been played."

Well, I guess it was pretty clear that they'd taken advantage of my absence to finally get through "Chapter Five: Gettin' Jiggy with Your Teen When They're Coppin' a 'Tude."

"Where are you, Kate?" my dad cut in. "I'll pick you up."

Seth's headlights swung onto Maddie's long driveway, illuminating what up until the past year had been my second home, sometimes even my only home. "I'm at Maddie's house."

"Hi, Mr. and Mrs. Lowry," Maddie's voice cracked from the backseat. I hadn't realized she was listening. Maddie offered a hesitant smile when I turned around in my seat.

"I'm going to stay with her. I'm sorry I scared you. I was just trying to help my friend." Even my slang-lovin' parents couldn't find fault in that.

I could practically see my mom rubbing at her tired eyes, staring at the clock ticking quietly on the wall. It was late, she was tired, she had to work tomorrow, she didn't have time for this, she wished it wasn't happening. I felt the same way.

"Never again, Kate," was all she said before she clicked the phone off.

I hung up the phone and twisted around in my seat. One look at Maddie and I knew I'd done the right thing. She was shivering, curled into a tiny ball with Seth's jacket laid over her like a blanket. She needed me right now.

"My parents can't know." She said the words so softly they were almost unintelligible.

"Shhhh…don't worry. We'll figure this out."

Seth shot me a doubtful look, and I could see where he was coming from. Smuggling a half-naked Maddie inside the house without Mr. and Mrs. Greene noticing was kind of a tall order. Especially when you considered the fact that she was fresh out of a rehab stint.

I sized Seth up. As usual his khaki pants were pristine, perfectly pressed, not a dirt stain in sight. Seth Allen had to be the only person on the planet who could make it through pitch-black underground tunnels without getting a speck of dirt on his pants, but give the kid a jelly donut, and jam would end up in places jam had absolutely no right to be.

There was one very obvious solution to this problem, but it involved me uttering four inconceivable words to Seth Allen. This was not going to be pretty.

"Take off your pants," I mumbled in Seth's direction.

"*What?*" Seth's voice was shrill as it cracked.

"Your pants. Take them off." I spoke louder now, impatient.

"But…I'll be naked and cold, and I still haven't had the chance to bulk up my legs at the gym so I'm just not sure…"

I cut Seth off with my best "Are you effing kidding me?" face and jerked my head toward Maddie in the backseat.

"Oh, right. I get it. Maddie needs pants and I have them, so I'll just go ahead and, um, well, strip down. Could you…" Seth's cheeks went up in twin flames.

I did my best to hide my smile and averted my eyes while Seth scrambled out of his pants next to me. I peeked and immediately wished I had some eye bleach to remove the image of Seth's blindingly white legs and equally bright tightie-whities. Apparently, looking at Seth Allen in his underwear was exactly like looking directly into the sun during an eclipse—ill advised unless your eyes are properly protected.

I reached over to Seth without looking and snatched his pants away. "Okay, Maddie, let's get you into these and that coat, and your parents won't notice a thing." I climbed over the center console and into the backseat, settling next to Maddie. Her frail shoulders felt more like a child's, and as I helped pull her arms through the sleeves, it felt similar to dressing a baby. Her arms and legs were limp, but her eyes were wide open and aware. Almost like she was having an out-of-body experience. After what she'd been through tonight, that wouldn't surprise me.

I ushered Maddie out of the car and did my best to keep my eyes away from Seth's underoos. "Thanks for everything, Seth." I leaned in to give him a quick kiss on the cheek before jumping out of the car.

To his credit, his eyes stayed focused on Maddie, and my impromptu show of affection didn't even make him blush.

"Just make sure she's okay, all right?" Concern was written all over his face as he watched Maddie swaying in the driveway. She looked like a strong wind would blow her up into the dark night sky.

"You got it, my friend. See ya at school tomorrow."

"Liam picking you guys up?"

I remembered seeing Liam standing in the crowd with the rest of the Brotherhood, just as complicit in Maddie's punishment as the rest of them. "Nah, we're busin' it."

I didn't wait for Seth's inevitable questions about my sudden fondness for school transportation. Instead I grabbed Maddie's elbow and walked her around to the back door. I breathed a sigh of relief when I saw it was still open a crack. Back in the day, we'd relied on that door as our late-night escape route. Only door in the house that didn't trigger the alarm. We used to wonder if the alarm-installation guys had done it on purpose, but tonight I was just happy that once upon a time I'd known Maddie well enough to remember all her tricks.

One look at the shadowed figure in front of me reminded me that I'd probably never know her that well again.

> To: GraceLee@pemberlybrown.edu
> Sent: Tues 1/13 1:02 AM
> From: KateLowry@pemberlybrown.edu
> Subject: Maddie
>
> Grace,
> I'm sitting here on my phone in the dark. Maddie is sleeping next to me, and everything is so messed up. I actually thought Maddie took Bethany. Is that crazy? Have we really changed so much that I could have believed she was capable of something like that? I guess so.
>
> Everything is just so different now. So wrong. She wouldn't be like this if you were still here. I wouldn't be like this. I so badly want everything to go back to normal. You've been gone over a year and this still doesn't feel normal. I wonder if it ever will.

Chapter 19

The next morning I woke up to the rich smell of coffee.

"Extra cream, four packs of sugar. That's still the way you take it, right?" Maddie was already dressed in her uniform. The purple half-moons etched beneath her eyes and the small green journal sitting on her desk provided the only evidence of her traumatic evening.

"I've actually downsized to two sugars. Trying to cut back." The words slipped out before I could even consider their implication, and I turned as red as Seth's hair, which with my new bright blue strands couldn't have worked well. Her features darkened and her shoulders slumped as she crumbled into herself, and I hated myself for trying to keep things light. I needed to be more aware. The constant reminders of how much we'd changed stood out in sharp contrast to the visible reminders here of our past life together.

Maddie's bedroom was no different. Plaid pink and kelly green comforters still graced her twin beds. Her mirror was still crowded with all the same photos of me, Grace, and herself mugging for the camera. Her stuffed animals were piled on the huge window seat overlooking her backyard, just like always.

But the thin, tired-looking girl seemed out of place in this cheerful room, like a guest who had overstayed her welcome. I wracked my brain for something to say, something to make things right. To give this morning some semblance of normalcy.

To avoid the thick silence, I leapt off the bed and made a beeline for the loose floorboard in Maddie's closet. Back in the day, we'd hidden our candy stash underneath so we'd have fuel for our late-night prank calls during the endless nights of our sleepovers. I had no idea if anything was still in there, but it was worth a shot. I tore up the floorboard and groped around in the cavern. A surge of happiness bubbled in my chest when my fingers met the crinkle of plastic. Twizzlers. I grabbed a Twizzler and almost cracked a tooth biting off the stale ends. I stuck my makeshift red straw into my coffee and took a long sip and was rewarded with a dazzling smile from Maddie.

"Eww. That is so gross." But she was laughing as she said it.

"Yup, some things never change."

Maddie's mom shouted for her to come downstairs. I guessed Maddie had a little explaining to do after our late-night entrance. They had been waiting for us when we opened the door. Just as her dad started yelling, they saw me and stopped. I'm not sure if it was my blue hair or my mere presence, a ghost from their daughter's haunted past, that was enough to silence a room. Either way, they stopped yelling and sent us both to bed, saying they'd hash everything out in the morning.

While Maddie muddled through some type of explanation, I helped myself to one of her uniforms, swirled around some mouthwash, and declared myself ready to face the world, or at least the bus stop at the end of Maddie's street.

By the time I got downstairs, Mrs. Greene was beaming at me.

"Oh, Kate! Maddie explained everything. I hope you're okay. I'm so glad you called Maddie last night in your…er…time of need. You know we'll always be here for you, honey. Whatever you need."

"Um, yeah. Sure." Mrs. Greene was using the voice people reserved for mental patients and death-row criminals, but as long as we weren't in trouble, I figured I'd just play along with whatever outrageous lie Maddie had conjured up.

"Oops, think I hear the bus! Bye, Mom!" Maddie plastered on a fake smile, kissed her mom on the cheek, and yanked me out of the house before I could say anything stupid. Girl after my own heart.

The bus arrived at the stop at the same time we did, and we both fell into the closest empty seat. Maddie stared out the window, the mask of her false happiness slipping off more the farther we drove from her house.

"Are you okay?" I knew that was the single most annoying thing you could ask a person who was so obviously not okay, but I couldn't seem to help myself. I had to know what she was thinking. I guess I just wanted to be prepared for what came next. If Maddie was going to fall apart, someone was going to have to pick up the pieces, and it sure as hell wasn't going to be Taylor or Bethany this time.

"I'm fine." She answered immediately, like people do in church when they've been brainwashed.

I elbowed her in the side, a gesture so achingly familiar, yet so foreign. Instead of meeting the soft flesh of her abdomen the way it used to, my elbow crunched right into bone and left me wondering if I'd cracked one of her ribs.

"No, really. I'm fine. Last night was awful, but honestly, I'm sort of glad that it's over. I knew they'd do something to me when I came back. It's actually easier now that I have it behind me. I can move on, you know? Start fresh. They talk a lot about starting fresh at…well, you know what I mean."

For the first time since Grace died, she actually sounded like the Maddie I used to know. And now that I looked at her more carefully, I saw that behind the tired eyes there was a spark. She really was going to be okay.

"I just hope that we can start fresh too. I've missed you, Kate. I can't even tell you how much. I'm so sorry for not trusting you. When I saw you with that page from my journal, I thought…well, I'm sure you can guess what I thought."

My eyes watered and I had to look away for a minute, because I'd done the same thing. I thought she'd come back for revenge, but really she just came back to make amends.

"But if we're going to be friends again, I need to know that you're starting fresh too. I don't want to talk about anything that's happened or hang out with anyone in the societies. I'm just not ready to talk about her or them or any of it."

My mind flashed to all of the pictures of Grace around Maddie's room. It seemed so strange to me that she could live with the pictures but couldn't even bring herself to say Grace's name. But if

I'd learned one thing over the past couple years it was that different people deal with things in different ways, and I was in no position to judge Maddie. But I wasn't ready to make any promises either.

An image of Taylor flashed in my mind, followed quickly by one of Bethany standing with Alistair and Bradley the night of Obsideo.

"How about we both just do our best, okay? I think that's all anyone can ask of us right now." It wasn't a lie, but it certainly wasn't the truth either. I was getting far too comfortable dealing in that shadowy area between the two.

"Deal." A hint of a smile, a real one this time, played on her lips as we shuffled off the bus and into the world of Pemberly Brown. We linked arms and walked into school together, just the way we did on our first day at the Academy all those years ago.

I slapped the bronze plaque that marked Station 1, the main entrance, but Maddie ignored it completely. I hoped someday I'd be brave enough to do the same, but I wasn't ready to test my luck just yet.

The loudspeaker crackled and beeped overhead, and I heard the school secretary's voice screech over the din of slamming locker doors and muffled conversations.

"Kate Lowry, report to the headmaster's office immediately. I repeat, Kate Lowry, report to Headmaster Sinclair's office immediately."

Maddie dropped her arm from mine and gave me a long, sad look. So much for my promise.

"Guess I should wish you good luck."

"Yeah, I'm gonna need it."

"Nah, something tells me you'll be fine." But she took a few steps backward, already putting distance between us. "Well, when you're ready, I'll be here," she said softly.

I nodded in response and wove my way to the headmaster's office. Sometimes it was better being alone…easier. Ever since Grace died I'd spent almost every day trying to believe just that, and I'd almost convinced myself.

Almost.

Chapter 20

Headmaster Sinclair was pretty much the embodiment of everything that was wrong with Pemberly Brown: a sexist little man with an ego bigger than all his students' trust funds combined. Pretty much your typical corrupt, power-hungry Brotherhood alumnus. Lucky for him, the Brotherhood's powerful network meant he'd always have a job at Pemberly Brown, one of the many perks of being a member. And lucky me, I'd managed to earn myself a special spot on his shit list. We had done our best to avoid each other in the months following the near destruction of the societies that ruled Pemberly Brown, like some sort of unspoken treaty.

Unfortunately, I hadn't been keeping up my end of the bargain lately, and I was guessing that Headmaster Sinclair wasn't too pleased about that. Or maybe he'd gotten wind that Ms. D. was trying to help us locate Bethany. Either way, I was pretty sure this wasn't an office visit informing me that I was on track to be valedictorian of my class.

He tapped a pen on his desk rhythmically, his back facing me as I walked through the door.

"Shut the door behind you."

I was pretty sure that was illegal, seeing that I was an underage girl, but I did as I was told. I had at least ten pounds on Sinclair, and he seemed like the kind of guy who only threw punches when he was sure he could win the fight.

"Kate Lowry!" At this he spun around in his seat for added drama, a wicked smile on his face. I swear to God, if he'd had a mustache, he would have been twirling it deviously. His beady eyes flickered over the length of me, evaluating my uniform for any breach of the dress code. Luckily Maddie's skirt fell just below my knee, and the shirt was a little wrinkled but perfectly acceptable. "We were rushing this morning, weren't we?"

My stomach instantly reacted to his mention of an "us," and I thought I might lose my breakfast. "No, actually, I took the bus." A silence lingered then and I wondered when he was going to spit out why I got called down here in the first place.

Reading my mind he said, "So, Kate, would you like to tell us why we have the pleasure of this meeting?" He rocked in his chair and stretched his arms behind his head, sizing me up.

It was the oldest trick in the book, and I wasn't about to fall for listing fifteen rules I'd supposedly broken to get sent to the headmaster. I hated when adults assumed I was a jackass. Two could play at this game.

"This has to do with Bethany Giordano, doesn't it?"

I had to hand it to him. Sinclair did an extra-good job of looking flustered. Either Ms. D. hadn't started negotiations yet, or his acting was coming along. He must have taken a community course or something. He'd make a perfect Claudius.

"I suppose it does." He narrowed his eyes and placed his elbows on the desk, folding his hands together Dr. Evil–style.

My pulse quickened and I wished I'd had the foresight to record our conversation. I had no idea what would come out of his mouth, but I was willing to bet Grace's pearls it'd be valuable.

"Ms. Richardson approached me the other day with some concerns. She expressed that you were wandering the halls during class. The entire staff is very well versed in your 'psychological accommodations,' Ms. Lowry, but cutting class is unacceptable."

I opened my mouth to respond but was cut off.

"I also want to take this time to remind you about the newest section of our handbook." He lifted a sheet of paper with a highlighted section of text. "Students caught participating in any type of secret, exclusive social club outside Pemberly Brown's affiliated groups will be punished and possibly expelled."

"But—"

"I can only assume that the business you were attending to as you cut class was 'secret-society' related, and this behavior will not be tolerated."

"I…" My cheeks were flaming, the anger coursing through my bloodstream like acid.

"There is nothing for you to say. It's very clear to me and your teachers how you operate, and you need to know you're being watched. You're on thin ice, young lady."

So much for school being a safe place. Not that I ever thought it was.

"Now if you'll excuse me…" He raised his thin eyebrows as

though *I* was the one who'd interrupted *his* morning. He shuffled papers on his desk, an important-looking set of blueprints revealed for a flash. It made me wonder what Sinclair even did all day. Threaten girls? Move papers around on his desk? Examine blueprints for some shady lair he was building?

As much as I felt defeated, as much as I wanted to hunch my shoulders and slink out of his office with my head hung low, I knew better than that. As my father was fond of reminding me, "Never let 'em see you sweat." I'd always thought it sounded more like an ad for deodorant than a source of inspiration, but in this moment the whole concept sort of crystallized for me.

I threw my head back, straightened my shoulders, and started for the door. And that's when I saw it. A creamy piece of stationery with a red seal and what looked like a B written in crisp calligraphy on the front. Without breaking my stride, I stepped on the paper and dragged it out of the office under my shoe in what I hoped looked like some type of dance move.

Lucky for me, I felt fairly confident that dancing my way out the door trumped that whole never-letting-'em see-me-sweat BS.

Chapter 21

The second I emerged into the bustling hallway, I bent down and picked up the envelope beneath my shoe. It was thick and textured. Expensive. I couldn't help but think that if the societies really wanted to fly under the radar, they'd use cheap printer paper for their communications like the rest of the world.

My fingers grazed Bethany's name written in small, square letters, then the embossed seal of the Brotherhood stamped in the corner. I lifted the flap carefully and a knot formed in my stomach. I wasn't sure if I was ready to know the truth about Bethany. What if there'd been another horrible accident? What if she was dead? How would I tell Taylor? How would we get…

All the questions racing through my brain were extinguished when something hard and expensive-smelling crashed right into me—Bradley Farrow's chest. The envelope fell to the floor, and I dove to grab it before Bradley could. When my fingers curled around the card stock, I breathed a short sigh of relief and shoved it under my shirt as nonchalantly as I could manage.

As soon as I lifted my chin, I met Bradley's golden eyes, which were focused a few inches lower than my own eyes, right down the gap in my uniform shirt. Apparently I'd popped a button in my haste to save the evidence. I felt a flush of warmth begin in my cheeks and move its way down to my chest. Oh, great…my boobs were blushing.

I stood up without adjusting my shirt. There was absolutely no way that I was going to give him the satisfaction of watching me scramble to cover myself up. And, hey, at least I wasn't wearing one of my tired-looking sports bras, so I could take some comfort in the fact that the girls were looking their best.

"No, really, I'm fine. No reason to help me up."

"Uh, last I checked you were standing in the middle of the hallway. Must have been a pretty interesting letter you were reading."

"Yeah, well, whatever. I've gotta get to class." So much for my razor-sharp wit. I decided to cut my losses and get the hell out of Dodge. Besides, I'd have to hurry to the bathroom if I wanted to read whatever was on that stationery before first period started.

"Wait." Bradley fell into step next to me. "I've been meaning to talk to you about last night." His voice dropped to a whisper, and a pained expression momentarily darkened his handsome features. "I know what you must think of me, but it wasn't what it seemed. I just showed up there with the rest of the guys. I have nothing against you or Maddie or anyone. I was just there."

"Hey, I have an idea," I said as Bradley's face brightened. "Why don't we sit down and talk about all of this?"

"Really? Because I'd love the chance to explain everything…" He stopped in front of one of the windows, and the winter sun bounced in his eyes, making them look like liquid gold.

Yeah, yeah, he was hot, but he was also a terrible liar. I didn't have time for this crap. Not today, not ever.

"Right, so tell me where Bethany is and I'm all yours."

Bradley's face went completely blank.

"Right. That's what I figured."

I ducked into the closest bathroom, ignoring Bradley's protests, and slipped past the row of girls jockeying for mirror space and obsessively applying lip gloss. I didn't dare retrieve the envelope from beneath my shirt until I was safely in the handicap stall.

A quick prayer came automatically as I lifted out the thick paper inside. Careful notes filled the page. I recognized the handwriting immediately from the countless labs we'd been forced to complete together. Ben Montrose. He'd written a series of times on the page, followed by what I assumed were Bethany's actions.

4:27—Arrived
4:42—First drink
4:57—Talks to Taylor and Co.

All leading up to the chilling scream. After that the notes stopped.

A picture of Bethany had been included in the envelope, a bright red cup in her hand. Her eyes glowed white, like a person possessed or an animal darting out of the woods. Clearly the picture had been taken at night. Obsideo.

But why the hell was my rocks-for-brains lab partner stalking Bethany? And more importantly, did this mean he'd know where they'd taken her? As usual, more information led to more questions.

"Find me."

A voice called from somewhere in the bathroom. The girl's voice was deep and raspy, like she'd smoked cigarette after cigarette the night before.

I scrambled to free myself from the bathroom stall just in time to see the door to the hallway swinging shut. Pushing through, I caught a tall, dark-haired figure turning the corner in the hallway ahead. It was Bethany; it had to be. I dropped my bag on the ground and raced after her.

Chapter 22

In. Out. In. Out.

All other sounds melted away except the whooshing of air in and out of my lungs. I pictured it spilling in like smoke, filling every crevice, and then pouring out again and dissipating. On repeat. The hallway narrowed as I ran, closing in against me, but I fought off the claustrophobia by hanging on to the image of Bethany. If I could only imagine her perfectly—her thick, black hair and olive skin—maybe I'd swing around the corner and bump into *her* this time. She'd act pissed and I'd pretend to be sorry, and this whole mess would be over as quickly as it had started. Like dodging a bullet.

My fingers trailed along the wall as I turned, the hallway opening up as the last few students slipped into their first-period classes with the bell. But none of them was Bethany. Instead, Ms. D. walked the hallway, shooing students out of bathrooms and away from lockers.

"Ms. D.," I said, jogging to close the space between us. "Did you see her?" I whispered, my eyes darting. It wasn't until after the words left my mouth that I regretted them. I shouldn't have admitted seeing anyone, not even to Ms. D. It'd only make things worse. The hallucinations, ghosts—whatever you wanted to call them—were back, and I had to figure out a way to deal with them that didn't involve tearing around the hallways of my school like some kind of lunatic. Preferably without having to take the awful pink pills that made me feel like I was sleepwalking through my life.

Ms. D. glanced at her watch, wrinkles lining the space between her brows. "First period already started, honey. Not sure who you're looking for, but it needs to wait."

I was already in, so I might as well dig deeper. Maybe I wasn't imagining anything. Maybe she was real. "It was Bethany. I swear I saw her running through the hallways."

Ms. D.'s face softened then, which made me regret not rushing to get to first period like everyone else. Why was I constantly chasing ghosts? What was wrong with me?

"Kate, I know you and Taylor are worried, but there's no reason you all need to be involved. Let me handle this."

I rubbed my tired eyes and wanted so badly to believe her, to let her take over. The radio at her waist crackled to life and she patted my shoulder, called away to some other emergency with the promise that she'd fix everything. I trusted Ms. D., but deep down I knew she was no match for Headmaster Sinclair and the Brotherhood. Turns out trusting and believing are two very different things.

My phone buzzed from my pocket, making me jump about a mile. Normally I kept it tucked in the front of my bag during school hours to avoid demerits, but I must have forgotten. I hesitated before sliding my fingers across the screen to read the incoming text. What if it was another picture of Bethany? What if they had another girl now? What if I was next?

But instead of an unknown number, Liam's picture popped up on my screen.

>We need to talk.

I deleted it almost instantly. He'd been there last night with all of the Brothers. However it had happened, he'd participated in Maddie's humiliation. And on top of all that, he was probably still pissed at me for ditching him during open period yesterday. So he'd spent all day avoiding me, and then when I caught him red-handed at a Brotherhood-sanctioned event, he suddenly wanted to talk? No thanks.

Defeated, I made my way back to my bag, only to find Taylor Wright standing there imperiously, reading the letter I'd stolen from the headmaster's office.

"When were you planning on telling me about this?" She spoke with quiet restraint, but the anger in her tone had the same impact as if she'd shouted the words at me.

"I just found it, and then I was in the bathroom and this girl, I'm sure it was..." I paused mid-sentence to consider my words carefully. The reality was that I had a history of seeing people that others didn't always seem to see. Dr. Prozac claimed it was an emotional response triggered by stressful situations, but I wasn't so sure. I mean, could an emotional response really run through gardens or the halls of our ancient school? Either way, Ms. D. already thought I was insane. There was absolutely no way I was going to let Taylor join the party. Better to focus on the concrete stuff.

"I found it in the headmaster's office this morning." Thank God. I got the words out of my mouth before I could say anything stupid.

"But what does it mean? Who wrote it? Do you think the headmaster is involved somehow?" Taylor quietly fired questions at me, her blue eyes trained carefully on my face, watching for the faintest flicker of a lie.

"I think that's Ben Montrose's handwriting. At least, I'm pretty sure."

"But he is not a Brother. Why would he be stalking Bethany at Obsideo?" Taylor wrung her hands and I noticed her signature ballet-slipper-pink polish, not a chip or smudge in sight. My own nails were bitten down, each painted a different color weeks ago but now chipped almost completely off. I realized then how much fingernails could say without words. Even during the most stressful days, Taylor's could remain intact, almost perfect. Mine were a hot mess. There was a metaphor in there somewhere.

"I have no idea. But that's exactly what we're gonna find out," I said, bending to grab my bag.

• • •

After a lengthy strategy session that took the better part of first and second periods, Taylor and I decided that rather than risk confronting Ben at school, it would be smarter to go to his house. I'd go in alone with the excuse that I had some Chemistry questions, and Taylor would wait outside as backup. Despite my deceptively tough exterior, my stomach had flip-flopped when the bell signaled the end of second period, or more specifically the end of the second class I'd cut.

When Taylor whipped out a very organized folder of crisp, signed late passes, I caught a glimpse of just what the societies had to offer and exactly how deep their connections ran at Pemberly Brown. And they weren't even operating on all four cylinders anymore. I couldn't imagine what life must have been like for the Sisterhood when they controlled the tunnels and their posh headquarters held pretty much every vital piece of information Pemberly Brown had to offer. No doubt membership had its perks.

After school, we drove to Taylor's house in her convertible, and I was mentally brainstorming excuses for my parents as to why I'd need another entire evening out. Ignoring six phone calls the night before hadn't done much for the trusting parent-daughter relationship we were all trying so hard to fake. I pressed "Mom Work" on my phone at least five times, hanging up each time before it started ringing. It was going to take more than a flimsy excuse about group projects to convince her that I should be allowed to go out on a school night.

"Here," Taylor said, after turning into an empty parking lot. She plucked the phone from my hand and pressed "Mom Work," letting the phone actually ring this time.

Butterflies fluttered in my stomach.

"Hi, Mrs. Lowry? No, no, she is fine. This is Taylor Wright, Kate's classmate at Pemberly Brown. I am the president of Concilium." She tapped her perfect nails on the leather steering wheel. If I knew my mom like I thought I knew my mom, she was thinking, "*That*

Taylor Wright," right about now. Even parents weren't immune to Taylor's far-reaching charms.

"I am not sure if Kate warned you, but tonight is the last night of our spring bake-sale fund-raising preparation. We have at least twenty more signs to make, which Kate is helping out with. I could sure use her help tonight, and my parents said it would be fine if she stayed for dinner." She paused, rolling her eyes. "She is sitting right next to me."

"Hi, Mom!" I called, unable to keep the smile from my voice. The girl was *really* good.

"We have pizzas for dinner, and we are going to make a night out of it!" Taylor raised her blond eyebrows at me. "Yes, yes. No problem at all. Do not even worry. I will drop her off when we are finished." She laughed at something obviously lame my mom said and ended the conversation. And that was that.

But parental consent did absolutely nothing for my nerves. The reality of confronting Ben was starting to hit me, and by the time we pulled into Taylor's driveway, my stomach was roiling with tension. Her house was set deep in the woods, down a winding driveway off the road. Even though we'd gone to the same school for the past ten years, the only part of her house I'd ever seen was the mailbox. I sat up a little straighter, straining to see out the windows as we carefully maneuvered through the snow and up the driveway. Most of the kids at Pemberly Brown lived in pretty big houses, but Taylor's was rumored to be obscene.

As it turns out, "obscene" was the perfect word for it. The Wrights' home was a modern monstrosity on a street where the money was so old that even the nannies wore Chanel No. 5. The entire exterior was constructed primarily of glass windows, and what wasn't a window was cream stucco. We walked inside and Taylor spun around, shutting the doors behind her and locking them with a click.

A wave of uneasiness settled over me as we shut out the world. The thing about locks was that even though you thought you were locking the bad guys out, there was always the possibility that you might be locking one in. "Um, I thought we were going to Ben's house?"

"I thought we decided to surprise him," Taylor said, pulling a bottle of water from her fridge and offering me one.

I shook my head. "Well, yeah…that's the idea."

"I have it on good authority that his parents will be home until they will be called out for an urgent meeting at the Shaker Nature Center at eight. Would you believe that someone took a chainsaw to the center's prized rose garden?"

"But how…"

Taylor put up a hand to silence my question, and she was right. Did I really want to know how she'd managed to destroy one of our city's most revered landmarks? Yet another uneasy reminder of the power the Sisterhood still wielded, not only at our school but also in our community.

The floor-to-ceiling windows might have seemed impressive from the outside, the afternoon sun making them sparkle like enormous diamonds, but from inside they were sort of terrifying. The back of my neck pricked with the sensation that someone was following our journey through the bright white hallway into the even brighter kitchen. The house was bathed in sunlight so bright that I reached my forearm up to shield my eyes.

The kitchen was all hard edges and clean lines. There weren't any nooks and crannies or hiding spots. My stomach unclenched a little at the idea that there weren't very many places for someone to hide.

"I can't believe you live here." The words popped out of my mouth before I could stop them. "I mean, I pictured you living in a typical mansion, you know? Bricks, ivy, traditional."

Taylor laughed a little. "Tell me about it. The neighbors tried to sue my father when he tore down the house that used to be here." Her phone looked out of place on the pristine, white marble countertop. "His company was going green, and he insisted that we live in a house that reflected their priorities. Mother refused to leave the neighborhood, so…" She shrugged.

"Are you here alone a lot?" The thought of spending the night by myself in this glass monstrosity made me shiver.

"It depends. When Tinsley and Teagan are home on break, it's not so bad. And we have Dee here sometimes." She pushed a series of buttons on a computer monitor, and I heard the shrill beep of an alarm turning on. "I still miss our old house, though."

Taylor led me through the foyer, her ballet-slipper flats barely making a sound on the bamboo floors while the heels of my riding boots clicked and left a trail of glimmering footprints in their wake.

"Oh, crap. I should have taken my shoes off."

Taylor waved a hand and kept walking. "Never mind. Dee will take care of it tomorrow."

As Taylor led me through the maze of white, I kept catching my reflection in the windows that lined the walls. My blue hair was pulled back into a knot on top of my head, but tiny hairs had escaped during the chaos of the day and now curled around my hairline. I kept doing double takes because the blue-haired girl walking next to the Homecoming queen didn't look like me. In fact, every time I caught a look at myself I felt like turning on my heel and heading back home to the safety of my medium-sized, non-glass house, complete with my ginger neighbor in the tree house outside.

Taylor led me into her bedroom. It was huge, but I was prepared for huge. What I wasn't prepared for was everything else. I guess I'd always assumed that the high priestess of popularity would live in a frilly pink kingdom, complete with a canopy bed and ruffled pink drapes, but I was *so* wrong. Nothing new there.

"Wow." It was the only word I could manage with my jaw hanging so low it practically touched my chest.

Taylor laughed. It was pretty and tinkling and sounded strange coming from her mouth. I realized that I'd never heard her laugh before. "Is that a good wow or a bad wow?"

"Um, a good one." Taylor's room was amazing. The far wall was a full-sized, black-and-white photograph of a ballerina practicing at her bar. But the wall closest to me was covered with vinyl records sheathed in plastic. She had everything from Mozart to the Beatles. I ran my hands over the cover of Cat Stevens's *Tea for the Tillerman*. "These albums. You must have hundreds. They're amazing."

"Music sounds different on a record player." She shrugged. "I learned that when I used to dance."

The rest of her room was an exercise in contradictions. A rustic-looking, white bed frame covered by a fluorescent pink bedspread over black sheets. A gorgeous vanity that looked like it had been painted with a million different shades of nail polish.

"I spilled a bottle of Vermillionaire and the rest is history," she explained as I ran my fingers over the glossy finish.

But the most amazing part of her room was that there were really only three walls. The fourth was nothing but a huge window overlooking the immense woods that surrounded the estate. In architecture magazines that wall would occupy a full-page spread, light sifting through the glass and spilling onto her dark hardwood floors. But something about the way the afternoon sun bounced off the snow-covered lawn made me feel like an actress overcome with stage fright and stuck in the spotlight. My skin crawled with the uncomfortable feeling of being watched again.

Taylor caught me staring and laughed. "Don't worry about the windows. They're tinted. No one is ever able to see in."

I coughed, embarrassed at my transparency. Of course the windows were treated with some million-dollar invisible glass tint. The Wrights probably had an electric fence hidden around the house's perimeter as well.

"I am going to change." She gestured at her Pemberly Brown uniform. "Not exactly getaway gear."

As soon as I heard the bathroom door click shut, I pushed a few buttons on the wall, attempting to lower the shades. It didn't matter how many times she mentioned tinted windows, I still heard my mom bitching and moaning that if I didn't close the shades to my room, the entire neighborhood would see me. The overhead light turned on, a fan, some music, but no shades. I walked back to the window, praying that I was just being paranoid about someone being out there.

Someone watching.

Instead, I tried to enjoy the view. Hundreds of towering trees hugged the property, and if I looked hard enough I could see shining water, a creek that cut the woods in half. I even saw a family of deer gathered around something that still managed to be green in the dead of winter. Taylor must have loved looking out that window. It was so peaceful and quiet, like a page from *National Geographic*. The only things that were out there belonged.

But then I saw one of the deer lift its head, the others following suit and standing stock-still. I tried to remember what preyed on deer, but all I could think of were cars and hunters. It's not like we had wolves roaming the woods in Cleveland. At least I hoped not. I wasn't in the mood to see some sort of deer ambush.

But then I caught movement. A hand reaching out to move away brush.

Then the flash of skin, a face maybe.

My arms and legs went numb and jittery with adrenaline. We weren't alone. People were out there watching and I didn't think they were hunters. I scrambled down the length of the window, hitting the wood floor hard and flattening out on my belly to watch. The forms huddled close together and then broke apart, bending close to the ground every few steps in unison. They wore dark clothes, blending into trees.

The Brotherhood.

"Taylor!" I whisper-shouted, my voice cracking in the middle. But it was useless. I could hear the water running in the bathroom. I needed to call the police. My phone was on the bed where I'd left it, and Taylor's cordless was farther off on the nightstand, but I lay transfixed at the window, unable to take my eyes off the shadowy figures in the woods.

Their movements were picking up now, closing in, and I thought back to Maddie's humiliation. The Brotherhood was taking this too far. Pemberly Brown's campus was one thing, but Taylor's personal property? As I watched them circle, I wondered what it all meant. Who were they sacrificing this time?

But I already knew. Bethany.

"Taylor!" I shouted again, louder this time. Nothing.

The harder I stared, the harder they were to see. The sunlight was playing tricks on my eyes, so I looked slightly to one figure's right, hoping that would help. There were two, closing in on Taylor's house with each step. The wind bent the trees, blowing harder this time, rustling what was left of the leaves and blowing back the hood one of the Brothers had pulled over his head. And before he reached up to replace it, I caught a glimpse of unmistakable red hair.

Chapter 23

What the hell was Seth doing at Taylor's house? I smacked my forehead against the glass when I noticed his partner in crime. The better question was what the hell was my boyfriend doing with him?

By the time Taylor disarmed the security system and pulled the heavy front doors open, Seth was standing in front of the gate, bent in half, hands on his knees, chest heaving, back rising and falling like he'd just finished some sort of street race. And behind him stood Liam.

"What the hell are you guys doing here?" I called, narrowing my eyes just to be sure I was seeing who I thought I was seeing. Not only was it surreal to be spending time with Taylor Wright, but now my worlds were colliding.

"I found him running down Courtland," Liam said, nodding toward the semi-main road. "I was afraid he'd get hit by a car or something."

"I couldn't"—*heave, heave*—"take the van"—*gasp*—"my mom's at the store."

A sheen of sweat covered Seth's pale skin despite the cold, and I noticed that he'd taken extra care in selecting some Under Armour lounge clothes that matched his running shoes. I would have thought biking or even taking a bus would have been a better option, but that was kind of irrelevant at this point. "When you weren't on the bus, I was worried. I used the GPS on your phone to track you here."

"You installed a GPS tracker on my phone? Seriously?" I was equal parts impressed and horrified. Apparently Seth's obsession with my whereabouts knew no bounds.

"You're always running off and getting trapped in dangerous situations. I installed it when we drove Maddie home the other night." Seth's voice cracked, and his face was roughly the same color as his red sweatshirt.

"Good lord, just get it off my phone, okay? The last thing I need is you following me around."

Seth looked wounded and I immediately felt guilty. The thing about Seth was that in spite of his early attempts to convince me to make out with him, he'd turned into a really amazing friend. And as sketchy as the GPS tracker might have been, he did sort of have a point.

Just as I was about to apologize and send the boys packing, Taylor shoved past me and yanked them both into the house. She slammed the door behind her and pressed a button to arm the security system.

Welcome to the house party of awkward.

"Actually we could use your help." I looked over at Taylor in confusion after she said the words. She was kidding. She had to be kidding. Taylor, of course, was dead serious. Seth stopped mid-turn.

"We're not here to help. We're here to bring Kate home. Whatever you've got her involved in, she wants no part of it." Liam had kept completely quiet up until this point, and he managed to keep his tone light, but there was nothing light about the way the tendons in his neck strained against the collar of his fleece.

"Kate is fine right where she is." Jesus, now he had me talking in the third person. "Why don't you go plan another humiliation ceremony?"

Taylor ignored me completely and addressed Liam. "What have you heard?"

Liam's eyes were on fire and seemed to be aimed primarily at me. "What the hell? I told you. I had no idea they were going to do that to Maddie. I just got this stupid text to show up at the auditorium, and after you ran out of open, I figured something was up so I showed up and…"

Taylor reduced the space between them in record time. I was starting to think that there was a ninja underneath all that pretty blond hair. Her face stopped just an inch from his. "You are one of them now? Where is she? What did you do to her?"

Liam jerked away, stumbling under his feet. The circular entry table wobbled as Liam bumped into it, a gigantic arrangement of flowers vibrating beneath the movement. A few petals rained down. I threw my arms into the air like some sort of deranged crossing guard and screamed.

"*Stop!*"

It worked.

Despite looking like he could take off at any second, Liam was still, every muscle in his body tensed and ready for a fight. Taylor looked like she was ready to pounce, but she'd twisted her head around. I could see the veins in her neck pulsating from where I stood. Seth, who had magically produced a bag of Cheetos, presumably from somewhere in his coat, stood with his mouth hanging open, a fresh Cheeto poised near his lips.

"He"—I nodded at Liam—"is not a member of the Brotherhood. I followed Maddie out of the house that night because I thought she might know something, but instead the Brotherhood held some sort of humiliation ceremony in her honor. I was pissed because Liam was there." As the words came out, I realized how angry I still was. Yeah, he wasn't in the Brotherhood, but he had been there. It was almost worse.

"Kate, I tried to tell you. I had no idea what was going on. I just got a text and showed up." He tossed his too-long hair out of his eyes and snorted. "If anyone should be pissed it's me. I mean what were *you* doing there? I thought you were done with this. With *her*." He jerked an arm angrily in Taylor's direction.

Ah, the classic defense mechanism. Liam loved deflecting the blame, especially when it had to do with me investigating anything involving the 'hoods.

I opened my mouth to defend myself, but Taylor beat me to it.

"As riveting as your relationship issues are, I would like to get back to my missing best friend." Her voice started out steely but cracked on the word "missing." It felt strange to hear her say it out loud, especially with other people in the room. I guess we were officially letting Seth and Liam in.

"Wait. What?" Seth held up five cheese-covered fingers.

"Bethany is missing. The Brotherhood took her. It happened the night of Obsideo." Taylor sounded exasperated already. I didn't have the heart to tell her how much patience was usually required when dealing with Seth.

"How do you know?" Liam asked quietly.

"What do you mean?" Taylor smoothed a nonexistent tangle from her hair.

"I mean, how do you know they took her? How do you even know she's missing?"

"Huh. Liam has a point. Her mom sent in a note about Bethany being out a week to study her chakras. They're even giving her extra credit in Anthropology." Seth's job working in the school office had many redeeming qualities when it came to investigating Pemberly Brown.

Hope flared in my chest. Maybe this was all just some huge misunderstanding. The thought of Beefany in the downward-facing-dog pose on a commune somewhere made me a little giddy. My shoulders sagged when I saw the look on Taylor's face, and I remembered the mess at Bethany's house, the police station, and of course the text with her picture.

"She's gone, okay? I heard her scream." Taylor's voice took on a hysterical edge. "How do you explain this?"

She pulled up Bethany's picture on her phone.

The boys squinted at the phone, and Seth grabbed it out of Taylor's hands and started manipulating the image with Cheeto-stained fingers. "Do you recognize where she is? Looks like a paneled room of some sort. A basement perhaps. Have you confirmed it's the Brotherhood and not that serial killer who talks girls into getting into his van to help him with a baby?"

"Pretty sure, Chester the Cheetah," Taylor snipped, eyeing the orange fingerprints Seth had left behind on her phone. Seth turned bright red.

"Lay off him, T." Taylor had no idea how lucky we were to have Seth on her side, and I wasn't going to let her make him feel like a jackass. "Besides, the real reason we're here is this." I handed over the paper from the headmaster's office.

"Who wrote this? How did you get it?" Liam had entered full-on protector mode.

"Ben Montrose. I recognize the handwriting."

"Chem Ben?" Liam sounded skeptical.

"Yeah. Chem Ben." Liam and I had nicknames for all the random people at Pemberly Brown. It was our thing, or at least it had been before.

"Well, there's really only one option then, right?" Seth licked his orange fingers and started walking toward the door.

"And what might that be?" Something told me Taylor was going to regret asking that question.

"Operation Save Bethany launches at nineteen hundred hours." Seth replied, licking the remaining Cheeto cheese from his fingers. "Now get me Ben's cell number."

"You think calling him is a good idea? You must be kidding."

Taylor looked like she was literally going to disembowel Seth, which would have been kind of awesome if Seth wasn't one of my best friends.

I immediately inserted myself between them. "No way you're calling Ben. We already have a plan. We're going to his house, and I'm going to ring the doorbell with some fake lab work for Chemistry, and then Taylor is going to set off his car alarm while I tear through his room looking for evidence."

"Wow. Great plan, Kate. Just out of curiosity, what exactly are you planning on doing when he comes back to his room to find you knee-deep in his secret Brotherhood bullshit?" Liam spat his words at me like nails.

"Oh, I'm sorry. Do you have a better idea? Ooh, I know. Maybe you could just call your brother and have him light his garage on fire or something." I knew as soon as I said the words that I'd taken it a step too far, and the hurt on Liam's face confirmed it. Arson was kind of a hot-button issue for the Gilmour family.

"Enough fighting, you guys." It was Seth's turn to step in and play peacemaker. "I've already got a plan and it's genius. I just need his number and a laptop."

Seth proceeded to pull up an Internet site guaranteed to deliver completely anonymous text messages. He typed in three lines that pretty much made him a poet, in my mind.

> Station 10 at 9. Bring the Bethany file..

We all stood there huddled around Taylor's laptop until Seth submitted the form that would send the text. The second it sent, he snapped the MacBook shut and stood up. "Now, go grab me some bedsheets and some beef jerky. We've got a missing girl to find."

Chapter 24

"Pull your hood tighter. I still see blue." Taylor yanked the hood of my makeshift black robe closer around my face.

"Last time I checked, the Brotherhood doesn't have any blue-haired members," Seth chortled. His hood was hiding his face, but I would have bet my imaginary trust fund that his lips were pursed into his ridiculous I'm-the-red-headed-Jerry-Seinfeld smile.

"Really? Last time I checked they also don't have any members under 5-foot-1 either."

"Whoa. Uncalled for, Kate. Totally uncalled for. Not to mention the fact that I was 5-foot-4 at my annual checkup last week."

Liam inserted himself between Seth and me and grabbed my shoulders. "You—put the hair in a ponytail. Now." After my earlier comment, I wasn't exactly in a position to argue with him, and before I had a chance to say something that might make things okay between us, he'd turned to Seth. "And you—there's no way you're 5-foot-4. If you're going to round up, at least go for something realistic, like 5-foot-2." Seth sagged a little in his robe, and

Liam quickly added, "But the robe totally lengthens you, man. You should think about wearing one more often."

"I hate to break up whatever it is you are doing over there, but I think I heard someone," Taylor hissed from behind her hood.

Sure enough, Ben was getting out of his BMW and heading toward Farrow's Arches. Operation Save Bethany was clearly a success. Cheesy code names aside, a couple things seemed clear:

1. The Brotherhood was involved, and
2. Ben was doing their dirty work.

The only thing we couldn't quite determine was a motive.

And that was exactly what we were going to figure out tonight. Oh, and get the information on Bethany. In my imagination, Ben handed over a detailed map to her whereabouts so we could go about bringing her home. Case closed.

"So, Kate. You know the plan?" Seth began, and I felt Liam stiffen next to me.

"She's just standing there, Seth. There is no plan," Liam said.

"We've been over this a million times already. It's going to be fine. I'm just going to be there as backup in case Taylor drops the file… or something."

Liam grunted, and without seeing his face, it was impossible to tell if it was an I've-got-your-back grunt or an I-hate-my-dumb-ass-soon-to-be-ex-girlfriend grunt.

"I am *not* going to drop the file." I knew from the tone of her voice that Taylor was rolling her eyes. "The Brotherhood always travels in groups. It is more believable if there are four of us there. Liam does all the talking." She turned to him. "You remember the Latin?"

"Of course. *Vir prudens non contra ventum mingit.*" I couldn't see his face because of the hood, but I could tell by the tone of his voice that he was completely serious. Or at least trying to be. I wrinkled my forehead as I attempted to translate.

"Wait a second," Seth said, pulling back his hood to demonstrate his utter confusion. "I thought their greeting was *Non ducor, duco.* 'I am not led, I lead.'"

Liam's shoulders began shaking just as I finished my rough translation. "A wise man does not urinate against the wind?" I pulled down my hood and looked at Liam. He winked at me, and it was pretty much the most beautiful thing I'd ever seen in my life. Normally, I'm very anti-wink when it comes to guys, but in this case it was a wink of absolution. It was a wink that meant Liam and I were actually going to be okay.

"You've been planning that all night, haven't you?" I reached over and squeezed his arm. It was the first time I'd touched him in at least twenty-four hours, and his strong forearm felt so good beneath my fingertips. When he grabbed my hand and quickly brought my palm to his lips, I felt all the air leave my body. As much as I hated to admit it, for fear of sounding like a ridiculous, boy-crazy damsel in distress, it felt good to have my boyfriend back.

Taylor whipped back her hood, her blue eyes icy. "I'm glad this is such a joke to you," she spat, clearly not in the mood for games.

Liam dropped my hand and sat up a little straighter. "Sorry, T., I've got it. *Non ducor, duco.* Don't worry."

She replaced her hood, gently tucking back a stray piece of her blond hair, while the rest of us followed suit. I couldn't resist shooting Liam a smile before I covered my face, though. With the way Taylor had had him practicing the simple Latin for the past two hours, it was pretty funny.

"Liam greets, I get the file, and then we all get out of there," Taylor finished.

"He's punching in the code." Seth's voice cracked with excitement and we all froze, knowing that if we missed our window into the tunnels, all of our plans would disintegrate.

Ben crouched underneath the arches in some sort of velour sweatsuit, enough product in his hair to style the entire *Jersey Shore* cast, and flung open the door to the tunnels. He took a quick look around the gardens and stepped into the hole in the ground and finally disappeared, closing the hatch behind him.

Taylor counted underneath her breath. "Five, four, three, two...*now!*"

We all ran for the hatch, but Liam got there first and swung it open just before the lock clicked.

He motioned for all of us to remain completely silent as we filed down the stairs, led by flickering gas lamps affixed to the walls. As usual, the walls seemed to inch together the lower we descended, my lungs constricting right along with them. The only thing worse than being underground was being underground alone, I reminded myself. I had my friends. I had backup. I needed to focus.

Ben stood alone at the bottom of the steps, clutching a thick manila folder to his chest. I lowered my chin, hopeful that the black sheet was effectively concealing my identity.

"*Non ducor, duco,*" Liam said, the Latin sounding strange on his lips.

Ben just bowed his head and cowered in response.

"Is that the file?" Liam wasn't wasting any time.

Ben nodded his overly gelled head and held out the folder, his hand shaking. The folder was thick and heavy, and his nerves forced the contents to the edge. Taylor must have noticed, because her hand shot out to grab the folder, but it was too late. Ben dropped the folder, and suddenly hundreds of photographs, folded notes, and even some personal items like lip gloss and pressed flowers littered the damp bricks of the tunnel floor.

I dove to the ground and started grabbing whatever I could get my hands on. I didn't think about anything except the photographs of Bethany. We finally had all the evidence we needed to find her. I could practically taste it.

I could also feel the frigid air on my bare cheeks. I heard the gust of cool air as Taylor swished past me in her robes. My hand flew to my head a second too late.

I looked up to see Ben staring at me, his normally squinty eyes as big as quarters. "Kate? What the hell are you doing here?"

Chapter 25

"WTF?" Ben yanked back Liam's hood, then Seth's, and finally Taylor's.

We all dove for the closest picture at the same time, but I got there first. I picked up the snapshot of Bethany, blurry headstones set behind her in the background, and flipped it over. It was embossed with a miniature wax version of the Brotherhood's crest. The lion. The key. *Fortes et liber*, "strong and free." It was all there.

Ben ripped the picture out of my hands. "I'm so frickin' screwed. Give me that folder. Now." His tone surprised me. I'd never heard him sound so authoritative.

"Where is she?" Taylor stepped in front of me, blocking Ben from making a grab for the folder.

He just shook his head. "Kate, you have to give that back." He lunged past Taylor and made a grab for me, but Liam was too fast for him. He grabbed Ben by his jacket and shoved him back against the wall.

"How'd you even get in, Ben?" I asked as he rubbed the shoulder that had slammed into the brick wall. There was a story here; I could smell it. Or maybe that was just some type of toxic black mold growing in the tunnels. Regardless, the Brotherhood was extremely exclusive. Only the most distinguished and the most popular students were tapped to join. And Ben was neither.

"Legacy," he whispered in a monotone voice, like he'd heard the question a million times before. "My dad was Class of '87."

"Where. Is. She?" Taylor's words were laced with acid. She inched forward in a way that barely counted as moving, and by the time the last word left her lips, she was practically on top of him.

"Who? Oh, you mean Bethany? I have no idea. She totally disappeared."

"Liar!" Taylor lost control and screamed the word like a curse.

If Ben's skin hadn't been tanned Oompa Loompa orange by however many minutes a week in his personal tanning bed or whatever man tanner he slathered on every morning, he would have gone completely white. Instead he turned the color of a melted Creamsicle.

"I'm not lying, I swear." His voice squeaked a little, and my gut told me he was telling the truth.

Guess Liam's gut must have told him the same thing, because he said, "But then what's with all the pictures?"

"It's some stupid initiation thing. *Viglio*. I think it means 'watching' in Latin or something." Ben ran his hand through his hair, which was actually kind of an impressive feat, given the amount of product on his head. "I had to follow her 24/7 for weeks. It's supposed to be their way of keeping track of the Sisterhood. They make the new guys do it because it's boring and if you get caught you look like a sex offender."

Something popped, the sound reverberating off the brick walls surrounding us, and we all spun around to find the source. The last thing we needed was company. Seth's cheeks were flaming, his jaw working slowly, an empty peanut shell near his feet.

"Low blood sugar," he said, holding out a fistful of nuts. "I keep 'em in my pocket, you know…just in case." Of course he did. But I was thankful for the distraction.

I had to get out of there with the file. I could see the stairs out of the corner of my eye, and even if Ben knew nothing about Bethany's whereabouts, there was bound to be something useful in here somewhere. There was no way I was going to risk Ben making a grab for it. Plus, I got the feeling that we were running out of time.

"How long did you watch her?" Taylor asked. Her carefully modulated voice was so dramatically changed that it verged on creepy.

"Months. Until all of a sudden she just disappeared. That's when they made me start watching Kate." He gestured vaguely at me.

"When was the last time you saw Bethany?" Taylor completely ignored the fact that I was being targeted by the Brotherhood. I inched farther up the stairs. A little closer to freedom.

"It was the night of Obsideo. Wait, I think…" Ben shoved past Taylor and Liam and came straight for me and his damn folder. I stood up and made a run for it, out the top of the hatch and into the night. I picked up speed, the cold fingers of the wind combing through my hair, and then slipped on a patch of ice. As I slammed to the ground, the folder bounced out of my hands, flinging hundreds of pictures of Bethany all over the wet snow. I made a pathetic attempt to start gathering the evidence, but everything in my body hurt at the same time.

Ben's patent leather loafers crunched past my head, and I watched as he grabbed a picture that lay a few feet away from me. Instead of taking off, he bent down next to me.

"They'd kill me if they knew I had this."

Bethany's dark hair was loose around her shoulders. Her scarf was wrapped in one of those twisty knot things that all the popular girls seemed to know how to do by default. The tiny hairs on my arms stood on end as I pulled the picture closer to my face to get a better look at her. An odd little smile lit her face. Like she had a secret.

"That's the last picture I got of her." He stared at it a little too long and finally looked at me, urging me to examine it closer without using any words at all. As much as Ben always seemed to trigger my d-bag radar, at this moment he couldn't have seemed further from it.

"Do you have any idea where she went?"

He shrugged. "I asked around at school, and everyone said she was on some retreat."

I plucked the picture from his hands to get a closer look. There was a shadow behind Bethany that I'd missed the first time I looked at the picture. I had been so focused on her that I never noticed there was someone standing behind her.

I lifted the picture up to the streetlight to get a closer look. Not just one figure, two. The second person was a few steps behind the first and dressed entirely in black, a ski mask obscuring his face. But the other figure hadn't put his mask on yet. In fact, if I looked closely enough I could see it dangling from his long fingertips just underneath his chin. If the camera had flashed just an instant later, I was sure his face would have been obscured.

I turned to Ben, who raised his eyebrows knowingly and then looked away. Apparently we both saw what was there. In the dim shadow behind Bethany's right shoulder I could just make out Bradley Farrow's face.

Chapter 26

"Bradley Farrow." Taylor had barely uttered the name before she headed back down into the tunnels. We had no choice but to file down after her. "Bethany! Bethany!" She screamed the name as she ran, and Ben kept muttering things about getting his ass kicked as we chased after her. I knew exactly where she was going, and I was terrified at what we might find there.

The heavy wood door to the Sisterhood's old headquarters was wide open. No key, no secret pass code to protect the nerve center of the society. Taylor stood in the opening looking like she was going to cry. All of their work protecting the secrets buried beneath Pemberly Brown, and the boys were too lazy to even install new locks.

I was shocked no one had made the breach up until this point. But then I remembered Maddie expertly punching numbers into a new keypad the night of her humiliation. Sure, the Brotherhood had altered the access points when they took control, but apparently they didn't monitor much else. I couldn't imagine how angry Taylor must feel. After months of being locked out of the tunnels, access to the headquarters was right beneath her perfectly manicured fingertips.

Taylor reached to the wall and flipped the light, illuminating the source of my posttraumatic stress disorder.

"What the…" The words escaped in one breath as she took a huge step back, knocking into me. The headquarters had looked like a professionally designed family room, but now it was completely empty. No flat-screen TV. No antique leather sofas. No shelves lined with books, and no information dating back hundreds of years. Most importantly, no files holding Pemberly Brown's most sought-after secrets. The Sisterhood knew everything from what questions would appear on this year's SAT to which teacher had had an affair with our vile headmaster.

"Is this a joke?" Taylor grabbed Ben's shoulders roughly, her face so close she could kiss him. The room was entirely empty. Every file drawer hung open. Empty.

"Um…no?" Ben stuttered, which wasn't going to end well. "We moved."

"Worthless!" Taylor screamed, slamming an empty file drawer closed. Seth gave Liam a knowing look and approached her as she hung over the drawer. But before he even laid a finger on her, she whipped around, ignoring him completely and zeroing in on Ben again. "Where is it? Where is all of our stuff?"

Ben's glassy eyes trailed upward toward the ceiling. One by one, we all did the same.

The Sisterhood buried their secrets underground. But unsurprisingly the Brotherhood had loftier ambitions. Apparently they'd decided to take everything to the top.

"Why is everyone looking up? There is absolutely no way you

guys could have moved everything. That is absolutely ridiculous." Taylor pronounced each word with careful, cutting restraint.

"Actually, they built a new headquarters. On top of the school. And now that they have these new secret passageways built behind the walls, they don't really use the tunnels anymore." Ben was rambling. "Headmaster Sinclair has had crews working late at night, weekends, holidays, whenever he can get them here without anyone noticing. All those new rules to keep students off campus are really just a way to cover all this up. Cool, right?" Clearly he was one of those people who felt it necessary to fill dead silences. His orange face lit up when he talked about the Brotherhood's latest endeavor.

Taylor just stood there watching him, letting him hang himself with his words. She would make a great investigative reporter someday.

When he finally stopped detailing the state-of-the-art security and the way they'd nested the new headquarters in between the four gables of the main building's roof, he looked at all of us. "I'm sorry, really."

Taylor turned and started walking toward the nearest exit. "You have nothing to be sorry about. Where is the best place for us to access the new headquarters?"

Ben looked like he was going to choke. He gasped a little and started coughing. His face turned red and his hands clutched at his throat. Actually, scratch that. Ben didn't look like he was going to choke. Ben was actually choking. The first thing I thought of was Seth's stupid peanuts.

Taylor just stood there watching him, her gaze never wavering. Clearly, she had no intention of helping.

Seth came barreling out from the empty room and embraced Ben from behind.

"Hang in there, buddy. I know the Heimlich. I am CPR certified after that babysitting…er…lifeguarding class my mom made me take." Seth folded his hands together under Ben's six-pack abs, which we'd all seen much more of than we cared to, and jerked him upward.

Something flew out of Ben's mouth and landed on the floor near Liam's feet. He leaned down to examine the object that had almost taken Ben's life. "Invisalign retainer. A cautionary tale for us all," he said, moving it lightly with his foot.

Ben coughed and sputtered, hands on his knees, trying to catch his breath.

"Well, what are we waiting for?" Taylor was already halfway down the hall. "Once I get in, I will find Bethany or at least figure out where they have her. If we can get her out tonight…"

"I can't." Ben's words still sounded like a cough. "I'm not a real member yet. You don't get to go into the headquarters until you're initiated." Ben's voice cracked, and I would have bet Grace's pearls that he was dangerously close to wetting himself. Not that I blamed him. Taylor was ten kinds of scary when she was pissed off, and I'd never in my life seen her this angry.

She took a step forward as Ben took a giant step back. "You are wasting my time." Taylor had literally backed him into a corner and he was shaking. It was kind of like watching a snake get ready to eat a baby rabbit. I had to step in.

"Look, he was just trying to help, Taylor. We ambushed him. He's not even thinking straight."

But Ben was shaking his head. "There is something…something you should see." His voice was raspy from choking, and watching him cower in the corner like some kind of kicked animal brought the words "man up" to mind.

"Well, what are you waiting for?" I inserted myself between Taylor and Ben and yanked him back toward the exit near Farrow's Arches where we'd entered.

"Wrong way," he rasped and started off in a different direction.

The tunnels down this way were damper and felt older than the rest of the system. I felt something brush past my boot and let out a little squeal.

"Do not tell me you are afraid of rats." Taylor laughed behind me.

My throat started to close up. "That was a rat?"

"Of course it was a rat. They love the tunnels. Some of the girls used to feed them. Like cats."

My stomach heaved, but I forced myself to keep walking. Liam pulled me a little bit closer. "You can't be afraid of rats, Kate. You're way bigger than they are."

"You know what else is smaller than me? Bombs."

Liam snorted and Taylor sighed disdainfully at what I'm assuming was yet another demonstration of our complete lack of maturity.

The tunnels grew darker and colder the farther we walked. I pulled my jacket up under my chin.

"We're under the cemetery now." Seth gestured up. "Bet that's why you're cold."

My heart began beating faster in my chest. I thought about the catacombs lined with bones we'd learned about in French class.

Coffins were buried beneath our feet; people were rotting away around us. Or maybe we were so far underground that they were actually above us. Just as I began imagining bones raining down on top of us, Ben gestured toward a stone staircase to our right and motioned that we should follow him up.

I heard the low moaning of chanting coming from the top of the staircase.

"It's the heart of Brown." He gestured at the door. The heart of Brown was one of the oldest buildings on campus. It had been part of Brown's original campus before the boys joined with the girls, but it was too far away and too old to be used anymore. So the Brotherhood had claimed it for their own.

"Please be quiet." Ben's watery eyes looked desperate. "I know you guys don't care if I get my ass kicked or not, but I'm trying to help you, and I can't help you with Alistair Reynolds's fist in my throat." I let out a little snort and Ben smiled at me gratefully. "Besides, you're not going to want to miss this. It's important."

We all huddled behind Ben as he cracked open one of the doors. I was worried they would hear us or see us, but the chanting was so loud and the room was so dark that we might as well have been invisible. The names of all the members of the Brotherhood shone on the wall like stars, and about twenty feet from where five heads peered out of a trapdoor built into the floor stood the Brotherhood.

Their togas were so bright in the black light that they appeared more purple than anything else. They moved in a circle, chanting.

"*Imperator. Conventus. Imperator. Conventus. Imperator.*"

Emperor. Unity. The Brotherhood had a new leader. The circle widened and a spotlight lit the face of the person sitting in the center on an elaborate throne. His teeth gleamed white and sharp in the strange light, and I felt a quick stab in my stomach. A stab that felt dangerously close to lust. Or maybe hate. I couldn't be sure which.

Bradley Farrow.

Chapter 27

Walking into school the next day, I realized it probably would have been more efficient to just sleep in one of the classrooms. The chants of the Brotherhood still echoed in my ears. Watching Bradley take the reins of the Brotherhood had created more questions than it answered. Was Alistair telling the truth? If he had nothing to do with Bethany's disappearance, maybe we needed to be talking to Bradley.

Either way, we were all exhausted, confused, and, with each passing hour, more freaked out. Every time I passed a boy in the halls I felt his eyes on me and wondered—is he a Brother? Did he send me the text of Bethany? Am I next?

When I saw Seth rushing down the hall toward me between classes, I was so excited to see a friendly face that I barely noticed the thick booklet of printed pages he had clasped in a death-like grip to his bony chest. But I should have seen the collision coming. Any time Seth so much as speed-walked, he either tripped or ran into something or someone. It was like he was walking on Bambi legs.

This time Seth looked left and a varsity football player veered in from the right after doing one of those shoulder-jerk fake-out moves meatheads are so fond of. Seth immediately tucked himself into the fetal position with the mysterious pages tucked beneath his chin. Jock Strap lifted his leg like he was either going to kick Seth while he was down or pee on him like a dog, but before he could make his move I slid between them.

"Anyone ever tell you you're not supposed to hit girls?"

"He's not a girl," Jock Strap growled.

"Wow, athletic and quick on the uptake. You must be a real catch." I gave him my sweetest smile.

"Yeah, right." Jock Strap laughed and then abruptly stopped laughing after he realized what he'd said. "I mean, the ladies love me and I'm smart and…God, Lowry, you're such a…a…" He turned and walked away.

"Well played, Jacques…Strap." I whispered the last word so only Seth could hear it.

"His name is Jeremy, Kate." Seth rasped from his tiny-man cocoon before sitting up and handing me the papers. "It's all here." His breath smelled faintly of sour-cream-and-onion potato chips. It was 9:54 a.m.

After we witnessed Bradley's little crowning ceremony last night, Seth had promised to approach his online buddy ConspiracyLuvR to determine exactly what was going down within the Brotherhood. Judging from the weight of the pages, Seth had gotten a ton of information, and I could have kissed him, sour-cream-and-onion breath and all. As hard a time as I gave Seth for trolling conspiracy blogs, facilitating chats, and theorizing with creepers who had screen names like AgntDbleOHvn and SkrtPlotMan, at moments like this I understood how lucky I was to have him.

Let's be honest, those geeks weren't about to give up their inside information to just anyone (especially a girl with bright blue hair), and because of Seth, we were all one step closer to finding Bethany before it was too late. I flashed him my first genuine smile of the day and tucked the pages into my bag.

"Thank you, Seth. Seriously. What would I do without you?"

He blushed, as usual, and nodded toward the clock, which offered us about one more minute before third period. "No biggie. You really should thank Mar…er…ConspiracyLuvR. I swear he was a member of the Brotherhood during his glory days."

I raised one eyebrow. Hard to believe anyone who maintained an online identity as ConspiracyLuvR had ever experienced "glory days," but I didn't have time to argue. McAdams was a stickler for the bell, so I'd have to run if I wanted to make it to class on time, and I hated running.

In addition to monitoring detention, McAdams was one of those old-school teachers who "taught" using transparencies of lecture notes created in the mid-'70s, showed occasional film strips (I'm not kidding) of war documentaries, and forced us to answer every question at the end of each textbook chapter, including the dreaded "Take It to the Field!" ones that required us to interview grandparents about the Great Depression or keep a journal from the perspective of a Native American.

The only thing that made him semi-popular was the fact that he hadn't updated his exams since his first year of teaching, which, judging from his sagging jowls, was sometime immediately following the Revolutionary War. So everyone knew exactly what was going to be on his tests before he gave them. The downside was that he always reported tardies to the office and timed all trips to the bathroom.

Sadly, it took me more than three minutes to pee (excuse me for actually washing my hands), and I'd already been given five demerits for being late to his class, so McAdams and I weren't going to be splitting a best-friend necklace anytime soon.

A fresh transparency of notes was already being projected and the bell was ringing as I slipped into my seat. The bulk of the class was already hunched over notebooks copying like mad, but I couldn't remember the date for the life of me and could barely read the words. Seth's notes were calling to me from the pocket of my bag. No matter how riveting the fifteen bullet points beneath "The Two Big Powers and Their Cold War" were, today it just wasn't happening.

I raised my hand. "Mr. McAdams?" He lowered the newspaper he was reading and scowled at me. My hair never went over well with the sixty-and-over set. "Can I use the bathroom?" I pulled the strap of my bag over my shoulder and patted it for good measure, implying that this was the time of the month a girl would need to bring a bag to the bathroom.

"Ms. Lowry, I am confident that you *can* use the restroom," he said, raising the paper again, the lumbar support of his computer chair squeaking beneath his weight.

I rolled my eyes. I hated when teachers made a big show out of "can" and "may." It was such a waste of time.

"Oh…er…may I go to the bathroom?" I adjusted the bag again in case he hadn't seen it. I thought about flashing him a tampon but figured that might be overkill.

Heavy sigh. "Three minutes. And take the pass."

McAdams was famous for his hall pass. It was a stuffed gray squirrel. Not a stuffed animal, but an actual live squirrel that had died and was subsequently stuffed. To call it disgusting was the understatement of the year. The thing's fur was matted and greasy at the same time, and its beady glass eyes always seemed to be begging me to set it free.

I gingerly picked up the squirrel between the tips of my two fingers, trying to make as little finger-to-squirrel contact as humanly possible. As soon as I set foot in the hallway, I tucked little Nutty (that's what I liked to call him) under my arm and booked it down the hall in an effort to both maximize my three minutes and put an end to my relationship with the scuzzy, STD-infested rodent.

I'd barely locked the stall door before whipping out Seth's pages.

ConspiracyLuvR: Hi.

SethaSaurus: Hi.

Oh my God, it was like a bad first date. I scanned down to where the conversation picked up a little and Seth asked questions other than "How are you?"

> ConspiracyLuvR: Sources indicate that the Brotherhood was first modeled off of the Republic of Rome.

Okay, based upon our viewing of their little toga party last night, this was not new information.

> ConspiracyLuvR: In the beginning, there was no set leadership, granting all members equal power. But back in the '70s, the society was gaining little traction while the Sisterhood maintained absolute political control over the school and much of the surrounding community.

Apparently the Sisterhood had some glory days of its own. I wondered what it had been like for them sneaking around below the school without any concerns of the Brotherhood invading their territory.

> ConspiracyLuvR: They needed leaders. As a result, three of the bigwigs decided to form a triumvirate and things slowly began to turn around. Many of the original leaders went off to serve in Congress and one made it all the way to the Oval Office.

I let the notes rest in my lap as I recalled the previous night, the Brothers circling their new emperor, chanting, honoring. Bradley was obviously selected as the Brotherhood's new leader. They had spoken about coming together, *Conventus*, joining as one. Apparently the Brotherhood was doing a bit of in-house restructuring. Perhaps that was why he ruled alone. Who needed three douche bags when you had one Bradley Farrow?

But I couldn't help but wonder how the other Brothers felt about Bradley assuming absolute power. I wondered if potential Brotherhood turmoil might in some way be connected to Bethany's disappearance. It seemed too big a coincidence for the two not to be connected.

The remaining notes from ConspiracyLuvR theorized about the new headquarters after Seth requested information about access to their rooftop lair. Nada. Apparently we were on our own if we wanted to get up close and personal. And we needed to get all up in their business if we were going to find Bethany.

Speaking of getting all up in business, my three minutes had come and gone.

When I slunk back into my desk, page three of the class notes was being projected and my last exam sat face up on my desk, a huge, red 63 percent scarlet letter mocking me at the top. Apparently having the old test only helped if you actually took the time to study it. Crap.

But worse was the chicken scratch below: "See me." Double crap. "See me" had to be the two most dreaded words ever to be written in red ink. I'd never experienced a time when a teacher wanted to "see me" to discuss the newest show on Bravo or Nordstrom's semi-annual sale, which under normal circumstances were pretty much the only things I'd want to discuss at great length. Something told me McAdams wasn't a closet Bravo junkie.

Four pages of incoherent notes later, the bell rang and I shuffled my books together to shove them in my bag. And that's when something sparkly caught my eye. My hand hovered over the sparkle-covered book, frozen and shaking. I knew exactly what it was before my fingers even touched the crinkled plastic cover.

Our slam book.

I ran my fingers over the glitter-puff, paint, and rhinestone-blanketed cover, and memories of Grace, Maddie, and me feverishly filling it in lower school washed over me. We had poured crushes, favorite outfits, hobbies, secrets, pretty much everything we could think of that held any sacredness into the joint diary.

It had been stolen months ago by the Brotherhood or the corrupt police or God only knows who, and now it was back. I gently lifted the cover and saw each of our names written in the bubbly, childish handwriting that had been replaced years ago with straighter, more grown-up print, devoid of the hearts and stars that used to dot our I's. Tears filled my eyes. How could something that was so lost so suddenly be found?

A grumble ripped me from my thoughts, and I carefully wiped beneath my eyes so my mascara wouldn't smudge. "Ms. Lowry?" Great. Now McAdams felt sorry for me. "Your test." Or not.

"Oh, right, Mr. McAdams, sorry."

"Tutor. You." He jabbed a meaty finger in my direction, and I wondered why I'd never noticed that he spoke Neanderthal.

I didn't have time for this. "Um…okay?" It didn't take a genius to know that I could be tutored in World History from now until graduation, but until Bethany lumbered home and took her rightful place beside Taylor and I stopped collecting mysterious droppings from my dead best friend, my 63 percent would remain a 63 percent. I had to straighten things out at Pemberly Brown before I could even consider tackling World War II.

Mr. McAdams then made a big show of unearthing a clipboard with the names of about twenty star pupils who made it their mission in life to impress teachers and earn above a 4.0, all in preparation for some fantastical *Good Will Hunting*–style academic debate at a college bar in a fruitless effort to finally get laid.

"How 'bout them apples," I whispered under my breath.

"Sorry?" McAdams furrowed his white unibrow in my direction.

I spotted Seth's name on the list he was holding. "Oh, I was just saying that he's my neighbor." I leaned in to point to his name, figuring Seth would be the least of all evils. He never met a conspiracy he didn't want to dissect, and the Bethany-Brotherhood situation would most definitely trump Cold War Russia.

But at the last minute I saw another name. A name that sparked an idea. A name that might just bring me one step closer to saving Bethany. A name that brought to mind togas and Romans and empires falling like dominos.

"Bradley Farrow. He lives next door," I lied. "He's helped me before."

Just like that, I was in. And I didn't even need a Trojan horse.

Chapter 28

The Farrows' house looked like it had been ripped from the English countryside and slapped onto a spacious lot in northeastern Ohio. I half expected Mr. Darcy to explode out of the hedges on horseback.

My hand shook a little as I reached up to pound the brass knocker against the huge front door that was probably made of wood recovered from a French monastery in the seventeenth century. I took a deep breath and tried to calm my frazzled nerves as I heard footsteps bounding toward the door.

It's just a study date. It's just a study date. It's just a study date.

Oh God, this was so much more than *just* a study date. I needed information. I had no idea where the Brotherhood was hiding Bethany, but there was no doubt in my mind that the answer was hidden in their new headquarters. If I could just figure out a way to get up there, I was sure we'd be able to find her.

Bradley's gorgeous sister, Naomi, answered the door.

"It's just a study date!"

"Huh?" Naomi stared at me like I had three heads. Good lord, I was a complete moron.

"I mean, I'm here to study with Bradley. McAdams said he's supposed to tutor me."

"Um, riiight. He's upstairs, I think. Come on in." Naomi was still wearing her school uniform, but somehow her ebony skin, golden eyes, and ridiculously high cheekbones made her look like a model strutting around in the latest vintage-inspired fashion. Meanwhile, I was a shortish, blue-haired, wrinkled mess. "Runway ready" was definitely not the term that came to mind when I caught a glimpse of myself in the huge gilt-edged mirror in their foyer.

"Bradley! Kate's here!" Naomi's voice bounced off the marble floors and up the stairs. She turned back to me. "Three words I never thought I'd say out loud."

"Yeah, apparently a 63 percent doesn't earn you the right to choose your tutor."

"Oh really? McAdams said you requested me specially." Bradley stood at the top of the winding wood staircase with an eyebrow raised.

"Busted." Naomi laughed and walked back toward the family room as I stood there gaping. Bradley's skin was a shade lighter than his sister's, and even though a massive staircase separated us, I could practically count each and every eyelash that fringed his golden eyes.

I was so busy debating with myself that his smile took me completely off guard. When Bradley Farrow smiled in your direction, it was kind of impossible not to smile back. Especially if you were unprepared. Luckily for me, I'd spent the better part of a year doing everything in my power to ignore his smile. My brain fought its usual battle with my mouth. And won.

He just shrugged, like he was used to girls going catatonic at the mere sight of him, and started back up the stairs. "Come on up. My books are in my room."

I used my time walking up the twenty-seven stairs to compose a proper retort.

"Actually, I tried to get him to pair me up with Seth, but he said you had a higher score." The words were out of my mouth before I'd even made it through the door of his room and came out sounding more like an excuse than a comeback. Not to mention the fact that they were approximately five minutes too late. I was off to a fan-freaking-tastic start.

"It's tough being perfect." His smile grew even wider.

"Actually it's pretty easy when you have all the tests."

Bradley's expression darkened. "Are you accusing me of cheating?"

"Everyone cheats on McAdams's tests."

"Right, so you got a 63 percent when you cheated? You must not be as smart as you look."

Wait, Bradley Farrow thinks I look…smart. That can't be a compliment.

"Very funny. I didn't cheat. Obviously. But I do need to get my grade up, so let's just get this over with." I threw my bag down next to a purposely beat-up couch that looked like it'd been torn right out of the pages of Restoration Hardware. He threw his body down into it and stretched out his legs, bending both arms behind his head as though he were settling in for some sort of show.

The alarm clock next to Bradley's bed read 3:23 p.m. If all went as planned, we'd get in approximately three minutes of studying before he got the call.

"So there's this country called Germany. It's in Europe. You might have heard of it." Bradley watched me carefully to see if I was going to take the bait, but I just ignored him. Two more minutes and I'd be able to search his room for information. I started looking around, planning where to start.

Bradley's bedroom was huge. Honestly, it looked more like a suite at a fancy hotel than a sixteen-year-old's bedroom. His king-sized bed was covered in a navy duvet with a thread count way higher than my IQ, and a huge rolltop desk was tucked in the corner near the window. A few feet away from the couch was a mini-refrigerator, which I assumed was stocked to the nines, and next to that, a shelf lined with every snack imaginable. My parents barely went grocery shopping, let alone outfitted my bedroom with a variety of healthy treats. Seth would have been in heaven.

A documentary about sharks was playing on mute on the flat-screen TV that hung in front of us, and that seemed fitting, considering my plan. After Bradley was called out, I'd start with the rolltop desk and then make my way into the closet. It was huge, but boys were always leaving things in their pockets. Maybe I'd find something...

"Uh, hello? Kate? You still with me?" Bradley fixed his eyes on me patiently. "Sorry if I was acting like a dick earlier. I just hate it when people assume…"

The clock turned 3:26 and I heard Naomi scream from downstairs. Right on time. I had to hand it to Seth; he was always punctual.

"What the…?" Bradley bolted up from the couch and ran for the door. I wasted no time, dodging for his desk and digging in. Old notebooks, pens, pencils, books. Crap. There was nothing even remotely helpful in here.

And then a creamy piece of paper with a hand-drawn crest caught my eye. If there was one thing I'd learned over the past year, it was that the secret societies loved heavy paper and a good crest. The word "Conventus" was scrawled above the unfamiliar crest. I folded the paper and stuffed it into the pocket of my uniform skirt. I didn't have time to analyze it now. There had to be something else.

The closet. I started ripping through clothes, checking pockets, flinging shoes. When my fingers landed on a soft fleece jacket, I stopped. I remembered the picture of Bethany laughing and Bradley lurking. This was the jacket he had on the night of Obsideo. I slid my hand into the pocket and felt something hard and square and covered in tiny crystals. I pulled out a phone and immediately flipped it over. Bethany's name was bedazzled on the back. I tried turning it on, but the battery was completely dead. Shit. I'd have to take it with me and hope that Bradley didn't notice it was missing.

I should have heard their footsteps on the stairs. Or the soft sigh of the bedroom door opening, the change in atmosphere as the air shifted. Or even the sound of their breath moving in and out of their lungs.

But I missed all of that. In fact, I missed just about everything up until I heard Naomi say, "What is she doing in there?"

Thankfully, I managed to slide the phone into my pocket before I puked all over the designer contents of Bradley Farrow's custom closet.

Chapter 29

"Oh God, get a bucket or something, Naomi!" Bradley shouted, his hands thrown into the air. I'm pretty sure if my vision wasn't blurred from the tears that filled my eyes, I would have shriveled under the look he gave me, which was one part shock and three parts horror, with a healthy dollop of disgust plopped on top. But I wasn't supposed to care what Bradley thought about me. I *didn't* care what Bradley thought about me.

That's how I managed to gear up for another round of make-me-puke. The game was all Grace's. She used to play before school when she hadn't studied for an exam or was having boy issues or was just plain tired.

"It's different every time. Sometimes I picture a maggot-and-stick-of-butter sandwich with microwaved mayonnaise poured over the top. Or last time it was being forced to suck on every single one of McAdams's hairy toes after he'd worn socks all day," she'd whispered into the phone. I could always imagine her shrugging her shoulders nonchalantly as she painted her fingernails or downloaded new songs onto her computer while the rest of us suffered through another endless day of school. It was such a Grace move.

And today she'd have been proud. Naomi arrived just in time with the bucket, and I puked inside for good measure. Once I started, it was kind of hard to stop. No matter how hard I tried not to think about licking the inside rim of one of the boys' toilets in the gym, the image still kept popping up.

And I had to admit, the puking was better than the post-puking. Especially when I'd just destroyed one-third of Bradley Farrow's closet while both he and his gorgeous sister looked on. Talk about embarrassing.

Luckily, I also knew how to cry on demand. Just another one of my many talents.

"Oh my God," I said, using my finger to wipe away the mascara-tinted tears beneath my eyes. If I'd known I was going to have to puke, I would have worn waterproof. "I'm so, so sorry. I didn't feel good all of a sudden and I thought this was the bathroom and by the time I made it inside, it was too late, and oh my God, oh my God. I can't believe I just did that."

"It's okay, seriously," Naomi said, stifling a laugh. "I'm just glad he's the history buff." She nodded toward her brother, covering her smirk with a hand.

Bradley shoved her and mumbled something that sounded like "It's fine" under his breath, even though it clearly wasn't fine. Naomi helped me up and handed me a tissue, and Bradley returned with a garbage bag, some towels, and an armful of cleaning supplies I was almost positive he'd never used in his entire life.

"I'll just catch up with you later," he said, his voice sounding more nasal than normal. Clearly he was trying to breathe through his mouth. I didn't blame him for a second. There was absolutely nothing worse than puke, and the thought of a random guy's puke splattered all over the contents of my closet made me feel the tiniest twinge of guilt.

But then I remembered Bethany. And the phone in my pocket. Puke was the least of Bradley Farrow's worries.

Naomi led me down the stairs like an invalid, her arm hooked through mine. "So, um, everything okay with you? That scream did not sound good," I said, reminding myself to take it slow, that I was supposed to be sick.

"It was the weirdest thing. I was just sitting and watching TV when this guy pressed his face against our window. But when Bradley came downstairs, there was no one outside. Come to think of it, he actually looked sort of like that redheaded neighbor of yours…"

"Oh gosh, I feel like I might be sick again." Amazing how potential puke can change the subject in a hurry.

Naomi rushed down the stairs ahead of me, ostensibly to avoid getting sprayed by rogue chunks of vomit. "Just hold on a sec. We're almost to the door."

As I wrapped up my own personal walk of shame, I hoped Taylor knew how much I was sacrificing in all of this. I didn't exactly see her puking on demand in front of two of the most popular kids in school. Granted she was *the* most popular girl in school, but still.

"Um…please tell your brother that I'm really sorry. I seriously don't even know what to say." I could barely look her in the eye.

My red cheeks were one thing that didn't have to be faked. No one ever forgot a puker. In lower school, Leif Anderson puked all over Penelope Townsend's desk, destroying the self-portrait she'd just completed during art class. To this day, you always left a little extra space between yourself and Leif.

I was never, ever going to live this one down. I patted the side of my skirt and felt the hard case of the cell phone beneath my fingertips. I hoped it was worth it.

"Meh." Naomi shrugged her shoulders. "Bradley floods a toilet at the club every time we eat dinner there. If he tries to bring it up, just tell him you know all about how our dad had to cover the cost of the men's bathroom renovation last year."

"Thanks, Naomi," I said, forcing a smile and slipping through the door.

I ran all the way to Liam's jeep, which was parked a block and a half over. Seth flung the back door open for me as though I was being chased and about to toss myself in the car, which would have been cool but overly dramatic considering there was absolutely no one outside in the dead of winter. Taylor sat shotgun but was twisted around in her seat, anxiety warping her features and highlighting the purple bags beneath her eyes.

"So?" Liam asked, letting me pull myself into the car before moving into first gear. Seth seemed disappointed at my entrance.

"Let's just say I had to play make-me-puke."

Taylor looked horrified, Seth laughed, and Liam appeared genuinely impressed.

"But, I got…this." I yanked the sparkly phone out of my pocket and held it up. For a second, I was so proud of myself that I forgot what finding the phone actually meant. Then I noticed the expression on Taylor's face. She looked like she was about to burst into tears. Her hand shook as she reached toward me, gingerly lifting the phone from my fingers.

"It's dea…er…out of batteries, but I have the same one. We can charge it at my house," I said, kicking myself for my initial choice of words. Liam flicked his blinker and made the turn in the direction of Seth's and my street as Taylor turned the phone over and examined the sparkly "B."

It wasn't hard to imagine how I'd feel if the roles were reversed. I'd been there. Except there was never any hope. The night of the fire, I just knew Grace was gone. I barely had time to understand what hit me. With Bethany, there was still hope. Except now, as Taylor turned the phone over in her hands, I could see that hope slipping between her fingers. And it was hard to watch.

The three of us marched into my house and rushed up the stairs to the charger. The phone gave a satisfying beep as we plugged it in, and we huddled around it, our heads almost touching. I resisted the urge to cheer it on. When it finally powered on, the series of beeps and vibrations it emitted made me afraid it was broken. But really, it was recovering hundreds of missed calls, texts, and voice mails. I thought of all the times I'd called Grace the night of the fire. The calls she never got.

"Do you…" I wasn't even sure what I wanted to say, but it didn't seem right for anyone but Taylor to be digging around in Bethany's phone. "Do you want to?" I lifted it and placed it in her hands.

She scrolled through the missed calls first. They were mainly from Taylor and a few of their close friends. I saw "Mom" and "Dad" and even a few of Bethany's brothers' names, but none from the boys we were expecting. The texts were the same. Text after text from contact after contact. I'd never considered how much a person could miss without their phone for three days. Especially if people were worried.

But Taylor quickly scrolled through the texts asking about the yoga retreat or wondering about cell service and a couple that just said "ommmmmmmmm," which I actually thought was kind of funny.

Taylor went right to the texts that came in on January 10th. The night of Obsideo. There had to be a hundred texts from that day, and almost every one of them was from Bradley Farrow.

> u think ur so smart

> they'll never believe u

> my word against urs. u know how that goes

> just wait

The phone slipped between Taylor's fingers, striking the hardwood floor and making all of us jump. But it didn't matter. The texts were seared into my brain. I just hoped we weren't too late.

Chapter 30

The school day was long under normal circumstances, but even longer that Friday. Watching the clock in every classroom tick away the minutes until I could interrogate Bradley Farrow was torture.

Under the new rules and regulations, by precisely 4:30 p.m. on any given day, Pemberly Brown transformed into a ghost town. The long marble hallways appeared desolate and abandoned, the parking lot cleared of all the expensive cars that occupied spots during the day. No extracurriculars, no detentions, no school meetings, no teacher planning sessions went past 4:00 p.m. Supposedly the school kept late afternoons free to ensure balance for the students. I always thought it was because too many mommies and daddies complained that school events were interfering with their happy hours, but according to Ben, the headmaster had his own extracurricular project he was attending to.

Normally I was the first one out the door when the last bell rang, but today I lingered at my locker and wandered the deserted halls long after most of the students and teachers had left for the day.

I heard whispers. The faint echo of voices trailing down empty hallways.

House party at the U, keg, college boys.

Peter Remington-Davis's parents are out of town. Pre-game.

My mom's stylist at Saks put it on hold, meet me there after school.

The 7:30 show with those kids from public.

Student parking was already empty. Even the office was dark behind its glass walls. The week was over. It was time to play. Liam thought I was with Seth; Seth thought I was with Liam; and Taylor thought I was with both of them. Even after seeing Bradley's name attached to the texts, after reading his threats to Bethany, after I'd spent hours imagining what he was truly capable of, he still didn't scare me. I was too pissed to be scared. We had a history, and I wanted to watch Bradley go down knowing I was the one who pulled the trigger. *Bang.*

And it wasn't because Bradley had spread the word of my puke-n-rally. He hadn't. Turns out Bradley can be a true gentleman in regards to humiliating bodily functions, even if they do destroy his designer wardrobe. I was angry because none of this should have been happening. I remembered the way his mouth felt on mine when he kissed me the night Grace died. The way my entire body had leaned into his, the way my lips had parted and my fingers had involuntarily wound themselves around his neck. But the moment I gave in was the same moment he'd pulled away. It wasn't until he'd left me sitting alone on the bench that I'd smelled the smoke.

And now Bethany's disappearance was history repeating itself. Only this time instead of sitting on a bench at the Pemberly Brown lake, giggling like an imbecile with butterflies fluttering thousands of tiny wings in my stomach, I was going to confront the bastard head-on. "Fool me once, shame on you. Fool me twice, I'm going to kick your ass." Wait, I don't think that's how the saying goes.

Regardless, a confrontation between me and Bradley Farrow was long overdue. And so I sat in front of his locker. Waiting. He could have pushed out through a side door or maybe the back, but his black Range Rover was parked where it had been all day, a layer of snow on the windshield reflecting the last rays of the late-afternoon sun. I knew there was a risk in leaving my post to search the empty school, that we might completely miss each other as he went out and I went up or vice versa, but I couldn't sit still any longer.

Plus, I figured walking around might help me formulate a plan. Which I clearly sucked at, hence my little puke-on-demand performance. My riding boots clicked along the abandoned hallways, the sound bouncing off the surrounding lockers, a few with doors still hanging open slightly after students rushed home at the end of a busy day.

For once, I actually had time to prepare, and I knew exactly how everything was going to play out. I'd quote a few of Bradley's horrible texts to Bethany so he'd figure out that I had her phone. And then I'd force him to confess to everything. Including where he'd hidden Bethany. After that I'd rescue Bethany and convince her to press charges and destroy the Brotherhood once and for all. It was so easy, it was sick.

Of course there was always the chance he'd confess right when he saw me, a silent understanding exchanged between both of us that this wasn't going to go any further, that I was here for the truth. Then he'd lead me to the Brotherhood's new headquarters, which also happened to be where they were holding Bethany, and I'd finally save someone instead of sitting around with my thumb up my butt.

Suddenly, my neck prickled with the knowledge that I was no longer alone in the deserted hallways. I whirled around, prepared to finally confront Bradley, but instead caught a flash of plaid and streaming black hair disappearing around the corner of the hallway.

Bethany?

I clutched the pearls wrapped around my neck. She was back. Or was I just hallucinating again? I chased after her. I had to know for sure.

When I turned the corner, the hallway was empty except for a small slip of paper in the middle of the floor. I didn't start trembling until I saw the familiar orange handwriting. Grace.

This time it had been Grace.

> Don't trust him. The lies bind.

But there was no time to process the note, because I finally heard his voice. It almost sounded like it was coming from within the walls.

"We're almost there. Yeah. No, not everyone. They're taken care of. I'll find out who. Uh-huh. Yeah."

There was a pause as though I was listening in on half a phone conversation. Inside a locker. I brought my ear closer to the metal grates, and sure enough, I heard the voice even clearer.

"No, not after Obsideo. No, no. She's gone. We're supposed to move forward with Conventus as planned. Yeah. Everything's in place."

I stepped back after the voice dropped off again, my hand over my mouth. I'd recognize Bradley Farrow's voice anywhere, but this didn't make any sense. What the hell was he doing in the lockers?

And then I remembered what Ben had said—I heard his voice clear as day. "And now that they have these new secret passageways built into the walls, they don't really use the tunnels anymore."

Just as my feeble brain finally began to put two and two together, I saw one of the handles of the lockers jiggle. I looked at the note in my hands, thought about the words I just heard, and I realized I wasn't ready to face Bradley. Not yet.

I whipped my head left and right looking for a place to hide. About three feet down, a locker door hung ajar, a heavy fleece preventing the lock from clicking into place. I ran toward it and sized up the space. Whoever used the locker wasn't exactly a neat person. An entire coat closet worth of jackets were looped over the hook, and textbooks were stacked with crumpled papers sticking out from between the pages. I didn't think even the creepy contortionist who had performed at Maddie's seventh-grade birthday party, made famous by his ability to fold himself into a small cooler, could have pulled this off. But I had to try. I put my foot in first, shoving the fleece and nylon back with my arm while my body temperature increased approximately fifteen degrees.

"Ahem."

At that moment I knew I'd rather be puking. I yanked my foot from the jaws of life, aka the most disgusting locker on the face of the planet, while working very hard not to make eye contact.

"You're not going to puke again, are you?" Bradley stood at the other end of the hallway, as far away as possible from the locker I'd just heard him speaking out of. Despite the fact that I was now questioning my own sanity, I did know one thing for sure. He had not emerged from behind that locker door. There was just no way. Empty or not. No one could fit into one of those. Especially not someone Bradley's size.

Before I could stop myself, another kind of vomit began spewing out uncontrollably from between my lips. And it was so much worse than a partially digested lunch.

"I saw the texts on Bethany's phone. I know you kidnapped her and I know she's in danger and I have no idea what you're planning on doing to her, but I swear to God, I will bring you down and destroy everything you love and I heard you talking in that locker and I don't care how you got in there but I am so sick of all these freaking secrets so bring me to her right now or…or…I'll…" I wracked my brain in the second it took to catch my breath and said the first thing that came to mind, raging lunatic or not: "Or I'll puke on you. I swear to God, I'll throw up right on you." I paused for dramatic effect. "And I had tacos for lunch."

Even with the distance between us, I could see Bradley's eyes widen. I watched as he pulled his head back as though he wasn't quite sure he was hearing what he was hearing. And then he lowered his head in his hands, his giant palms covering his face. I thought for a second that a confession was forthcoming, that I'd finally brought the king of the Brotherhood to tears. But then I realized this was an emotional breakdown of a completely different variety.

Bradley wasn't crying; he was laughing, the huge, shoulder-jerking, can't-catch-your-breath kind of laughing that Grace, Maddie, and I used to spend entire summers doing.

I probably should have been scared for my own safety, considering I was alone in an empty building with a person clearly crazier than myself, but I was too pissed off for fear.

Instead, a burning rage coursed through my veins, and my fists clenched and unclenched. I was going to get the truth out of Bradley Farrow, even if I had to rip it out of his throat. I rushed at him with every intention of wrapping my hands around his neck and doing just that.

Triumph burst sweet and bitter, like sour candy in my mouth, the moment my fingers met his neck.

Chapter 31

Bradley pried my fingers off his neck, one by one. He wasn't even breathing heavily. Apparently, the nickname Kate "the Strangler" Lowry wasn't in my future.

"What the hell is wrong with you?" The note of genuine concern in his voice only stoked the anger burning in my gut.

"Just tell me where she is. I know everything. There's no point in lying." I was practically begging. So much for maintaining control of the situation.

"Are you off your meds or something?" Bradley leaned in close to examine my pupils, and his warm breath lapped at my cheek. He grabbed my hand. "You should sit down. You don't look so good."

When his words finally sank in, I jerked my arm away from his. Unbelievable. Who did he think he was fooling?

"I'm fine." I wanted to take a few steps back. I wanted to scream at the top of my lungs and let out all the frustration, let it echo through the empty hallways. But I couldn't let him see that I was rattled. I had to hold my ground. "I just want answers."

"You're kidding, right?"

I shook my head. "I know you guys have her. Just tell me where she is."

"You really think I *kidnapped* Bethany?"

"I saw the texts you were sending her. I found her phone." I sort of wished I'd brought it with me now, but I couldn't risk Bradley taking the only evidence I'd been able to find so far. Been there, done that. I'd locked the bedazzled phone in the small safe under my bed at home. No one knew the code to that safe except me and Grace, and even if she was still haunting the halls of Pemberly Brown, I was pretty sure she wouldn't be helping out the Brotherhood anytime soon.

Bradley shook his head and swore under his breath. "I know you have absolutely no reason to trust me, but someone is setting me up."

I snorted. I couldn't help it. How stupid did he think I was?

"Bradley?" A deep voice called out from down the hall and we both jumped a little.

Bradley narrowed his eyes as he peered down the hall. "Oh, um…hey, Dad."

Mr. Farrow walked toward us with a tight smile on his face. He was handsome in the most intimidating way possible, all ebony skin and taut cheekbones. It should have been reassuring to have an adult present, but the knot that formed in my stomach when Mr. Farrow towered over me was anything but.

"Did you get what you needed?" Mr. Farrow shot his son a meaningful look.

"Uh, yeah. I got it." Bradley's cool confidence completely

disappeared in front of his father. Not that I blamed him. I think if I'd had a full bladder I probably would have peed myself.

Mr. Farrow turned his sharp eyes on me.

"Hello, Kate. What's keeping you here so late?" I was pretty sure Mr. Farrow's question could be loosely translated as: "What the hell are you doing snooping around in my son's business?" and I didn't exactly have an answer on the tip of my tongue. Thankfully, Bradley beat me to the punch.

"Kate just forgot one of her books. She didn't see…I mean, I just ran into her on my way out to my car."

Mr. Farrow did not look convinced. Not even close.

"Are you sure there isn't something you want to tell me, Bradley?"

I opened my mouth to speak. The hell with this. Mr. Farrow should know what his son and his friends have been up to. It was time to lay all my cards out on the table. Now or never. "The truth is…"

"We're dating," Bradley interrupted.

"Huh?" I looked over at Bradley. "Are you on…"

"It's okay, Kate," Bradley interrupted, gently placing his fingers over my mouth. "I was going to tell him anyway. I don't want you to get *hurt*." Bradley had a strange look in his eyes, and his emphasis on the word "hurt" convinced me that it might be in my best interest to nod along with his scheme, as opposed to biting his fingers, which would have been my next move.

I ducked away from Bradley's fingers. "Well, I've always liked Bradley. I'm not sure if he told you that." I fluttered my eyelashes in Bradley's direction and swallowed the bile in my throat. "It's embarrassing but true!"

Mr. Farrow stiffened. And Bradley started talking fast to cover up my social ineptitude.

"Right. It's just one of those things. You know…love at first sight. Or maybe first barf." Bradley gave me an awkward half hug and smiled winningly, but the look faded as soon as he met his dad's eyes. Anger flashed across Mr. Farrow's face, and I was reminded at once of his power.

"You'll forgive me for being a little shocked. Bradley seems to think most everything is a joke. He forgets how quickly things can become serious."

"Actually, I'm reminded every day," Bradley mumbled under his breath.

Somehow I got the feeling we weren't talking relationships anymore.

"Sometimes when you've had everything handed to you on a silver platter, you need a reminder of what it means to actually have to work for something." Mr. Farrow winked at Bradley, mocking his son. It reminded me of that song about fathers, sons, and (randomly) a cat in a cradle that always made my dad cry. Dr. Prozac would have a field day with this little display.

I shifted uncomfortably on my feet and stumbled into the locker behind me. Mr. Farrow jerked his head in my direction and gave me a long, hard look starting at the tips of my beat-up riding boots and going all the way up to my blue hair. "Kate, you'll be happy to know that we've teamed up with the Lees to contribute to the new wing in Grace's name. I know you've been doing everything in your power to keep her memory alive."

My stomach clenched when he said her name, his words sounding more like a challenge than idle small talk. Sweat ran down into the small of my back. The mere mention of Grace and a subtle hint at my failed investigation were enough to put a crack in my performance as Kate Lowry, perfect girlfriend.

"Grace was my best friend. I can't let anyone forget her. I'm sure you understand."

Mr. Farrow smiled, but the smile didn't quite reach his eyes. "Of course, it's easy to rewrite history when we lose a loved one, isn't it? Sometimes we only remember the things we want to remember."

The truth of his words felt like a knife in my heart. That was the story of my life, wasn't it? Everyone remembering the stuff that they wanted to remember, ignoring the facts, fudging the truth.

Bradley slung his arm around my shoulders and gave me a quick squeeze. I shrugged his arm off in disgust before I remembered we were supposed to be dating. Or something.

"Well, the good news is that I remember everything. All of it." I grabbed my bag from the floor and swung it over my shoulders. "It was kind of my job to know her secrets."

Mr. Farrow cleared his throat and looked a little shocked. The expression that flickered over his handsome face somehow made him look even more like Bradley.

"You've chosen well for once, Bradley. At least this one seems loyal."

Our strained conversation officially fell into awkward territory as Bradley and I stared at our feet, the hallway completely silent except for the low hiss of the heat kicking on.

I leaned my head against the locker next to me, and that's when I heard the voice.

"She's as good as dead. It's all over for the Sisterhood."

I froze, Mr. Farrow stiffened, and Bradley jerked to attention. Guess Bradley and I weren't the only ones who decided to stay late tonight. There was someone else in the passageway, and they were talking about Bethany. They had her in there. I was sure of it. If only I could figure out how to get to her.

"Well, this place still has the strangest echoes, doesn't it, Kate?" Mr. Farrow wrapped his strong fingers around my elbow and started to drag me toward the main doors of the school.

I nodded mutely. Unable to think of anything except the words I'd heard behind the lockers.

"Some people even say it's haunted. What do you think, Kate? Do you think the school is haunted?"

"Maybe." I finally found my voice. "But something tells me there are scarier things than ghosts at this school."

Mr. Farrow laughed and Bradley joined in, but his voice was an octave higher than it normally was.

"Ah, well, you might be right, Kate." Mr. Farrow patted me fondly on the back. "After all, ghosts can't tell secrets."

To: GraceLee@pemberlybrown.edu
Sent: Fri 1/16 7:11 PM
From: KateLowry@pemberlybrown.edu
Subject: (no subject)

Grace,
I'm so sorry. I feel like I'm letting you down all over again. Our slam

book showed up in History. It was like opening a time machine. All I could talk about then was Bradley freaking Farrow. Yeah, the same guy who distracted me from saving your life and kidnapped Bethany. What a charmer. And now I've somehow managed to become his beard or whatever it is they call fake girlfriends for guys who have an unhealthy amount of fear for their fathers.

Bradley is like this walking, talking reminder of the Kate I used to be. The girl who followed boys around school and doodled their names in her notebooks. And I hate that girl. Or maybe I just want to hate her because I can't. Not totally. I mean, that was the girl who was your best friend. She couldn't have been all bad, right?

Chapter 32

As a result of my unfortunate encounter with the Farrows, I was in no position to be spending my evening anywhere but in my room, where I could work through everything that had gone down. I had a hate hangover. I couldn't stop thinking about Bradley texting Bethany those horrible things and then turning around and trying to save me (or himself) from his father. And then there were the notes from Grace and her belongings slowly finding their way back into my life. Something just wasn't adding up.

Maybe that's why I kept screening Liam's calls. I'm not sure why I didn't feel like talking. It's not like Liam did anything. Things had been almost normal between us the other night, but I just couldn't bring myself to answer.

Instead, I lingered over the email I'd just written to Grace, deleting and retyping lines, watching the cursor eat letter after letter and then resurrecting each word, one by one. It was therapeutic somehow, filling the space and then emptying it, addicting. I considered who I'd be in ten years if the strange obsession continued, possibly featured on some messed-up documentary with girls who ate their own hair or guys who collected toenail clippings. Kate: the girl who typed and deleted the same one hundred words around the clock. Just another head case.

So it was no wonder I didn't feel his presence until too late. By the time I turned around, he was hunched over a few inches behind me, his eyes narrowed, taking in every letter I'd typed to Grace. Every private Bradley-doused letter.

"Oh my God, you scared me!" I threw my hand over my heart to demonstrate, but the action was wasted as Liam continued to stare at my computer, his face all scrunched up. I quickly minimized the email. If I didn't look guilty before, that action pretty much sealed the deal.

Liam stood straighter then, his lips pinched together in a line. I wished he would talk, because the longer the silence lingered, the more time I had to think about my course of action—and at a time like this, thinking was the enemy. I determined the need to take one of two possible avenues: get pissed at Liam for snooping in my private business or play dumb.

"Are you hungry? I'm starving. We have no food in the house. Let's go out!" If that wasn't dumb, I'm not sure what is. The smile I'd managed to swipe across my face threatened to consume the rest of my features in one gigantic bite.

"When were you planning on telling me that you are now dating Bradley Farrow?"

I briefly considered playing super-dumb and suggesting a restaurant, but the hurt in Liam's eyes stopped me in my tracks. "It's not what you think."

"Which part? That you used to be obsessed with him or that you're talking to him again?" Liam flinched as though the words burned coming out. If only he knew how much they hurt on my end too. The worst part was that in these types of situations, no amount of explaining could ever fix things. Everything was out there, displayed on some billboard situated right where the only person I'd ever want to hide it from was standing. I was screwed.

I opened my mouth to say something, even though I wasn't quite sure what it was going to be yet, and the Amicus private-message tone sounded on my computer. I squeezed my eyes shut as Liam looked beyond me, intercepting the message before I could do a thing about it. I spun around and opened one eye, praying, "Please be from Seth, please be from Seth, please be from Seth," and saw Bradley's name in the message box. Naturally.

> Meet me at the club in 30. We need to talk.

"I'm out of here." Four words. It only took four words from Liam to break my heart. It was official. Bradley Farrow was destroying my life for the second time.

"Liam. Wait! I swear I can explain. I hate him! He's awful and I hate him." Tears welled in my eyes as I said the words to Liam's back.

"I thought something was wrong. You weren't answering your phone. But it makes sense now."

"Liam, it's not like that. I ran into Bradley at school and…"

"Oh, when you were supposed to be with Seth? Yeah, I saw him at the McDonald's drive-through. Without you."

"Just let me explain. I heard him talking…from a locker." I said this as though it would explain everything, defend my email to Grace, and justify Bradley's private message about the country club.

But Liam was already halfway out the door.

"Liam!" I jumped up, cursing my computer, the message, Bradley, Taylor, even Bethany. "Liam, wait!" I ran to the top of the stairs.

Liam opened the front door and then, without turning around, said, "I'm not going to watch you self-destruct. I just won't do it. You want to hang out with assholes who kidnap girls in the name of some lame-ass secret society, go for it. But don't expect me to be there for you when everything falls apart." He turned around then and met my eyes, his own a steel gray. "Grace is dead, Kate. She's gone. You're not keeping her memory alive. You're following in her footsteps."

The door slammed and my mom's voice trailed up the stairs. "Kate?"

She was the absolute last person I wanted to talk to right now. We didn't exactly have the sort of mother-daughter relationship where she knocked quietly on my bedroom door wielding a pint of Ben & Jerry's and offering a soft, understanding smile.

I stood at the top of the stairs, Liam's words hanging in the air like black smoke, burning my lungs and stinging my eyes. Maybe it was clear that he cared about me, that he couldn't handle the risk, but in that moment the only thing that made any sense was my anger. I might have even hated him a little bit for what he said about Grace, because hating him was so much easier than understanding him. He obviously felt the same way.

I wasn't going to apologize for confronting Bradley on my own.

As much as Liam and Seth loved our whole *Mod Squad* routine, did they honestly think that Bradley Farrow would tell them anything? It was up to me to get him talking. And I definitely wasn't going to apologize for working out my feelings through an email to Grace. It was practically prescribed by Dr. Prozac, and Liam had no right to take that away from me. Even if he didn't like what I had to say.

When my phone vibrated on my duvet, I cursed myself for hoping to see Liam's name on the screen. He didn't deserve that hope right now.

But instead of Liam it was a text from a number I didn't recognize.

> R u coming or what?

My powers of deductive reasoning led me to one name.

Bradley.

At this point, all the valued relationships in my life were total crap, so I might as well make it worth it. I wondered if blue hair was against the club's dress code. Probably.

> On my way.

The moment I sent the text, I regretted it. Then again, it's not like I had anything to lose.

Chapter 33

I'd only been to Bradley's country club once, for Camille Youngblood's eleventh birthday party in lower school. My parents claimed that they didn't subscribe to the culture of exclusivity that country clubs perpetuated. Their words, not mine. Personally, I think they probably just couldn't get in.

Either way, no one ever turned down an invitation to the country club, no matter who was doing the inviting. And tonight the invitation came with the added bonus of a "we need to talk," which clearly meant Bradley had something to say.

And I was willing to bet that that "something" was related to a certain missing someone. An image of Bethany wrapped in a blanket and being led to safety by yours truly flashed in my mind. If I saved Bethany, Liam would see how stupid he was being about the email. He'd see that I was just using Bradley for information.

The club was exactly how I remembered it. The black sign with gold engraved lettering hung on a wrought-iron post, lightly dusted with snow. Trees hugged the property and were lit individually with spotlights, the snow sparkling like a collection of diamonds. Add a horse and carriage and some kid rolling snowballs, and I'd be staring at a Norman Rockwell painting.

When the clubhouse came into view, I pulled the hood of my winter jacket tighter around my chin, tucking a stray lock of blue hair behind my ear. As much as I loved my whole rebel-with-a-cause vibe, a tiny part of me wished I could walk into the club as a boring brunette wearing ballet flats and an A-line skirt. It was the kind of place that made you want to fit in. Desperately.

I walked into the lobby and kept my eyes trained on the green carpeting, praying my scuffed riding boots screamed "Vintage!" instead of "Charity case!" But after only a second, I felt a pair of rheumy eyes fall to the top of my head, work their way down past my perfectly broken-in jeans, and finally land on the salt stains lining the toes of my "vintage" boots. No. Such. Luck.

"May I help you, dear? You look lost." Her voice was laced with disgust.

Enough of this crap.

I yanked off my hood and revealed my bright blue ponytail in all its glory. It felt a little like giving her the middle finger. The old biddy gasped and my lips twitched up in a smile.

"I'm here to see Bradley Farrow." I did my best to match her haughty tone.

"I believe you'll find him downstairs in the café next to the gym. That's where all the young people seem to congregate." She sniffed once, pulled her long fur coat tighter around her shoulders, and paraded out the front door.

"Friendly here, aren't they?" I whirled around to see Naomi Farrow smiling at me from one of the couches surrounding the massive fireplace, textbooks and papers spread all around her.

"Just lovely. Think she'll write me into her will?"

"Doubtful. Rumor has it she's leaving everything she's got to her horrible little dog."

"Of course she is."

Naomi gathered up a few notebooks and gestured for me to sit.

I glanced down at my phone and shook my head. "I'm actually meeting someone…" That someone being your brother, who I once had a socially crippling crush on and who most recently appears to be hiding missing girls in lockers.

"Interesting." The word was heavy with judgment. "He's downstairs. As usual."

"Thanks, Naomi." I made my way toward the huge spiral staircase to the left of the sitting room.

"Kate?"

I swiveled my head back to look at her again. Her hair fell down her back in soft waves; her honey-brown skin glowed in the firelight; and her fingers twisted the Sisterhood's crest around her necklace. "Be careful."

I nodded. I had no way of knowing how much Naomi knew or whose side she was on, but I couldn't exactly argue with that little piece of advice.

I found Bradley sitting at a café table with a coffee. He raised his eyebrows in greeting.

"Took you long enough."

"Yeah, well, I wasn't sure whether I should come." The words were out before I could stop them.

"Why?" His golden eyes burned into me. It was kind of a loaded question. There was no way I was going to admit he'd caused a rift between Liam and me.

"Where is Bethany?" Always answer a question with a question. Wasn't that an old detective trick? Or maybe it was just a really annoying habit I'd picked up after spending too much time with Seth. Too close to call.

He eyed my phone on the table and his smile evaporated, his eyes clouding over and losing their signature shine.

"Do you really think I kidnapped Bethany?"

I had to hand it to him; Bradley Farrow did not mess around.

"Yes." Honesty had to be the best policy at this point.

"How do you even know she's missing? I thought she was at some yoga retreat."

I started picking the remaining polish from my nails underneath the table. I wanted to bite them so badly, but there was no way I was going there in front of Bradley. "Well, her house was ransacked and I got a text of her all tied up. And I found her phone in your closet and there are all these crazy texts from you. Just tell me where she is before I go back to the police."

Bradley raised an eyebrow and I sighed. He knew as well as I did that the police weren't an option.

"Where's the phone?"

I made the mistake of looking down at my bag on the ground. I'd thrown the phone in at the last minute. It sounds stupid, but I'd thought I might need proof. Before I could even process what was happening, Bradley's arm shot out and snagged my bag. He had Bethany's phone in his hands before I could even manage to string together a decent curse.

I jumped up from my chair and tried to grab the phone back, but Bradley was too fast for me. He had already moved across the café and was scrolling quickly through the texts.

"These aren't from me." He shook his head. "I mean, they have my name on them, but they're not…" His fingers danced and slid across the screen of the phone until he looked up at me with triumph in his eyes. "I didn't send these texts."

I rolled my eyes. "Whatever, Bradley. Just give it back, okay?"

"No, seriously." He tossed the phone in my direction. I watched it spiral through the air, hoping against all reason that this was one of those slow-motion moments where I'd extend my arm and revel in the moment of electronic-to-palm contact, even if it meant sliding on the floor on my belly. Unfortunately, when the phone struck the shiny, hardwood floor, it made the type of sound that can only be described as "broken."

"Shit!" Dropping the phone felt exactly like missing a fly ball after being exiled to right field for an entire softball game. Crappy with a heavy dose of humiliation.

I scrambled to put the phone back together and held my breath waiting for it to power on. I was such an idiot for coming here. For practically handing my prime suspect my only piece of evidence. What was wrong with me? Where was my judgment? Why did Bradley Farrow always manage to turn me into some kind of half-witted idiot?

The screen of Bethany's phone lit up, and the breath I'd been holding came out in a big whoosh. I grabbed my bag, tossed the phone in the side pocket, and booked it toward the stairs.

"Hey! Where're you going?"

I ignored Bradley completely and kept moving. Time to cut my losses.

"Wait up!"

I was halfway up the stairs.

"Kate!" I felt an arm on my shoulder. Bradley whirled me around.

"I didn't send those texts."

"Super. Thanks for sharing. I totally believe you." I turned around and started walking back up the stairs.

My phone vibrated in my pocket and I pulled it out. A new text.

The #s don't match

I froze. Bradley had texted me from this number earlier, and based on the fact that he was standing two stairs down from me with his phone in his hands, he had just texted me again now.

I clawed around in my bag for Bethany's phone and quickly pulled up Bradley's texts. I clicked on his name, bringing up the cell number he'd been texting from. It was a completely different number from the one on my phone.

Either Bradley had a super-secret cell phone he used to send threatening texts to missing girls or he was actually telling the truth.

Chapter 34

"But how…"

I looked down the stairs at Bradley and he just shrugged. "Someone's setting us up."

Us. The way he said it sent a chill up and down my spine, which subsequently triggered goose bumps, as usual. I promptly rubbed them away. I promised myself that it was just the idea of being in it with someone else, that it had nothing to do with Bradley and his smoothly shaved head, his golden-brown skin, his straight teeth and soft lips. Because I already had the boy of my dreams; he just happened to be beyond pissed at me *again* at the moment.

"You're freezing. Let's sit in the parlor. There's a fireplace, and after you warm up, I'll drive you home."

We walked back into the Norman Rockwell painting that doubled as the clubhouse lobby, but I barely felt the warmth of the roaring fire. Something wasn't right. Somehow I wasn't entirely convinced of Bradley's innocence. A few minutes by the fire with him might reveal something interesting.

I ran my fingers along the wall as we walked. The wallpaper would have been tacky anywhere else, but somehow the random collection of horses and dogs and mallards and trees seemed perfect, even stylish, at the country club. Because the club was so exclusive, you naturally assumed that all of the furnishings were rare and expensive. A tattered sofa transformed into an elegant antique, and tacky wallpaper became a statement instead of an eyesore.

Ahead, a grouping of old ladies who were clearly besties with the old hag I'd scandalized upon my arrival not-so-subtly gave Bradley and me the once-over. My blue hair obviously clashed with the overall décor of the club in that it was neither old nor expensive.

I almost stopped dead in my tracks when I felt Bradley's hand move down over my arm. His fingers clasped my own, and I had the overwhelming urge to apologize for walking too close and accidentally forcing our hands together. But his hand didn't fall away. Instead, the closer we walked to the women, the tighter he held on, determination hardening his features, his grip borderline hurting my hand.

"Mrs. Portney, Mrs. Howard, Mrs. Jacobson." He gave each of the women, whose mouths now hung open ever so slightly, a curt nod as we strolled past, and I couldn't help but smile at their shocked faces. They obviously thought Bradley was slumming with some tart with blue hair. Meanwhile my hand was on fire with…friendship.

"Sorry, that was just too easy. Mrs. Howard remembers the good ole days when the only black people around here were watering the golf course." Bradley leaned close, his breath moving the tiny hairs around my ear.

"And here I thought they were just admiring my hair." I fluffed my ponytail and Bradley snorted, our heads practically touching as we entered the parlor.

"Oh…" Naomi said. Her eyes zeroed in on our hands, still firmly clasped. I yanked my hand from his and wiped it across my jeans for good measure. "I was just leaving." She busied herself gathering together her loose papers and shutting textbooks with a thud. Clearly she wasn't anywhere near finished.

Bradley didn't seem fazed by his younger sister, but my stomach clenched at the thought of Naomi misunderstanding anything between her brother and me. Not only was it common knowledge that Liam and I were together, but she'd just told me minutes before to be careful. She wasn't stupid. She wasn't jealous. She'd given me fair warning.

"Meet you by the valet in ten?" Bradley said as he threw himself onto the overstuffed couch closest to the fire.

"Nah, I'll call Mom." And then Naomi was gone, rushing off without ever making eye contact with me or saying good-bye.

Awkward. I wondered for the millionth time if maybe I was talking to the wrong person in all of this. As I lowered my body onto the fluffy couch next to Bradley, suspicion strangled me all over again. I decided to model Bradley's way of doing things and cut right to the chase.

"How do I know you're not setting me up?" And the second the words were out of my mouth, everything sort of crystallized in my mind. The phone in his pocket, the switched texts, the Amicus message, the hand-holding.

"I have no idea how to convince you of anything, Kate. All I know is that according to you, Bethany is gone. And according to everyone else, she's at a yoga retreat." His voice trailed off a little, but I still caught the last part. "Not that I'm surprised."

"What's that supposed to mean? Not that you're surprised?" He lowered his head a little and avoided my eyes. He was hiding something. I felt a new resolve. "What do you know?"

I was going to find something out. I was going to get somewhere. Something was going on. We weren't crazy. This was all worth it. The problem was that everything was so muddled and twisty that sometimes it felt like every time I got a new piece of information, I ended up more confused than I had been before. One step forward, five million steps back and all that.

"It's nothing." I didn't even have to roll my eyes or snap at him for him to pick up that his answer was not going to fly. "Well, it's Conventus. She's against it, so I could see why someone might try to get rid of her. You wouldn't understand. It's society stuff. But with the vote on Tuesday, I'm not surprised she's gone. Taylor shouldn't be either."

And a bell went off. Conventus. The word was important. I'd heard it as we watched the boys circle Bradley. I'd found it in his room, heard him whisper about it in the hallway. It meant something.

"What's Conventus?"

He shook his head quickly and didn't even consider letting me in. "Listen. Don't worry about Bethany. She can take care of herself." He shut down. Again. But I wasn't going to let it happen. Not this time.

"I don't believe you." I lowered my chin and fought the humiliating urge to cry. It was so stupid. But the more I tried to fight them, the more I felt the tears gather along the edges of my lashes, the burn snake its way up my esophagus. The entire night had been such a waste. I'd lost my boyfriend, and I hadn't even made any progress in the process. It was a throwaway, a wash. And the cherry on top was apparently going to be me bawling like a baby because some stupid boy wouldn't tell me what Conventus was.

Screw that. I zipped up my jacket and grabbed my bag from the floor. I didn't need Bradley Farrow to tell me about Conventus. I had other resources, other options.

"Kate, wait." *Ignore*. I mentally pressed the button and shut out Bradley's sickeningly smooth voice like I would a phone call from my mom or dad. "Wait!" He gripped my upper arm and spun me around, placing his phone squarely in the center of my palm. "Check my messages. I really don't care. I swear to you I'm not hiding anything. There are just things I can't tell you. I'm sorry. I really am."

As much as I tried to avoid his golden eyes, they locked in on my own, urging me to scroll through his phone, to look through a window into his personal contacts.

So I did.

But not before walking a few feet away. Reading someone's personal messages felt a little like reading a letter in front of the person who wrote it to you. Mega awkward, so a little distance was mandatory. I scrolled right through to the days before Bethany's disappearance. There were all sorts of outgoing messages—a few to Bethany about random plans the group had made and even one from Bethany about Econ homework. Either he had deleted any incriminating messages immediately after sending them or he was telling the truth. But with completely neutral messages from Bethany coming in around the same time as the much more violent ones on her phone, I found it hard to believe he was responsible.

Someone was hiding something, and for the first time all night, I felt confident it wasn't Bradley.

And then his phone vibrated.

> Did u take care of her yet?

Alistair. I frantically deleted the message before walking back to the fire. Clearly Bradley couldn't be trusted, but he didn't need to know that. Something told me I'd be better off if he thought we were friends. I tossed the phone back to him.

"You win. I trust you."

He smiled his toothpaste-commercial smile and slung his arm around my shoulder as we walked out to his car. The old ladies tittered, and that uncomfortable heat burned through my thin sweater and coiled down my back again.

You know what they say: "Keep your friends close and ridiculously gorgeous guys who should be your enemy even closer."

Chapter 35

After Bradley dropped me off at my house, I briefly considered throwing on my coat and walking over to Seth's, but that would have required answering a lot of really annoying questions from Mrs. Allen. Plus there was always one place you could count on finding Seth after 10:00 p.m., and going there required a computer. I was about to do something I swore on my life that I'd never, ever do. But if there's one thing I've learned over the past couple years, it's never say never.

I pulled up a new window and typed in the web address for TwiChat.com. When prompted for a screen name, I decided to go with the old standby, "BellaBlows." If nothing else, I'd definitely stand out.

The chat was in full swing by the time I got in. Judging from the flurry of responses, tonight's topic was something about Edward's desire to keep Bella a mere mortal. Just as I was getting ready to type in a quick comment about Edward being a misogynistic asshat, I saw someone with the screen name WereWolfEdwardWhenBellaNeededHim. It had to be Seth. He's the only person who would possibly come up with a screen name that involved.

I figured a private message would be my best bet.

BellaBlows: Jacob rules, Edward drools.

WereWolfEdwardWhenBellaNeededHim: I tend to agree, but what's up with your screen name? Bella is a goddess.

BellaBlows: Bella is a weak damsel in distress who is completely reliant on supernatural male creatures to avoid walking off a cliff on a daily basis.

WereWolfEdwardWhenBellaNeededHim: Kate????

BellaBlows: HA!

WereWolfEdwardWhenBellaNeededHim: What are you doing here? I'm supposed to be moderating the chat, and EdHard and Jacob4Hire are at it again.

BellaBlows: We need to talk…

WereWolfEdwardWhenBellaNeededHim: Can't this wait?

BellaBlows: Do you really think I'd be in this chat if it could?

BellaBlows: Please?

I waited for a minute and got nothing but a flashing cursor as a response. And then I heard something skitter across my window.

When I opened the shade, I saw the familiar red ringlets and Seth's sheepish smile below. I jerked open the window.

"You're here."

"Aren't I always?"

I couldn't help but laugh, because that was the thing about Seth. Whenever I really needed him, he was always there. And despite the fact that I was constantly giving Seth a hard time for his incessant questioning, he always avoided the right questions. As much as I'm sure it drove him crazy not to know, he didn't utter a word about Liam. And I could have kissed him.

Seth made a big show of attempting to climb up the trellis on the side of our house before I finally convinced him to come in through the front door like a normal person. My parents had left to go to a fundraiser, but even if they had been home, they would have been thrilled to see our neighbor. He fell squarely into their "good influence" friend sector. There's a lesson about irony in there somewhere.

It didn't take long for me to explain the entire Bradley story to Seth, detail for detail. Well, except for the email to Grace and the goose bumps. This wasn't a romance novel. As I rambled, Seth shoved the last of a king-sized Butterfinger bar in his mouth and wiped his lips with the back of his hand.

"So, Conventus, huh?" He raised an orange eyebrow.

"Yeah, I mean, I definitely don't trust Bradley, but there's got to be some connection. It keeps popping up."

Seth nodded and I could almost hear the gears grinding in his brain as he tried to figure out exactly what we needed to do next. "I think we need a third-party assist."

I rolled my eyes, reading his mind. "Seth, I don't have time to wait for ConspiracyMother to check his email."

Seth was involved in an absurd number of online communities, his most active being the Northern Ohio Association of Conspiracy Theorists (NOACT—an appropriate acronym for a group of guys who consistently saw *no action* in every sense of the word). ConspiracyMother, as I liked to call him, was one of Seth's online buddies and knew a crap ton about the secret societies that ruled our school.

"It's Conspiracy*Luv*R," Seth said, drawing out the "Love" part to be sure I got it, "and I know we don't have time to wait. That's why we have to go to *him*."

"Wait, you know where he lives?"

A blush crept from Seth's ears to his cheeks, hiding his freckles for a minute. "I interviewed him for an I-Search paper one time." Seth pushed red curls back from off his forehead. "And I'd cool it on the criticizing. You need my help, remember?"

Seth was the only teenager I knew who used the words "cool" and "it" in that order. Seventeen going on forty. But he was right. Who was I to argue? I whipped my hair into a messy blue ponytail, pulled a sweatshirt over my head, and slipped my feet into my boots.

We were going in. Er…technically we were going out.

"Uh, so are you going to borrow your mom's van, or what?" I asked as we walked out into the frigid January air.

"We don't need a car. ConspiracyLuvR is closer than you think." Seth smiled and began walking across the street.

I was slightly horrified when we walked approximately one block down our street, and then Seth steered me up a long, winding driveway that led to a somewhat neglected-looking house.

I grabbed Seth's arm before we got any closer to the house. "Wait, so ConspiracyMother lives on our street? How have you failed to mention this in the past?"

"Well, you never asked. Besides, the first rule of Conspiracy Club is that you don't talk about Conspiracy Club. And the second is that you never, ever discuss a member's true identity."

"I think you've watched *Fight Club* one too many times."

"Look, do you want to talk to him or not? He's our best bet at this point." Seth raised his eyebrows and looked at me expectantly.

"Yeah, yeah, let's go."

I shuffled my feet as he rang the doorbell, wondering for the five hundredth time that day what I'd gotten myself into. Some sort of a scuffle ensued behind the heavy door, and I heard a scream, a few cries of "Mom!" and what sounded like an inordinately large person knocking into furniture.

"He's one of four," Seth whispered as a man with over a week's worth of stubble threw open the door. He was wearing a dirty, gray robe that had probably once been white and a stained undershirt with what appeared to be some type of long johns. A thirty-something-year-old woman shoved into him, jockeying for position, and he pinched her arm, eliciting a sharp cry.

"It's for me, nerdzoid," the man spat at the woman, who took one look at us and turned away.

"Have fun with your loser friends, dickwad," she called over her shoulder.

The man opened the screen door and in an oddly professional tone of voice said, "Seth, man, what's happening?"

"Hey, Mark," Seth said. "I have a huge favor. Are you busy?"

"Not at all. Come on in." Mark, aka ConspiracyLuvR, opened the door wide enough so we could fit and led us through the living room and into the house. I was immediately assaulted by the smell of bacon bits and maple syrup.

Knickknacks covered every square inch of the place, and I had the sneaking suspicion that this thirty-something-year-old man-child still lived with his parents. And apparently so did his sister, who was currently lounging on the couch in what looked like adult-sized footie pajamas or a Snuggie. I wasn't sure which was worse. She lifted her middle finger at me as we headed up the stairs. Classy.

We entered Mark's room, which featured *Star Wars* wallpaper, bedding, and even action figures positioned on shelves. Mark headed toward a desk and sat behind a fancy-looking computer, his hands clasped behind his head.

"What can I do for you?"

Seth elbowed me in the ribs as though we were approaching the Wizard of freaking Oz, as opposed to a haggard-looking, middle-aged computer geek who clearly lacked an appreciation for general hygiene.

"So this thing called Conventus keeps coming up with the societies, and I sort of need to know what it means." I launched right in. The smell that permeated this entire house was making me nauseous, so the sooner we were done here, the better.

"Conventus, conventus, conventus..." he said, tapping the desk lightly as he thought. Recognition dawned as he typed furiously on his keyboard, nodding his head and mumbling to himself.

As I tried to make out what he was saying, his bedroom door flew open. His sister pushed her head in and yelled, "Hey, butthead. Mom says it's your turn to unload the dishwasher." I tried to remember the last time I'd heard the word "butthead" used in a sentence, and I was 99 percent sure that it was in reruns of '90s MTV cartoons.

"Nice try, Patty. I did it last time." He threw a ball at her head as she slammed the door back shut. I could hear her yelling for her mom behind the closed door.

Where the hell were we?

"It means unity, right?" Seth chimed in, looking nervously at the door.

"Au contraire, my friend," Mark said. "Au contraire." He raked his fingers through the thinning hair on his head, making it stand at odd angles. "'Conventus might mean 'unity' in Latin, but it is the single most divisive issue among the secret societies to date. You see, the Farrows have long advocated for the merging of the two societies that divide their family. That's commonly referred to as Conventus. As students, Mr. and Mrs. Farrow fought hard to form a union but failed." He folded his hands together to emphasize his point.

My eyes widened a little. "Wait, so they want to merge the Brotherhood and the Sisterhood into one society?"

"Precisely," Mark said while typing something into his computer. He pulled up some sort of archive on the screen and punched in a password. I glanced at all of his *Star Wars* paraphernalia and figured it was probably something like "skywalkersdabomb" or "lukeiamyourfather." But when I noticed the Harvard diploma hanging on the wall, I decided it might be something closer to "CrimsonIntheCrapper."

"They've been working on negotiating a truce and a union ever since their respective terms leading the societies."

This was getting interesting. I walked closer to his computer screen and sat on the stool beside his swivel chair. On the screen were row after row of what appeared to be senior pictures but were really Sisterhood membership photos. They wore pristine white shirts featuring the Pemberly crest. I recognized Mrs. Farrow right away. She looked almost exactly like Naomi. I narrowed my eyes at another familiar face, trying to place her.

"Who's that?" I pointed to the screen at the gorgeous blond.

"That's Catherine Richardson. She single-handedly destroyed Conventus when the Farrows tried to push it through in '83."

Mark continued talking but I could barely hear him. I couldn't tear my eyes away from the familiar face in front of me. I knew without a doubt who I was looking at. But I couldn't stop myself from asking ConspiracyMother to say her name out loud.

"Do you know her married name?"

He slapped his forehead, "Oh, duh, I should have told you from the start. That's Catherine Wright. You probably know Taylor and her sisters, Tinsley and Teagan."

Uh, yeah.

Chapter 36

"Hello? Earth to Kate?"

I felt one of Seth's sharp elbows jab me in the ribs, but I was too busy trying to put all the pieces together in my mind to care. Taylor had left out some pretty important information in her efforts to protect the Sisterhood. If Mrs. Wright had destroyed Conventus back in the day, I imagined that Taylor wasn't exactly on board with a resurrection. So if Bethany and Taylor were trying to stop the societies from joining, that was a pretty clear motive for the boys to kidnap Bethany. I just couldn't believe that Taylor hadn't told me.

"Do you have any other questions for Mark? He's got some business to attend to." Seth nodded at what looked like an old television with tinfoil-covered antennas furiously beeping in the corner. "Last chance."

"Uh, no, this has been so helpful. I think I'm good for now. Thanks, ConspiracyMoth…er…Mark?" I held out my hand for a good old-fashioned handshake, but the man who I will forever think of as ConspiracyMother stood up and dove in for a hug.

I tried to breathe through my mouth but still got a major whiff of Bac-Os that emanated from his nasty-ass robe. Thankfully, I managed to cover my dry heave with a polite cough.

Seth leaned over and murmured something I couldn't quite make out while gesturing at the beeping television. Then he initiated this weird set of hand movements that ended in what had to be the most awkward chest bump of all time.

Where's the eye bleach when you need it?

ConspiracyMother slammed the door to his room as soon as we emerged into the cluttered hallway. Guess we'd have to see ourselves out.

"Whatever you do, do *not* make eye contact if you see his mom," Seth warned as we raced down the stairs.

"What? Wait! Why not? And why are you just mentioning this now?" I spotted a large woman in some kind of muumuu making her way out of the kitchen as we wandered down the stairs.

"Just trust me." Seth grabbed my hand and yanked both of us out the front door, ignoring the shrill cry of, "Oh, Gingersnap, Gingersnap!" that followed us out into the night.

Seth sprinted once we were on the grass, and I wasn't about to be caught by the ConspiracyMother's redhead-loving mama, so I took off right behind him. He didn't stop until we were back in front of my house.

"So…what…next?" He had his hands on his knees, his chest heaving. He finally looked up at me expectantly.

"We talk to Taylor. Bradley specifically said that Bethany was anti-Conventus and that there was going to be some kind of vote next week. Lame-ass blood oaths aside, it's time for Taylor to come clean."

"Well, at least it doesn't sound like Bethany's in any real danger." Seth shrugged.

I thought about that for a minute. I remembered Taylor's panic at losing her friend. The text message. The notes from Grace.

"I'm not so sure about that."

When it came to absolute power, there was nothing the societies wouldn't do. I knew that firsthand.

Chapter 37

After our Conventus revelation, I went home and tried to call Taylor more than was socially acceptable, even for me. I sent her three personal messages on Amicus, which remained unanswered when I checked first thing the next morning. I waited impatiently for the clock to strike nine so I could call Seth and get him to drive me over to her house. Our knocking and ringing were ignored, so we decided to keep an eye on her house. I mean, she'd have to leave sometime.

Six painfully slow drive-bys later, we saw a neighbor peek her head out behind a curtain, ear to phone, presumably calling the cops and forcing Seth to peel away in the van. It. Was. Awesome. But Taylor was still MIA.

This could mean one of two things:

1. Taylor had been kidnapped right along with her BFF.
2. She was royally pissed because she found out about my fauxmance with Bradley.

I knew definitively that my relationship with Liam could not withstand an additional kidnapping—one could actually argue that we weren't surviving the first. Liam still wouldn't return any of my phone calls or personal messages, no matter how I tried to spin my Bradley tale. And all signs were pointing to Taylor following suit.

During our seventh drive-by, we saw a flash of T in the dining-room window, and I was almost positive she wasn't being held hostage in her own house. Plus, she'd logged into Amicus five times in the past twenty-four hours. I figured the Brothers would have forbidden that, so I officially removed kidnapping from my list of reasons Taylor was MIA.

Based on the power of deductive reasoning, it seemed pretty clear that Taylor was avoiding me. It was like Bradley Farrow had given me a raging case of social leprosy.

Everyone was avoiding me. Well, except at the Allens' house. They were always happy to see me, and there was no better place for Seth and me to hide after Taylor's neighbor presumably filed a restraining order against us.

"Kate, sweetheart, would you like another muffin?" Mrs. Allen stood in an apron, oven mitts on each hand, a genuine smile plastered across her face. Looking at Mrs. Allen was like peering through a window into 1952. Although it wasn't exactly the future I'd choose for myself, I had to hand it to Mrs. A. —she was a bitchin' housewife.

"No, thank you," I said, bringing a napkin to my lips to wipe away blueberry remnants. Between the two of us, we'd already consumed an entire pan full, and Seth didn't appear to be stopping any time soon. His mom just kept mixing. At the Allen house, you could count on many constants—company, warm baked goods, organic milk, and organized meals, to name a few.

"I just have to say, you two, I'm just thrilled you're spending so much time together." Mrs. Allen bent down to retrieve a pan from the oven. I wasn't sure what she was implying, but the smell of warm blueberry muffins was so intoxicating that I might have agreed to just about anything. "You just look so cute together."

Hmm. Maybe not quite *that*.

Seth smiled widely, a blueberry covering one of his front teeth. "I knew Kate would eventually come around." He winked at me, and even though the gesture was completely full of cheese, I couldn't help but crack up. I shook my head and rested it on my arms. I had to admit it was nice to have a distraction.

But then an All-School message buzzed through on Amicus, and I was brought back to reality so quickly that I swear I felt whiplash.

> Don't forget…Concilium is holding its annual bake sale this afternoon during the varsity basketball game against Reserve. Come hungry and support PB!

I rubbed my neck and eyed the fresh pan of Mrs. Allen's famous muffins. In all the drama of the last few days, I'd completely forgotten about the bake sale everyone had been droning on about during the Concilium meetings I was still forced to attend. Not only was I supposed to have made something, but I was also supposed to show up.

"Um…Mrs. Allen?"

Mrs. Allen stopped humming and turned the faucet off, placing a freshly washed spatula on the drying rack. "Yes, honey?"

"Is there any way I can borrow some of those muffins for the bake sale today? I completely forgot I was supposed to make something, and I'm sure they will raise a lot of money for Concilium."

Mrs. Allen looked like she was about to cry. She placed her hand over her heart and cocked her head, shaking it slowly back and forth. "Oh, Kate, there is nothing I'd like more." She batted Seth's hand away from the plate without even looking and rushed to cover them with foil.

The one silver lining of having to participate in Concilium was that it'd force Taylor out of hiding.

There was no avoiding me now.

Unfortunately, when we walked into the rotunda in the late afternoon, Seth decked out in PB gear—a hat and a sweatshirt with a crisp PB tee beneath—and I approached the long Concilium fundraising table with my tightly wrapped plate of blueberry muffins in hand, Taylor was nowhere to be found.

"Didn't you say she'd be here?" Seth whispered, his gleaming white sneakers squeaking against the floor.

"Yeah…this isn't good." All sorts of terrible thoughts raced through my head. Maybe she really was missing like Bethany. Then what? If Taylor, president of Concilium, was absent from a sponsored event, it had to be bad. I put my muffins down with the rest of the treats and began asking around. They hadn't seen her. They hadn't heard a word, didn't know where she could be.

Meanwhile the Pemberly Brown Lions were kicking some serious butt on the basketball court. Cheers erupted from the gymnasium, and I listened as the cheerleaders performed another routine, celebrating an additional three points.

"I'll go check the bleachers." Seth adjusted his hat proudly and disappeared into the crowd. I didn't have the heart to tell him that one piece of PB paraphernalia would have been more than enough, too much even. It was kind of an unspoken rule, like having your parents drop you off a block away from any given social event or never buying a T-shirt at a concert and wearing it to the actual show. Ah, well, at least he'd be easy to spot.

And then Ben Montrose rolled in, a desperate-looking first-year girl attached to each overly tanned arm. He wore a tight turquoise shirt with the collar popped as though he had been plucked straight from some seedy Jersey beach bar, as opposed to attending a January basketball game in northeastern Ohio. Although I had to hand it to him. Ever since our little rendezvous in the tunnels beneath Pemberly Brown, he'd inadvertently taken it down a notch. Sure, he still fake-n-baked, name-dropped, and wore ridiculously bright colors in the dead of winter, but I hadn't seen his abs in over a week, and we'd been spared his tired break-dancing routine altogether. Apparently, being duped underground had humbled our good friend.

He tossed a dude-nod in my direction and ushered his lady friends into the crowded gymnasium just as a buzzer sounded. And out came Maddie. She spotted me, looked away, looked back at me, looked at the ground, offered a hesitant smile, and finally approached the Concilium table.

"This all looks really good," she offered meekly.

"Oh…um…thanks. Do you want anything?" I fumbled with a few plates, adjusting their position to occupy my hands.

She flushed. "I didn't bring any money."

I immediately regretted offering. Stupid. She was a recovering anorexic, and I'm sure she felt like everyone was watching her like a hawk every time she approached anything edible. She definitely didn't need to feel judged by her former best friend.

Maddie looked down at her shoes, opened and closed her mouth a few times as though she were about to speak, and shifted her weight from leg to leg. It was clear she needed to say something, something potentially awkward or serious, which made my stomach clench. A confrontation with Maddie was pretty much the last thing I wanted to involve myself in right now.

"Um…" I began, instantly cut off as Maddie spoke at the same time.

"You…need to be careful." We both turned bright red, and I felt like we were in a hallway doing that terrible dance when one person goes right and you go right and then the other person goes left and you go left. Brutal. "I mean…I don't know what's going on with Taylor, but I've seen you guys together and I just want you to be careful."

My stomach twisted further. I didn't know quite how to say it, but Maddie was sort of the last person I was going to take advice from regarding Taylor Wright.

"Okay," I managed.

"I just don't want anyone to get hurt."

An image of Bethany bound and gagged flashed in my head. And then I thought of Taylor, broken and lost without her best friend. No one believed her. She'd lost her voice. Maddie was so concerned about me getting hurt by Taylor that she couldn't see that Taylor was already the one hurting.

"That's exactly what I'm trying to prevent," I said, knowing on some level it was way too late for that. My phone buzzed in my pocket, jolting me away from the conversation. I appreciated the diversion. "Sorry," I mumbled, looking down at the screen.

Taylor.

I had to hand it to her, the girl had great timing. A breath I hadn't realized I was holding slipped through my lips. I turned away from Maddie and knew without a shadow of a doubt that when I turned back around, she'd be gone. But like with everything else, that was a risk I was willing to take.

I answered without bothering to say hello. "We need to talk." I wasn't really in the mood for pleasantries.

For a second there was nothing but the sound of Taylor gasping for breath, and regret rained down over me. What if she really was in trouble and not just avoiding me? What if that was the last thing I ever said to Taylor Wright…ever?

"Taylor? Hello?"

"I saw her." Her voice cracked, and I realized the gasping sound was sobbing. "They sent me a new picture. And everyone is talking about you and Bradley, and I have no idea if I can even trust you anymore. But I need to find her now, Kate. Before they…" A choking sound came over the phone.

"Where are you?"

"At school."

I looked around, confused. "Where? I'm in the rotunda."

I heard a smack and pictured Taylor cupping her hand over her mouth. If she was anything like me, she hadn't stopped looking at the picture since it'd come in. She was obsessing over it. Zooming in on it. Staring.

"Just stay where you are. I'm on my way." I turned back around, and as predicted, Maddie had vanished. But in her place was Seth in all his school-spirited glory. "She's not in there," he said, helping himself to a chocolate-chip cookie. I didn't even have time to shoot him a look.

"We've gotta go."

Seth nodded his head, shoved the rest of the cookie in his mouth, and turned on his toe. No questions. No judgment. No nothing. Just pure, genuine support. I had to take a second because, if I really thought about it—and it was too late for that since my brain was going a mile a minute—I would cry. Liam wasn't even taking my phone calls; Taylor needed my help but refused to trust anyone outside of the Sisterhood; and Bradley was clearly manipulating me. But Seth. Seth was on board without even batting a ginger eyelash.

I rushed after him, touching his shoulder to stop him as we walked the hall.

"Thank you." My voice was thick, and I knew if I kept talking, the tears would come.

Seth appeared confused at first but then smiled wide.

"Seriously. Your friendship…" My voice cracked again and I stopped short.

Before I could even attempt to finish, a pair of wet, chocolate-sweet lips were on mine. I jerked my head back and gave him my if-you-kiss-me-again-I'm-going-to-castrate-you-before-you-actually-complete-puberty look. Yeah, I've got a patent pending on that bad boy.

"Can't blame a guy for trying."

This time it was me who leaned over and kissed him. On the cheek. The truth was, I could never blame Seth for anything.

Seth made a strange squeaking sound and smiled so big that I thought his face might break into a million little pieces. I felt a surge of something I couldn't quite put my finger on, but I hoped it'd be enough to take care of everything once and for all. As much as I loved my blueberry muffins with a heaping side of drama and my friendships with a layer of deceit, I was ready for some milk and honesty.

Chapter 38

We roamed the halls of Pemberly Brown in search of Taylor. I had absolutely no idea where I'd find her. In the headmaster's office? Crouched with a knife in one of the darkened classrooms and ready to pounce? Shaking near the front entrance in some sort of comatose state?

But I should have known. After all, if it had been me, I'd have camped out in front of Grace's locker too. As soon as I saw Taylor, her back resting against Bethany's locker, her bedazzled phone glowing beside her, I forgot how mad I was at her for not telling me about Conventus. In that moment this had nothing to do with feuding secret societies or even revenge. This was about a missing girl and the friend who loved her.

Seth hung back respectfully while I approached and gently took the phone from Taylor's vise-like grip. The picture of Bethany flashed on the screen.

And it was bad.

Her hair was matted down by something dark, I'm assuming blood or dirt or both, and there were dark circles under her eyes.

A black cloth had been tied around her mouth like a gag, and she had dried blood crusted across her face. I couldn't see her arms, but it looked like they were bound behind her back. Her once lush cheeks looked sunken from lack of food and water, and her eyes screamed at us to save her. All at once I was pulled back in front of that burning chapel with the knowledge that my best friend was trapped inside and there wasn't a damn thing I could do about it.

I wondered if Grace's eyes had looked like that when the smoke billowed around her, when she realized there was no way out.

Society politics aside, Bethany needed us. And according to the accompanying text, *Vote For or die*, we didn't have a lot of time.

I used my two fingers to zoom into the photo, waiting as the pixels reconfigured. The background was slightly blurry and looked mainly like a darkened room, no identifying photos or people to indicate where Bethany was hidden. But as I zoomed further and further, shapes began to take form behind her. An exceptionally blurry horse, part of a duck, a tree. It didn't take long for me to place where I'd seen them. It was the gaudy wallpaper from the club.

"Let's go," I said, holding my hand out to Taylor. "I know it's hard to remember, Taylor, but this isn't over yet."

Taylor continued to rock back and forth. "I saw you with him. At the club," she said, picking at one of her nails. I noticed a chip then and it seemed so out of place, so unlike Taylor. "Is that over?"

"Don't you get it? I was there trying to get information about Bethany. It's not what you think, and you can believe whatever you want to believe, but I'm going to go try to find her. I haven't given up yet, Taylor, and neither should you." She met my eyes, brown versus blue, a standoff, and for a second I didn't think she'd relent. But then she blinked.

Taylor finally pushed up from the hardwood floor and used a hand to steady herself against the locker. Seth shuffled awkwardly in an attempt to remind us of his presence, and I shot him a look that roughly translated into "Stop staring at her and *do something. Now.*" For the second time tonight, he proved he was fluent in the complex language of Kate's angry looks, because moments later he was at Taylor's side, helping me guide her to his mom's van.

Taylor continued to stare at her phone, her eyes empty and cold. I was pretty sure she was in shock. Meanwhile I leaned forward, straining against the seat belt. This was it. Our moment. I knew without a doubt that the picture had been taken at the club, and if Bethany was still there, we could end this. Tonight.

"Taylor, since you're a club member, no one will find it weird for you to be there." Seth tapped his fingers on the steering wheel to an old-school Celine Dion song while we waited for the light to turn green. "But, Kate, we'll have to work on blending."

This coming from the kid with flaming red hair to the girl with bright blue.

Taylor completely ignored him. "I can't believe I didn't notice the background first." The sound of her voice startled me. "This was taken in the billiard room. Those chairs look like the ones that are in there."

I didn't have the heart to tell her that Bethany probably wasn't gagged and bound in plain sight. Whoever had snapped the pic was probably smart enough to hide her away within the club or, more likely, at an entirely different location.

Seth parked the car, and the three of us ran into the club and up the huge, winding staircase in the center hall. Luckily it was getting late and a light snow had begun to fall, so the place had pretty much cleared out.

Including the billiard room. It was completely empty. I felt the hope wheeze out of my chest in a short whoosh. I should have known better, but I couldn't help the disappointment. We were so close. Smoke still hung in the air and trailed from the butt of a cigar someone hadn't stubbed out all the way. A few glasses littered the tables, ice cubes melting into brown liquor. Chairs identical to the one in Bethany's picture dotted the room. The familiar hunting landscape adorned the walls, slightly faded and tattered looking. I wondered how long ago they'd left, whether anyone had seen them take the picture, and if a girl with cloth covering her mouth drew any red flags for members or employees.

But none of that really mattered, because Bethany was gone. Again.

Taylor slumped into a chair while I searched the ground, on tables, in closets, behind the bar for anything that might lead us back to Bethany. Seth snacked on trail mix and offered a handful to Taylor, who shot him the most disgusted look I'd ever seen one human give another.

And then I saw it. It was almost like divine intervention, as though the clue had been put exactly in this place for me to find.

The map was hand drawn, crumpled after being folded and refolded, shoved into pocket after pocket. It featured the main building and had stars marking stairways at seemingly random locations—the boys' bathroom, the showers in the gym locker room, the headmaster's office, a custodial closet, a locker. But contrary to the map of Pemberly Brown we'd uncovered months earlier, these stairs did not lead down.

They led up. And they began exactly at Bethany's locker.

Chapter 39

It didn't take Nancy Drew to figure out our next move. The three of us piled into Seth's mom's van and were back at Pemberly Brown standing in front of Bethany's locker before the clock struck seven.

"Now what?" Getting the door open was cake, but the next step had us stumped. Seth had all but climbed into the locker, but it was just a steel and metal box. No key pad. No secret trapdoor. Just a locker. Taylor elbowed her way past him and wedged herself inside, feeling along the walls for something, anything that would let us in.

"Well, at least we have a motive, right?" Seth squeaked next to me.

"What do you mean?" I couldn't keep the edge out of my voice. I had no patience for Seth's questions. I just wanted to get Bethany and be done with this.

"I mean, the Brotherhood had a motive for taking Bethany. She was obviously against Conventus, right, Taylor?"

"Of course she was. All the Sisters should be."

"But why? Hasn't all of this gone too far? One girl is dead and another one missing. All of it would stop if you guys just joined forces. One happy secret society." I'm sure my words sounded naïve to Taylor, but I didn't care. The answer was so obvious. They both had access to information, exceptional connections, and, of course, the power to do just about whatever they wanted within the hallowed halls of PB and even beyond. If they combined their resources, they would be unstoppable.

The thought gave me pause. The omnipotence of a single society was actually kind of scary. Just like in government, Pemberly Brown needed checks and balances, and like it or not, the two societies kept each other in check.

Taylor stepped out of the locker, blue eyes blazing. "Conventus is just a fancy way for letting *them* win. For letting *them* take over. I mean, look at this. They've built a new headquarters. You think that we'll have a big ceremony, sing 'Kumbaya,' and then they will hand us the keys to some shared kingdom? Think again."

I was too tired to argue with her. All this society crap had to stop, but first we had to find Bethany.

We checked all of the other locations on the map with stars, but we couldn't find the hidden stairs in the locker room, the bathroom, or the custodian's closet. Soon we found ourselves back in front of Bethany's locker, and after spending the better part of an hour trying everything short of taking a blowtorch to the metal, we all sat down on the window seat in front of the bay of lockers and stared at the locker blankly.

"Look, this clearly isn't working. We need a Plan B." You could always count on Seth to state the obvious.

Taylor leaned across me to give Seth one of her more withering glares. "She is up there. I can feel it. We just have to figure out a way to get to her."

I nodded thoughtfully. Taylor was right. If we wanted to save Bethany, we had to get up to the headquarters, but we couldn't just walk right up to Bradley or Alistair and ask them for the key. Nope. The Brotherhood was like a bunch of rats. To find their nest, we'd have to lure them out of hiding and set a trap.

Fortunately for me, I had the perfect bait.

"We need to have a party. Tomorrow night. A big one."

The look on Taylor's face made me relieved that she wasn't holding any sharp objects when I said those words.

"I know, I know," I said, scooting a little bit away from her. "But think about it for a second. We need the Brotherhood to come out of hiding and play, right? What better way to get them moving than the promise of a keg and half-naked girls?"

"Kate, in case you have not noticed, it is January. And we are not living in a Super Bowl commercial. Last I checked, Pemberly Brown does not have a beach."

"We've got something better than a beach—we've got the Underground."

Although the name might sound like a British rail system, Pemberly Brown's Underground was something else entirely. Back in the '50s when the school was originally founded, they had no room on campus for a pool and no budget for a new building. But the poor little rich girls had wanted to swim, so someone's daddy coughed up the money to convert one of the dormitory basements into an Olympic-sized pool.

Even though PB has since converted the dormitories into classrooms and built a state-of-the-art rec center, complete with a brand-new swimming pool, the alumni kept the Underground open for the little old ladies who liked to come and swim laps and do water aerobics on the weekends, but it was strictly off limits to students. Naturally, we snuck in every chance we got. Late-night skinny-dipping sessions and impromptu parties in the Underground were practically required activities for all incoming first-years.

I could practically see the lightbulb go off over Taylor's head. "So we get them to a party and then what? I don't see how drunk swimming gets us any closer to finding Bethany."

"Getting them out is half the battle. Once we've got them here, we create an emergency. Make 'em scramble. Luckily for the Brotherhood, they'll know exactly where to go when the shit hits the fan. Even luckier for us, we'll know exactly where to wait to watch how they get in."

"And once we are in…it is all over." Taylor's voice went up an octave. Clearly she was excited about this plan.

"Well, maybe. We're still not sure Bethany is up there."

"Oh, she's up there. She has to be. You are a genius, Kate!" Taylor threw her arms around me. "I cannot imagine how I would have done this without you." Her eyes were glassy with tears, and I couldn't help it. I was touched. It felt good to have Taylor's approval. Maddie was pissed at me; Liam hated me; and Seth was practically my brother. But Taylor was different.

"And lucky for us, I still have a couple of tricks up my sleeve."

She whipped a cell phone out of her pocket. I recognized the case almost instantly.

"Is that?"

"Bradley's phone? Why, yes. Yes, it is." Taylor waggled it in front of my face victoriously.

Seth's eyes practically fell out of his head. "But how did you get it? And if you've had it all this time, why didn't you—"

Taylor cut Seth off. "I saw it lying on the floor at the country club, but I was not sure what good it would do us. I mean, there is not any new information on here." She paused to start swiping and typing on the phone. "But I think the boys are much more likely to show if the invitation comes from their king, am I right?"

She *was* right. Seth and I just sort of nodded dumbly and let Taylor do her thing. Clearly, our work here was done. I mean, sure it was my idea, but when it came to actually planning a party, I was completely clueless. I had a sum total of three friends at this school, and two of them weren't speaking to me.

Most girls probably would have started an elaborate pity party, complete with tears and tantrums, but I wasn't most girls. Justice came at a price, and feeling sorry for myself was a luxury I couldn't afford.

My phone buzzed in my pocket, and I willed it not to be my parents. I'd specifically checked in with them four times already to avoid this exact scenario. But when I swiped my phone to life, an unknown number appeared on the screen. The lump that formed in my throat was instantaneous. I bit my lip as I tapped on the text. The picture of Bethany exploded onto my screen, and I just barely managed to choke back a scream. Seth, who clearly had been reading over my shoulder, let out an actual high-pitched shriek.

Taylor rushed over to us and grabbed the phone out of my hand. Her face froze as she took in the image, pain darkening her features. When she closed her eyes, two fat tears leaked out of the corners.

I gently pried my phone out of her hands. The picture was almost too much to bear. Bethany was collapsed on a dirty floor, her eyes blank, unseeing.

>Too late for B. End the Sisterhood or you're next.

Taylor looked at me, her eyes glassy.

"It is over."

I put my arms around her and felt her body convulse with silent sobs, and then all at once she grew very still. For a second, I thought she'd passed out, but instead she straightened her legs and slowly stood up.

"This ends tonight."

"I don't know, Taylor. I think we need to go to the police. I mean, with evidence like this, surely…" You had to hand it to Seth for at least trying to be the voice of reason, but Taylor was in no mood.

"The only way this will ever end is if we end it. Now."

"Tonight? But it's almost eight. There's not enough time." I wrinkled my forehead, wondering exactly how Taylor planned to rally anyone on such little notice, posing as Bradley or not.

But sheer determination skewed her features as she texted from Bradley's phone. Apparently the party was on.

Chapter 40

Three hours later, the scene was set. My hair frizzed in the thick humidity of the Underground as I sat on a wooden bench, straining my eyes to see through the darkness. A line of candles flickered beside me, five or six positioned on each wooden bench lining the perimeter of the pool. In the darkness the effect was almost magical. Every so often, a cell phone illuminated like a firefly, but the only other source of light came from the pool, a blue diamond dazzling at center stage.

The water churned as body after body jumped, splashed, dove, and dunked. A couple flirted in the corner of the pool, the guy splashing water lightly toward the girl, who squealed in delight. I thought of Liam and felt sick. He had said things to me that he would never, ever be able to unsay, and I hated him for it. But in that moment I missed him too. I missed the way I knew he'd sit down next to me in his perfectly broken-in jeans and super-soft T-shirt. He'd tousle my hair and call me "babe," and I'd roll my eyes just because and he'd laugh. And then *we'd* laugh. I missed having someone to genuinely laugh with.

I wished I could go back and undo everything. Go back to the other night and delete that email to Grace for good. Go back to Obsideo and save Bethany from the Brotherhood. Go back to the night I lost Grace and find her before it was too late. I wanted so badly to start everything over from the beginning so I could finally get it right. But life didn't come with a rewind button.

I promised myself that this would all be over soon. When Bethany was found alive, I could get some closure, go back to being normal. Maybe the normal Kate would even be able to figure out a way to forgive Liam for what he'd said. Then I could bow out, back away, wipe my hands of anything and everything society-related, and retreat into a little corner with my amazing boyfriend and friends. But first I had to finish what I'd started. I had to find Bethany.

I finally caught Seth's eye, and he threw up what looked like some kind of gang sign, curving his fingers into a heart shape across his chest. I guessed this was my signal to get moving. When I'd spoken with him earlier, he'd refused to tell me how I would know when he was about to sound the alarm. He'd only say that it would be super subtle and that I'd know it when I saw it. Well, at least he was right about one thing, the subtlety.

I started moving toward the exit. The plan was that I'd hide next to the window seat in front of Bethany's locker to watch how the Brotherhood accessed the headquarters. Once we knew how to get in, we'd rescue Bethany. That part of the plan was still sort of hazy, but we'd figure something out. Together. As crazy as it seemed, Taylor, Seth, and I made a pretty good team.

"Kate?" I was so lost in my thoughts that it took my brain a second to place his voice. Or maybe I was just distracted by the way tiny droplets of water clung to his light brown skin, pooling down into the waistband of swim trunks hanging low on his narrow hips. Surely someone this hot couldn't be a cold-blooded killer. Dangerous, yes. Manipulative, absolutely. But a killer? No way. Wherever he had Bethany, she had to be alive.

"Oh, hey, Bradley. What's up?" It was a small victory that my voice didn't crack when I said his name.

His smile took up half his face. Clearly our pool-party trap was doing its job.

His fingers, still dripping water from the pool, closed around my forearm. "I wanted to tell you I did some digging around about Bethany." I jumped a little when he said her name. It felt like he was reading my mind. He ran a hand over his shaved head and rubbed his jaw. "I hated the idea of someone on my side going to such extremes. I know you don't believe me, Kate, but I'm doing everything I can to end all this crap."

"Conventus, right?"

I was pleased by the look of shock on Bradley's face.

"How did you…" Shock had quickly been replaced with concern.

"It's not exactly a secret that you want the Sisterhood to disappear, Bradley. I guess I should really be applauding you for your creativity."

"You *have* to believe that we don't have Bethany. I swear to God, Kate. The Brothers would never do something like that."

"Not even Alistair Reynolds?" I said his name with such certainty that I shouldn't have even bothered asking.

Bradley smiled crookedly. "Yeah, you're right. This is exactly the kind of crap the old Alistair would have pulled. But he's changed, Kate."

I rolled my eyes. I couldn't stop myself. The idea that Alistair Reynolds had changed was just too much. I looked into the pool, where he was chicken-fighting with an all-girls team. Changed, my ass.

"Okay, okay, you're not buying it. I get it." Bradley grabbed my hand. "But things are different now. I can prove it."

His hand should have been shriveled and pruney from the pool, but I felt nothing but heat when his fingers wrapped around mine. A tiny shriek escaped my lips, and I pulled my hand away as though I'd been burned. Liam would have called me on my "telltale squeak." But Bradley didn't know me that well. Thank God.

And then the fire alarm ripped through the silence, echoing off the tiled walls and floors. It didn't matter that I knew it was coming or that it wasn't real, that Seth had pulled the alarm next to the pool door. It still sent a shot of adrenaline racing through me.

Bradley rolled his eyes. "Why do people feel the need to pull the alarm when everyone's having fun?" He reached his hand out again. "Come on. We've gotta get out of here."

People spilled from the pool, water cascading off fronts and backs like waterfalls, feet slipping on the slick floor, tiny screams emitting during the dash to the locker rooms, through doorways, and up stairs. The response was immediate—absolute chaos. And it was only then that I realized I'd missed my all-important cue.

Chapter 41

Crap.

There are few things more humiliating for a girl than being so distracted by a half-naked boy that she loses track of time and misses her opportunity to infiltrate his secret society's headquarters. Okay, so maybe this wasn't exactly the typical embarrassing moment for a fifteen-year-old girl, but I'd essentially caught myself in my own trap, and it sucked. Big time.

"Now, Kate." Bradley's eyes flashed in the darkness, and instead of waiting, he gripped my fingers and pulled me to standing. A candle tipped over across the room, and I had the overwhelming urge to blow out each one. The last thing we needed tonight was a real fire. I said a prayer to Grace just in case, although I knew the pool deck was now covered in at least two inches of water. Before I knew what was happening, Bradley grabbed me, pulling me toward the winding staircase that led to the familiar halls of Pemberly Brown.

Moments later, we both stood in front of Bethany's locker, and I couldn't help but cast a longing look at my hiding spot by the window. Taylor and Seth were going to kill me when they found out how badly I'd botched our master plan. Worse, my hand still tingled from Bradley's touch. What was wrong with me?

"Can I trust you?" They were words that were meant to be said with some kind of intense burning glance, but Bradley was too busy looking around the hallway to ensure we were alone.

"Yes." I wish I could say that the word tasted like a lie, but it rang with an odd sort of truth that was impossible to ignore. The word was barely out of my mouth when he twisted the combination on the locker next to Bethany's. As it turned out, I hadn't botched the plan after all. In fact, infiltrating the headquarters *with* Bradley was so much more efficient. I mentally gave myself a pat on the back.

23-54-25

Before I even had time to process exactly what was happening, three lockers swung open like a door, revealing a staircase. Bradley took the stairs two at a time, leaving me gaping at him from the hallway.

The stairs in front of me were not dimly lit or lined with bricks, and there weren't cobwebs in the corners like on the ones that led to the tunnels. These were wide and constructed of swirled marble. Etched into the marble between each step was a different Latin phrase, similar to the ones carved into the bronze plaques around campus. *Ab initio*, "From the beginning." *Labor omnia vincit*, "Hard work conquers all." *Palma non sine pulvere*, "No reward without effort."

I climbed slowly, letting the ancient words guide me up toward the bright light at the top. It felt like the stairs were talking to me, reminding me that I had to uncover the truth. I wondered what the words meant to Bradley as he bounded up the stairs.

Moonlight spilled into the room at the top of the stairwell, so bright we didn't even need the lights. The ceiling was domed with a large circular window at the top. I expected to see Bethany bound and gagged in some corner, but the room was completely empty. Was it possible that Bradley was telling the truth? That the Brotherhood had nothing to do with her disappearance? Maybe a serial killer had Bethany. Or Headmaster Sinclair. Something about being here with Bradley made me second-guess everything, and I hated myself for it.

Massive columns lined the perimeter of the room, and I was overcome with a creepy sense of déjà vu, like I'd been here before in a past life or a dream or some sort of out-of-body experience. And then it hit me. The Pantheon. The new Brotherhood headquarters was a mini-version of ancient Rome's Pantheon.

Large marble statues of various gods were nestled in the boxes that led up to the window at the tip of the dome. Jupiter, Apollo, Hercules—their eyes tracking me. How was this even possible? Three months ago, the Brotherhood had set up shop in the Sisterhood's underground lair, and now they'd built an empire? They must have hidden the dome between the turrets that lined the roof of the school. I had to admit that it was sort of genius. I thought back to Ben's explanation—that the headquarters had been constructed in secret after hours, over holidays, and on the weekends. I'd heard of hiding in plain sight, but this was ridiculous.

"Pretty impressive, right?" Bradley's smile stretched across his face as he leaned casually against the marble wall. It killed me to admit that he looked pretty god-like himself. A lying, powerful, cocky god.

"What is all this?"

"It's basically a new beginning, a clean slate. When we finally pass Conventus on Tuesday, we're going to unveil this new headquarters to the girls." His eyes sparkled as he pushed away from the wall. "You see, the artist who created the gods for us is waiting for word, and he'll start on whichever goddesses the girls choose, although Naomi has her opinions already, of course." He pointed to the beautiful statues and couldn't keep the smile off his face. It was hard not to match his excitement. "And did you notice some of the stairs were missing phrases? Well, that's up to the girls as well."

"But what if it doesn't pass?" I couldn't help it. He had to know that was a possibility. Especially since, according to Taylor, Conventus was all a front to destroy the Sisterhood. Although the way his face dropped after I asked the question, it was hard to imagine he had anything but good intentions.

"There are only one or two against, so it shouldn't be an issue." He gave me a hard look. The well-intentioned Bradley disappeared before my eyes. If Bethany was as against Conventus as Taylor claimed she was, Bradley's comment was as good as a confession.

And all of a sudden I felt like my arms were being pulled in two very distinct directions. There was Taylor pulling hard on one side, reminding me that the Brotherhood had destroyed my life and was currently destroying her own, and then there was Bradley with his enthusiasm and this idea that he could end the war between the societies forever.

Bradley was wrong. Taylor was right. This was supposed to be easy. Black and white. But nothing was ever easy. Not for me anyway. I always got stuck in the grays.

"Not an issue because you're removing them from the equation?" I said the words, my eyes fixed on his face, examining all of the intricacies, the twitches, any changes in that split second as my question registered.

His brows pulled together, his forehead wrinkling in response. And the only way I could describe his face was hurt. I might as well have slapped him.

"I don't know how else to tell you I have nothing to do with Bethany. Or Grace. Or whatever else it is you're accusing me of. I thought I could prove it to you by bringing you here, but that was clearly a mistake."

He started to walk toward the stairs, and I should have let him go. I knew how to get in now. Enough was enough. It was time to leave.

And that's when I saw it. It was just a gray scarf, nothing really remarkable about it. It could have easily belonged to one of the Brothers. Except it didn't.

It was Bethany's. The scarf she'd been wearing the night of Obsideo. The same one she'd worn in all the pictures they'd sent us. And right next to it was a black strip of fabric. This must have been the blindfold they'd wrapped around her head. I delicately touched the hairs. Whoever had ripped this off her head hadn't been gentle. Hot anger snaked its way up my throat.

"Didn't have anything to do with Bethany, huh?" I waved the

blindfold at Bradley before sticking it in my pocket and grabbed the scarf up off the ground. I had everything I needed now.

Just before I reached the stairs, Bradley grabbed my shoulder roughly and turned me around to face him.

Maybe not.

"What the hell are you even talking about?"

"This." I pulled the blindfold out of my pocket. "As of 7:13 p.m. tonight, this was wrapped around Bethany Giordano's head. You almost had me, Bradley." I pulled up the picture of Bethany on my phone and waved it in his face.

His dark complexion went a shade or two lighter, the color draining from his face.

"Who sent you this?"

I shook my head. He was either telling the truth or was a fantastic actor, but at this point I couldn't have cared less. Someone had had Bethany in this room at some point this evening, and I was going to find out who. I pushed past Bradley and started down the stairs.

"Kate, wait! I have no idea where this stuff came from, but there's a camera at the base of the stairs. Let's pull the footage. We'll find her."

Something in his voice made me turn around. It almost sounded like he actually wanted to help.

"Fine. Pull it." I couldn't get access to the video footage without him.

We walked over to a computer monitor, and Bradley began tapping on the keyboard. Almost instantly a picture of the hallway outside Bethany's locker popped up on the screen.

"Cool." I couldn't stop myself from whispering the word. I mean, it was pretty badass. They had video that monitored the comings and goings at the headquarters, but they'd also caught some other interesting stuff on camera. I noticed that as he zipped through the footage pulling up the images from last night. One of Pemberly Brown's custodians danced across the screen without his pants on.

"Um, eww."

"Tell me about it. You should see what he wears to wax the floors."

Bradley continued to fast-forward through the footage, through streams of students switching classes in a blur, teachers coming and going, and all the other normal Pemberly Brown activity.

"Ooh, stop." I couldn't help myself. Bradley backed up a few frames and we watched Porter Reynolds amble down the hallway, his guitar slung across his chest as usual. He walked backward, playing what had to be one of only four songs in his repertoire as a bevy of giggling first-years followed close behind. "You've got to be kidding me," I said, shaking my head.

"You're really surprised? First-years eat that crap up."

Bradley continued whizzing through the frames when I caught a flash of a dark-haired girl.

"Wait."

Bradley pressed Play and sure enough Bethany filled the screen. Someone was guiding her roughly up to the stairs. She turned directly to the camera, blindfold securely in place, but I could feel the panic radiating off her in waves.

"Holy shit." Bradley breathed the words. "I'm going to freaking kill them."

"Told you." I leaned in for a closer look. It was definitely Bethany, but she didn't look nearly as bad as she had in the picture. I looked at the little clock in the upper right-hand corner of the screen. 6:23. I guess a lot could happen in an hour.

"Who's she with? Can you zoom in?"

But Bradley was already typing commands furiously into the keyboard, his face set in hard, angry lines.

"I can't believe they'd do this. It goes against everything…" He let his voice trail off and he shook his head. He really *didn't* know anything about this. He hadn't been lying after all, but someone wanted Conventus to happen even more than he did. Someone was willing to kill for it.

The shadowed face behind Bethany slowly came into focus, and I wish I could say I was surprised, but I wasn't. I guess if I'd ever really taken the time to think about it, I would have known that only one person at school was capable of pulling off something like this, and he just happened to be Bradley Farrow's best friend.

Alistair Reynolds.

Chapter 42

Alistair's face was dark and blurry and pixilated, but I would recognize his brooding stare anywhere. With all the emoting he was doing, it was almost like he knew he was on *Candid* freaking *Camera*.

He led Bethany up the stairs and slammed the door behind him without even a glance around the hallway. There was no one else with him. It was just Alistair.

Bradley kept zipping through the footage, and panic hit me like a bolt of lightning. If they monitored everything that happened outside the door of the new headquarters…

And just like clockwork Taylor, Seth, and I showed up on the tape at seven o'clock. I jumped up from the chair and tried to make a break for the stairs.

"What the…" Bradley jumped up too, and grabbed me. "What the hell are you playing at, Kate?"

I slipped out of his grip and took the stairs two at a time. Even if I did believe that he hadn't had anything to do with whatever had happened to Bethany, it didn't change anything. It couldn't.

He stopped at the top of the stairs. "I have no idea what Taylor told you, but it's all a lie. We can fix this. Find Bethany, end the feud. You need to do this for Grace. In her memory. That's all she ever wanted—to be remembered. She even wrote it in that book."

I froze at the bottom.

"What the hell are you talking about?" I said the words slowly, enunciating each syllable.

"Her book, the beat-up paperback by…" Bradley's voice trailed off, and he realized his mistake.

"It was you? You were the person taunting me with Grace's stuff?" My voice was hysterical, and the tears started to come fast and furious. There was just too much going on. The second I started to trust Bradley, to actually believe that he gave a shit about finding Bethany and ending this pointless war before it hurt anyone else, he revealed himself to be an even bigger jerk than I ever could have imagined.

I stood up and ran down the stairs and into the hallway. I could barely see where I was going through the tears, but it didn't matter. Well, it didn't matter until I tripped over a freaking "Caution, Wet Floor" sign outside the girls' bathroom and face-planted into the marble tile.

"Kate! Are you okay?" Bradley helped me up before I remembered to push him away. "I wasn't taunting you with her things. I swear. When we moved the headquarters, I found a box of her stuff and I thought you should have it, but I had no way of giving it to you. You look so sad sometimes, and I just thought that maybe if a little piece of Grace showed up on a bad day, it would help.

It started at the memorial. I knew her jacket was in the box, so I figured I'd just put it on your chair or whatever.

"And then you gave that speech, and I don't know, I just had to do something. So I left the book in your room. And then that day in History, you just looked like you needed a piece of her back. So I left the notebook. You can have everything else too. It's all up there." He ran his hand across his head and pulled at his neck. "I guess I just thought that if I was missing somebody that much, I'd want to feel like they were still around, like pieces of them were still out there." He shrugged his shoulders and looked down at his feet. "I'm so sorry."

The weird thing was that I could actually see how his theory might have worked in his head. I did miss Grace, and I desperately wanted to keep her alive somehow. Wasn't that why I was constantly writing her those emails?

"You kept me from her that night. I should have been able to save her, but if you hadn't...and you thought leaving me pieces of her was going to make it all better?" I let my voice trail off. We both knew what he'd done to keep me away from Grace that night. I still remembered how amazing his lips had felt on mine, only to be completely humiliated seconds later when he ditched me. And then to think of everything that had happened while I sat on that bench, how I never had the chance to save her—it was too much. It was still too much.

"I'm sorry, Kate. I had no idea what they were up to, and I never would have agreed to it if I hadn't thought you were cute."

Cute? Seriously. I wanted to punch him, but instead I managed a curt, "I've got to go find Alistair."

"Kate…wait." But I pulled away, his footsteps trailing my own, my name reverberating off the marble, his hand finally grabbing mine as I came to the end of the hallway.

He jerked me back to his chest and my body tumbled into his. I froze a breath away from his face, our noses almost touching. For a second I couldn't breathe, let alone move away from him.

"I liked you, Kate. I still like you."

I took a big breath, prepared to tell him exactly what he could do with all of his ridiculous "like," but before I could say a word, his lips were crushing mine. His mouth opened just slightly as I felt his hand slip from my shoulder and down the length of my back, nudging me closer, urging me. And then I made a decision that I regretted almost instantly.

I kissed him back.

For just one second I forgot about Bethany. I forgot about Taylor desperately worried about her missing friend. I even forgot about Grace. For a few long seconds, the only things that existed in my world were Bradley Farrow's lips. And his hands. And his legs.

And then I heard an all-too-familiar voice calling my name. Shock and anger made it sound more like a curse.

Liam.

I pushed Bradley away and turned to explain. But Liam was gone.

Anger boiled up inside me from a place so deep and dark and scary that it felt as though it might explode, taking me with it. I hated Bradley for understanding why I needed to keep Grace alive. I hated Liam for not. I hated both of them for making me feel so completely out of control.

But a bright, blinding light interrupted my fit and I was forced to throw my arm over my burning eyes. Both Bradley and I turned our heads to the side as if we could escape the painful, white light before we realized there was absolutely no way out.

And then we heard the clicks.

At first I thought Headmaster Sinclair's dress shoes were clicking along the shiny hardwood floors. He'd flipped the lights and broken up our party; he would threaten us and force us out. But by the time my eyes adjusted and I was able to focus, Headmaster Sinclair was nowhere to be found. Instead the president of the Pemberly Brown school board's high heels were clicking ominously down the hallway toward us, Ms. D. trailing behind her in tennis shoes, a triumphant smile on her face.

The president shoved past me, barely even sparing me a glance, and grabbed Bradley by the elbow.

"Thanks for the invitation, Bradley. You sure know how to throw a party."

Bradley opened his mouth but no words came out. He must have been just as shocked as I was. "What are you talking about?" he finally managed.

"The invitation you sent out for the pool party, of course. We've gone ahead and turned on all the lights, and by now most students are being removed from the premises. But I was disappointed not to find you down there. I wanted to thank you in person for the invite. Thankfully, Taylor Wright told me I might be able to find you up here."

"But I didn't send that invitation. I mean, I saw it on Amicus and

I came, but I'd never send…My phone. I lost my phone this afternoon. Someone else must have sent the invitation using my name. Taylor. She's trying to get me in trouble. Kate, you have to tell her!"

"There will be plenty of time for explanations, Mr. Farrow, but in the meantime I think you'd better show me what's going on up there." She nodded toward the staircase hidden behind the lockers, and Bradley's entire face crumpled. It was all over. He knew it. And I knew it.

"Now, if you'll please do me the honors." She gestured for Bradley to lead her up the stairs, and I watched them ascend to his headquarters.

The second they disappeared up the stairs, Ms. D. rushed over to put her arms around me.

"You did good, Kate. I'm so proud of you." She enveloped me in one of her signature hugs.

"But what about Bethany?" My voice cracked and I leaned forward, insistent. "You can see the headquarters later. It's Alistair Reynolds we really need to talk to."

Ms. D. pulled away and gave me a long look. "She's fine, Kate. I'm sure of it. I promise we'll figure all of that out tomorrow. But tonight, we need to deal with this." She jerked her arm toward the hidden staircase.

"But she's hurt! I got another text! We have to go now and get her. What am I going to tell Taylor?" I was frantic now, shocked that the only adult I trusted at Pemberly Brown was turning her back on me.

"Trust me, Kate." She smiled sadly and started up the stairs.

"Wait, let me show you." I began digging through my bag,

desperately searching for my phone. Finally I just dumped the contents on the floor. Pens rolled, one stopping at the base of Ms. D.'s sneaker. A container of lip gloss lost its cap as it hit the ground, and my wallet spilled open, change clattering to the floor. I didn't care about any of it. I just needed my phone. But after every last pocket in my bag was emptied and I still hadn't found it, the vein on the side of my neck began to pulse. My heart pounded.

I stood and shoved my fingers into my pockets, praying that I'd feel the smooth plastic case of my phone. A dull ache began to spread from each temple as Ms. D. lingered at the base of the stairwell, a sympathetic look on her face.

"Kate." Ms. D's voice was gentle. "I don't have time for this now, but I promise we'll work this all out tomorrow. I've got to go. They're waiting on me up there." She turned and left me with tears streaming down my face.

The hallways felt empty, like a house after a party or a littered street after a parade. Show's over. Everyone had moved on. Everyone except me.

"Looking for this?"

At first I thought I must have imagined the voice from the blackened classroom, that I was officially going crazy.

Again.

"I'm late, aren't I?"

The moonlight shone in perfectly straight lines through the panes of glass along the back wall. It gave the empty classroom a peaceful, serene appearance. I'd always imagined that was what heaven looked like. Only without the desks.

From the bright lights of the hallway, it was difficult to see in. My eyes hadn't quite adjusted, and my pupils were manic from all the changes. But there was definitely someone there. I could see the shape of a person.

I knew that voice.

The form moved forward, coming closer.

I recognized the outline of that body.

And closer.

There was no mistaking that hair.

Bethany.

Chapter 43

I stepped backward, my butt hitting a locker. It sounds ridiculous, but I was sure Bethany must be a ghost. A ghost who was probably about to kick my ass for messing up everything and getting her killed.

But as she stepped into the light, coming clearly into focus, she looked like the same old Bethany. She didn't glow. Or float. And there weren't even dark circles under her eyes. She was holding something, extending her arm, offering it up.

My phone.

I couldn't form words, because the whole thing was too much to process. As it turns out, talking was completely unnecessary. Another form entered from behind us, around the corner, this time a head shorter and about a million shades lighter. I didn't have to wait for her to speak; my eyes didn't have to adjust. I knew who she was.

"Thanks for everything, Kate," Taylor said, smoothing her already perfectly smooth hair.

I opened my mouth to say something, anything, but again I

found no words. I just stared at the two girls in front of me, waiting for one of them to burst into tears, to thank me for all of my hard work, to hug me for not letting it happen again.

Because I honestly couldn't imagine this ending any other way.

But then I saw my phone again. How had Bethany gotten my phone? Why?

"I mean, I've always thought you were sort of useless. But Taylor was right. There's no way we could have pulled it off without you." Bethany's words hung in the hallway for a moment as my brain struggled to remind my mouth how to speak.

"Pull what off?" I found my voice, but just barely. It came out a whisper. A squeak. I hated myself for the way it sounded.

Taylor laughed the kind of laugh that usually made people cry, as though she thought the whole thing was so hilarious she couldn't contain herself. "Destroying the Brotherhood. Obviously."

Bethany smiled smugly. "They're finally done. And you know what that means, right?"

My throat tightened in response, burned like the time in lower school when I'd had strep throat and could barely swallow soup. I knew it didn't matter if I said anything. I knew they'd tell me.

"The Sisterhood owns Pemberly Brown. Again." Taylor raised both of her blond eyebrows and cocked her head to the side. I wondered if this whole exchange had been rehearsed. The moonlight spilling into the pitch-black classroom behind them, the play of their lips, the jut of their chins, each smile and every word. The scene was so perfectly delivered that it had to have been choreographed.

Bethany closed the space between us and placed the phone

in my hand. I didn't have to scroll through to know that it had been wiped clean. It was almost as though nothing had ever happened. And it occurred to me that Bradley was probably feeling the same way as he watched the headquarters he'd built get systematically destroyed.

Taylor linked her thin arm through Bethany's muscled bicep.

"We owe you one, Kate." They walked down the bright hallway, their shapes darkening more with the distance they put between us. "We have waited forty-eight years to officially take back the school and destroy the boys." She smiled at me again. "It's finally happening, and we owe it all to you."

"But the fortune cookie, the texts, the messages in the hallway. You were bleeding." My hands shook as all of the events of the past several days flashed before my eyes.

"I know, right? Bethany deserves an Emmy for her performance as the damsel in distress, don't you think?" Taylor elbowed her friend and laughed.

"No way. Your forgery skills are what really sealed the deal. You never would have gotten involved if it weren't for that fortune-cookie message Taylor wrote in Grace's handwriting, right, Kate? I paid off three servers at that dump to plant the cookie."

"But Alistair? How did you…" There was nothing I could do to keep the shock out of my voice.

The girls just looked at each other and laughed. Bethany got control of herself first. "Alistair thought he was working with us to stop Conventus. I can't wait to see the look on his face when he finds out what happened to their precious new headquarters."

I just stared at them blankly, not wanting to really process what they were saying. The Sisterhood had strung me up by pulling strings, throwing voices, and watching while I jerked and danced for their entertainment.

All this time I had thought I was saving another girl from Grace's fate, but I was no hero. No savior. I was nothing more than the Sisterhood's puppet.

> To: GraceLee@pemberlybrown.edu
> Sent: Sun 1/18 1:42 AM
> From: KateLowry@pemberlybrown.edu
> Subject: (no subject)
>
> Grace,
> I was just trying to help. To make things right. I figured that since I couldn't save you, I could save someone else. I thought I was saving them from your fate. No one should have to go through losing a best friend. Not even Taylor and Bethany. But now…Oh God, Grace, what have I done? What the hell have I done?

Chapter 44

The only ghost to arrive at school Monday morning was my own. I floated through the hallways completely detached, voices washing over me, no doubt rehashing everything that had gone down in the school over the weekend. Everything that I had contributed to. I felt tricked, used. But at the same time, could I really blame them? They'd finally done it. They managed to destroy the Brotherhood and the people responsible for Grace's death.

But what about the Sisterhood? They weren't completely blameless. Not by a long shot.

Eventually I found myself returning to the same spot in front of Bethany's locker where time seemed to stand still, and I was able to pinpoint the exact moment where everything had gone so terribly wrong. I was frozen.

What the hell had I done?

"Kate!" Liam's voice snapped me out of my thoughts, and I stared at him blankly. My mind could barely process the past twenty-four hours, let alone the state of our relationship. I was in no way ready to talk, but when I opened my mouth to explain this to him, his mouth crushed down upon mine before I could even utter a word.

His lips were warm and inviting as always, but my mouth was still pressed into a firm line. Detaching my mind from my body did not come nearly as naturally as it had with Bradley the night before. I hated myself for pulling back, but I did it anyway.

"I'm so sorry, Kate. I heard about the Brotherhood. You did it. You finally did it."

I just stood there staring at him, completely conflicted. Part of me wanted to let him make whatever assumptions he needed to make to forgive me. But the other part of me remembered what he'd said about Grace, the judgment in his eyes.

"Liam…I…" I started to try to explain but lost the words.

"Don't apologize. I know why you kissed him. I know you had to do it to get into the headquarters, and I know how important it is for you to put a stop to all of this. For Grace. I get it." He grabbed my hands and laced his fingers through mine. "You did it, Kate. You finally did it."

"Apologize? You think I'm going to apologize? You're kidding, right?" All the anger, all the helplessness and regret that had been pent up inside me since Saturday night erupted. I wished I could feel bad about the pain in Liam's eyes. I wished I could get past what he'd said about Grace, but I wasn't there yet. I wasn't sure I ever would be. "I just can't do this right now, Liam. I need some space."

We were interrupted by the squeak of new tennis shoes racing down the hallway. I didn't even need to turn around to know that Seth would be standing there, red-faced and out of breath.

"Guys, we've got a problem," he said.

"A big problem," a second voice boomed.

Bradley and Alistair looked out of place standing beside little, old Seth. Having all these boys in the same place at the same time felt like a collision of worlds.

"What the hell, Seth?" Liam looked furious.

"You need to hear them out."

"This is all my fault. I trusted them. They said if we set Bradley up to make it look like he'd abducted Bethany, that we'd be able to put a stop to Conventus." Alistair coughed, and I was pretty sure he was trying to cover up actual tears.

I had to clench my hands into tight fists to stop from pretending to play a little violin to accompany his sob story. A lovely habit I'd picked up from my father.

"No one cares," Liam growled.

"Well, you're about to start caring," Bradley retorted.

As if on cue, a woman's voice crackled on the loudspeaker. "Liam Gilmour, Seth Allen, and Alistair Reynolds are to report to the headmaster's office immediately."

Seth went completely pale. He'd never done anything except file papers in the headmaster's office. "What the…"

"It's starting." Bradley sighed.

"What are you talking about?" I took a step closer to him. I couldn't help myself.

"We're all going down. One by one." He looked at Seth and Liam. "Good luck in public school."

"But Seth and Liam weren't even in the Brotherhood. There's no way they'll be kicked out." My voice was getting increasingly shrill. This couldn't be happening. It didn't make any sense.

"Doesn't matter. They've appointed a new headmistress. Some chick who used to be in the Sisterhood. It's their word against ours now." Alistair stuffed his hands in his pockets and began the long walk toward the main office. It looked like a death march.

"But what about you?" Seth squeaked. For a second I was sure he was going to lock his arms around one of Bradley's legs and refuse to go.

"Let's just say this wing wouldn't exist if I wasn't here, so they can't really do much about me."

"But they can't do this. The new rules from the school board—there's no way the president would let this happen. Not after what happened to Grace." I moved another step closer to Bradley, and I felt Liam's eyes digging into my back.

"This is only the beginning. They're going to destroy this school. Just wait till they start recruiting."

The bell rang and students flooded the hallway. I was vaguely aware of being jostled back toward the window. I sank down on the window seat and watched the students hustle toward their lockers, talking, laughing, gossiping about the party. Instead of falling into line with the rest of them, I made my way to the office. This was some kind of mistake. It had to be.

Faber est suae quisque fortunae. Station 3. "Every man is the artisan of his own fortune."

As I ran my fingers over the Latin, I wondered how the words would apply today. It didn't feel like I had any control over anything in my life, let alone my fortune.

Behind the glass walls of the office there was a constant stream of motion that could only be described as change. Furniture was being rearranged, some even removed. The paintings that normally hung on the wall were stacked and leaning against the corner. The wall plaque beside Headmaster Sinclair's office that displayed his name was now blank. I should have been celebrating, overcome with excitement that Headmaster Sinclair was finally gone, but instead I felt an overwhelming sense of uneasiness.

My hand was on the door handle before Mrs. Newbury even noticed I was there.

"Hey, wait. You can't…"

I tuned her out and threw open the door.

At first I didn't recognize the woman sitting behind the huge mahogany desk. She had perfectly coiffed silver hair and wore an impeccable black power suit, her face brightened by a strand of milky white pearls at her throat, but I'd recognize the determination in those steely gray eyes anywhere.

It was Ms. D.

Chapter 45

"Well, hello, Kate. How nice of you to pay me a visit in my new office. What do you think?" She gestured gracefully at the walls, or maybe the expensive fabric of her suit jacket just made everything look graceful.

"I don't understand." Tears welled in my eyes.

"Oh, don't worry. I'm going to redecorate." She laughed at her little joke and jerked her head in Seth's direction. In all of my shock I hadn't even noticed him sitting in the chair in front of the desk.

"Mr. Allen, you are dismissed. I assume you'll remember what we spoke about and steer clear of dangerous influences in the future. Please do close the door behind you.

Seth nodded mutely and gave my arm a quick squeeze as he brushed past me. "Be careful."

"Now, Kate, I know this must be confusing for you…" Ms. D. started talking the second the door clicked shut.

"Confusing? You were supposed to be helping me! I trusted you. Did you know what they were up to this entire time?" My voice shook with anger. Never in my life could I remember feeling this betrayed. This hurt by someone who I thought I could trust.

"Please calm down. You know as well as I do that things could not continue as they were. We needed to do something to control the Brotherhood, and people far more powerful than I decided that this was the best course of action." Ms. D. stood up, made her way around the desk, and put her hands on my shoulders. She towered over me in blood-red stilettos, which seemed so out of place on Ms. D. In the past I'd always found her size comforting, like a sturdy grandmother. But in her new clothes, her size was intimidating, scary. I couldn't help but think that if she wanted to, this woman could crush me like a bug.

"I learned a long time ago not to question what I can't control, Kate. It was a lesson hard won, but I'll never forget it." She let her arms drop to her sides and walked over to the window. "Please don't do anything you'll regret. I can't protect you. Not anymore."

I shook my head, desperate to ask her what had happened to the old security guard that I'd come to love over the past couple of years. But I already knew the answer to that question.

She was gone.

I let myself out of her office and nodded briskly at Alistair on my way out.

Outside the office, students laughed and gossiped, texted and jostled. They had no idea what had really happened. How could they? Most of them didn't even know that either society existed.

And that's when I saw them. Bethany and Taylor, arms linked with a first-year. With her long, black hair and her almond eyes, she was a dead ringer for Grace. And that's when I knew that my fight wasn't even close to being over.

But this time I knew exactly what I had to do.

I threw my shoulders back and walked straight toward them. Bethany's mouth turned down at the corners, her eyes narrowed into two slits. But Taylor broke into a huge smile when I linked my arm through hers.

"So what's next?"

"Oh, we have big things planned, Kate. Huge."

I pasted a smile on my face and fell into step next to them. Taylor shot me an approving look and I gave her arm a quick squeeze, but the muscles in my stomach tensed. She had no idea, but I was getting ready for the fight of my life. I was done doing battle from the sidelines. I'd played the pawn long enough.

"So is that invitation still good?" I asked.

"You have no idea how long I have been waiting for you to ask that question, Kate." Taylor kept walking, not missing a beat, but Bethany fell a step behind.

"I can't wait to finally be one of you." My teeth ached as the overly sweet words slipped between my lips.

If I'd learned anything over the past week, it was that the rules were constantly changing, shifting so subtly that most people never even noticed. I didn't like following rules, and I wasn't about to start now.

But that whole "rules are meant to be broken" thing? Total crap. The real secret is to make your own.

Acknowledgments

None of this would have been possible if our dear major agent, Catherine Drayton, hadn't taken a chance on two sister-writers in Cleveland, Ohio. We'll be forever grateful for your honesty and guidance.

We can say with 100 percent certainty that this book would have completely sucked if it weren't for the editorial stylings of Leah Hultenschmidt and Aubrey Poole. We moaned and groaned our way through all of your notes, but we would be lost without you ladies.

A huge thanks to the team at Inkwell, especially Nathaniel Jacks and Alexis Hurley, and to everyone at Sourcebooks, especially Todd Stocke, Kay Mitchell, Derry Wilkens, Kelly Barrales-Saylor, and Kristin Zelazko. We are so lucky to work with people who love books and who have worked so hard to put Kate out into the world. Thank you, thank you, thank you.

To all of our amazing writer friends, especially Loretta Nyhan, Lee Nichols, Elana Johnson, Gretchen McNeill, and Beth Revis. You've all been just an email away whenever we need a friend to laugh with or bitch at—or mostly to bitch, then laugh. We'd be certifiable without you.

To all of our amazing real-life friends and family for putting up with our incessant book chatter and for helping us follow our dream. Especially Stacey, the third, most talented Roecker, for not getting annoyed with us and for designing custom creations at the drop of a hat; Joni Roecker for her daily updates on all things publishing; and Mike Roecker for the most random emails ever.

And none of this would be possible without the support of our husbands and kids. John and Ken, we promise this will all be worthwhile. Someday. In the meantime, at least you guys get to drink beer and make fun of us. Jack, Mia, Lydia, Ben, and James: believe it or not, we're writing these books for you. While the chance of you falling in love with a neon-haired detective remains slim, we hope all the hours spent watching us at our computers will show you that if you work hard, sometimes dreams really do come true. If not, we'll pay all your therapy bills. Promise.

About the Authors

Lisa and Laura Roecker are sisters-turned-writing-partners with a passion for good books, pop culture, and Bravo programming. Not necessarily in that order. Lisa has always been a phenomenal liar and Laura loves to write angsty poetry, so writing for young adults seemed like a natural fit. The sisters live in Cleveland, Ohio, in separate residences. Their husbands wouldn't agree to a duplex. To learn more about *The Liar Society* series, check out www.theliarsociety.com.